A Grave in Autumn

by

Donald Gorman

authorHOUSE™

1663 LIBERTY DRIVE, SUITE 200
BLOOMINGTON, INDIANA 47403
(800) 839-8640
WWW.AUTHORHOUSE.COM

© *2005 Donald Gorman. All Rights Reserved.*

No part of this book may be reproduced, stored in a retrieval system, or transmitted by any means without the written permission of the author.

First published by AuthorHouse 01/17/05

ISBN: 1-4208-2215-2 (sc)

Printed in the United States of America
Bloomington, Indiana

This book is printed on acid-free paper.

DEDICATION

This book is dedicated in loving memory to my father, Dr. William Gorman (August 6, 1928-October 27, 2004). His patience, love and support have always been a great inspiration. He has always been there when needed. He will be missed by many.

TABLE OF CONTENTS

CHAPTER 1.....
AUTUMN_____

He stepped out of the kitchen. He carried the plate down a narrow path between boxes. He sat on the sofa. It was one of the few standing pieces of furniture in the room. The plate fit comfortably on his lap. He lifted the sandwich to his mouth. His dark eyes surveyed the mess around him as he chewed.

He took another bite.

It was too quiet.

He drank cola from a can he had placed on the hardwood floor.

Sunlight beamed mercilessly through uncovered windows. It washed unobstructed over the bleak jungle of cardboard containers that filled the large room. Shadows hid in silence. The imposing late morning sky was too bright.

He couldn't see much from his present position. There wasn't much to look at. He sighed before taking another bite.

The doorbell rang before he could swallow. He raised his head in surprise. "Who even knows I'm here?" he mumbled beneath his breath.

He wiped his mouth with a napkin as he rose to his feet. He made his way to the front door. The knob felt cold in his hand. But, the door opened gracefully without a sound. The couple on the porch was older than he. However, their expressions were friendly. They each carried food.

"Can I help you?" he asked politely.

"Good morning," said the man. His warm smile creased his weathered face. "We're the Burgdorfs. I'm Jerry, and this is my wife, Maria. We live two houses down the road."

"Pleased to meet you," said the host. "My name's Russell Wilburn. I'm new here."

"So we've noticed," replied Jerry. "We're sort of the self-proclaimed welcoming committee on the block. We saw the moving vans last night."

"We thought we'd give you the evening to settle in," Maria added.

"But, we wanted to extend a warm welcome to the neighborhood," her husband continued. "We bring you gifts. I have my wife's famous Meatball Surprise."

"It can be heated for dinner tonight," she said. Her smile was also wrinkled but inviting. "It's very nourishing. And, I have the Bundt cake."

"Thank you," he said awkwardly. "That's very kind. Where are my manners? Please come in."

The couple thanked him as he allowed them passage into the building. "You'll have to excuse the mess," said the host. "I'm not sure you'll be able to find a place to sit. Let me relieve you of that cake, Mrs. Burgdorf."

He took the gift from his guest as she said, "It's Maria, please. And, don't worry about the mess. We understand."

Jerry followed his host to the kitchen with the Meatball Surprise "We're not too old to stand," he said. "Where are you from?"

Russell told him to put the pan anywhere. They were headed back into the main room before he answered, "I'm originally from Yonkers, New York."

The older couple accepted his invitation to sit on the sofa. However, they declined his offer of refreshments. He took a seat on a sturdy box beside his lunch.

"So, what made you decide to move to Rhode Island?" Jerry asked.

"And, where's the rest of your family?" Maria added. "I'm sure a handsome young man like you has not been able to escape the blissful bonds of holy matrimony."

Russell sighed. He glanced down at the floor. Finally, he replied, "My wife was killed in a car crash about five years ago."

The Burgdorfs' smiles vanished. "Tough break, son," he said.

"We're sorry," she said. "Were there any children?"

"No," Russell said. "We were only married two years. They say the man in the Global Freight Express truck was driving drunk. Of course, he walked away with hardly a scratch. It seemed like the court case lasted forever. But despite their best attorneys, I won the lawsuit. I made enough money to buy this house, and a struggling little store downtown to keep me busy. One way or the other, I'm financially set for life. But, that's not much consolation for losing my Kristina."

"Of course not," Maria said. "How old was she?"

"She was 23 when she died," he said. "I moved here to get away from everyone and everything that reminded me of her. I just wanted to leave it all behind and start a brand new life. Even with all the legal mumbo jumbo, I was able to close on this house just before my thirtieth birthday."

"Well, congratulations on that, anyway," Jerry said. "And, happy birthday, by the way. How did you decide to move to this particular town?"

"I didn't want to be completely cut off from Yonkers," he replied. "I still have family ties there. But, I wanted to be far enough away that I could forget as much as possible. And, Autumn is such an intriguing name for a town. I had to check it out. And once I did, I was hooked."

"Yes," nodded Jerry. "This is a quiet, pleasant town. It's not too big. You can drive to the coast in less than half an hour. And, legend has it that the first people to settle here named this town in October. The brilliant colors of fall set the surrounding hills ablaze every year. It's really something to see. But, you'll be able to judge for yourself in a month or so. The leaves will be changing by then."

"Plus, you certainly chose a cozy little house here," Maria observed. "It will be the perfect place to start a family someday....when you're ready. I assume Mrs. Kellerman showed it to you. Did she tell you everything about this place? Or the town in general?"

"All the usual necessary stuff, I suppose," Russell said. "Why? What do you mean by 'everything'? Is there something extraordinary I should know about?"

Jerry and Maria glanced at each other. "Not at all," she said quickly. She toyed with her graying, curly hair. "A little dry rot, maybe. But, nothing you need to worry about."

"Did you say you bought a small store downtown, son?" the husband added suddenly. "Which one?"

"The Golden Eagle General Store on Thornton Ave."

"I know the place," said Jerry. "Is it still open? I haven't seen anyone in there in a while. Not that I stop by there very often."

"Yes," he said. "To the best of my knowledge it's still open. I have yet to go down there to acquaint myself with the staff and the daily routine of the operation. I'll be doing that next week, so I can see what we need to do to save the place. From what little I've seen, bad management is the main problem. Luckily, I got my Business degree before my wife died. I'm sure we can turn things around in there."

"I hope so," Maria commented. "That's a sweet little store. And, it would be nice to see you start off your new life here on the right foot."

"Thank you. Keep your fingers crossed."

Suddenly, the conversation seemed to die.

Russell absorbed the awkward silence with curiosity.

"We should go," Jerry said as he stood. He gestured toward the door. "You have a lot of unpacking to do. We've taken up enough of your time."

"Yes," his wife agreed. "I'm sure you're too busy to stand around talking to us. Besides, we interrupted your lunch."

"It's just a bologna sandwich. You really don't have to go."

"We have a hectic Saturday afternoon planned," Jerry explained.

The guests were nearly at the front door, when she said, "Nice to meet you, young man. Again, welcome to the neighborhood. Enjoy the Meatball Surprise."

"And, the cake," her husband added as he reached for the doorknob.

As his guests departed, Russell called after them, "Thanks for everything. I'll return your pans to you as soon as I can, Mrs. Burgdorf. I promise."

"Please. Call me Maria."

"Wait," he called. "I didn't get your address."

They were already disappearing into the shadows of the trees, which lined the road. He watched for a moment from the shade of the porch. Only the unprotected lawn dried up in the sun.

"They're pretty spry for their age," he muttered to himself. Then, he went back inside. He sat on the sofa. He tried to forget about his curious visitors as he slowly finished his sandwich.

Unpacking became tedious. A few hours' work didn't make much of an impact on the imposing chore that still loomed before him. The fan in the window could not provide enough relief from the oppressive, stagnant heat.

He checked his watch. It said 4:02. The phone rang. It was the hollow echo of a ring between bare walls. He wiped the sweat from his face as he searched the floor for the phone. Another hollow ring sounded. He wondered who it could be as he searched.

The ring echoed through the room again.

He found the phone. He almost dropped the receiver on his race to speak into it. "Hello," he said.

There was no reply.

"Hello?" he repeated.

The consequent silence was as thick as the heat in the room.

Finally, he gave up. He put the receiver back in its cradle. His impatient scowl didn't last long. "At least I know the phone works," he reasoned. "Sort of."

After a short break, he showered and dressed. He drove down the hill and into town.

He drove past the tidy middle-class homes and manicured lawns of this comforting locality. He navigated cleanly paved streets past fresh, green oak trees. He entered a bourgeois paradise of jump ropes, skateboards and retail shopping offered by cozy little storefronts. The sun cast its bright spell of warmth over the busy residents of a pleasant small town named Autumn.

Marshall Ave. was a broad thoroughfare that defined the length of the commercial district. He rode leisurely down its course in search of a dinner that sounded more appetizing than Meatball Surprise. Rush hour traffic permeated the streets. Still, the gentle sounds and smells of late summer accented the peaceful surroundings.

His casual search finally drew him to an appealing establishment called Fehr's Steak and Ale. He enjoyed a fine meal in a charming, hardwood atmosphere. Then, he sat at the bar for a quick drink. The same radio still offered pop music as a mild distraction. Empty barstools were easy to find. The bartender was a tall, stocky man in the obligatory vest and bow tie. He was rinsing glasses as his new customer took a seat. "Good evening, sir," he offered in a professional tone. "What can I get you?"

"A gin and tonic, please."

"Very good, sir."

He glanced around as the bartender made his drink. "This is a nice place," he observed.

"Yes," said the bartender. "The owners take good care of it. I take it you've never been here before."

"I just moved to town," he said. "I don't know anyone or anything about the area. I stopped in here because it looked nice from the outside."

"So, why did you move to this town?"

"It's a long, sad story," he said. "I'd rather not go into it."

"Okay," said the bartender. "Then, what part of town are you living in now?"

"Not too far from here," he replied. "I'm moving into a house on Agnes St."

"I know that neighborhood," the bartender said. "Isn't that one of the roads that runs up the hill to the old cemetery?"

"That's right."

"Yes. That's a decent part of town, mostly."

"Mostly?"

"Well," the bartender said. He placed a drink on the bar. Then, he took his payment to the cash register. "Every block has its weirdoes."

He rolled his eyes. "I think I already met the ones on my block," he said. "And, I only moved here yesterday."

"Is that so?"

"Some old couple in their mid-fifties visited me today," he said. "They seemed friendly, but a bit strange. I never got used to the idea of complete strangers invading someone's house with food offerings. She seemed very motherly. He was a goofy old guy with a bad comb-over."

"Yes," the bartender nodded. "I know the type. We get a lot of those people in this town. They're just plain nosy. No life of their own."

"That was my impression," he agreed. "I have a feeling I'll be seeing much more of them than I'd like."

The bartender excused himself. He had customers to attend. When he returned, he held out his hand. "By the way," he said. "My name's Deke."

"I'm Russell," he replied as they shook hands. "Nice to meet you."

"So, what line of work are you in?"

"I just bought The Golden Eagle General Store."

"That place on Thornton Ave?" Deke asked. "That used to be a nice little store. Is it even still open?"

"Yes."

"Good," said Deke. "That's great. Good luck turning that place around. Not that you'll need luck. You must have some money if you bought that store."

"I do all right for myself," he said. After a sip of his drink, he changed the subject. "Listen, what can you tell me about my neighborhood? You had a tone in your voice when you said it was 'mostly' okay. Is there something I should know?"

"I had a tone?"

"Maybe I'm just being paranoid," he admitted. "Believe me. I'm looking forward to starting a new life in this town. But, my new neighbors made me a little nervous. Anything you can tell me about the area would be appreciated."

Deke watched him sip from his glass. "There's nothing to tell, really," he replied. "But, if neighbors with bad combovers make you nervous, I have to wonder why you moved so close to a cemetery."

"Do cemeteries bother you?"

"No," Deke said. "But, every graveyard has ties to its local history."

"Would you care to elaborate?"

Deke watched him take another sip. "Well, I don't know," he finally answered. "Take the street you live on. As I understand it, Agnes St. was named after the original matriarch of the Van Pouck family. They were some of the first settlers in this region. They were a rich Dutch family that owned a good share of this town at one time. They were in the import business, real estate and they were demons in the stock market."

"What happened to them?"

"The Great Depression hit them kind of hard," Deke explained. "That began the downfall of their dynasty. There were a few suicides. Some of them moved away. A few of them weathered the storm. They were able to maintain their lifestyle and regain some of their fortune. But, the town bounced back better than the Van Poucks did. And, we managed to flourish without their help."

"Are any of them still around?"

"Just one," said Deke. "Elliott is the last Van Pouck alive in this town. He's a crazy old man. He's got to be pushing seventy by now. As a matter of fact, I think he lives on your street. It's a big, gray mansion just a few blocks from the cemetery. The place is getting kind of run-down. Nobody's made an effort to keep it up. He lives alone in there. And, he almost never comes out or speaks to anybody. If he's even still alive, he could die in there and no one would know.... possibly for months."

"Didn't he have a family?" Russell asked. "A wife or kids?"

Deke watched him finish his drink. "He used to," he said. "Or so I'm told. Once he had a beautiful wife and three kids. Would you like another drink?"

"Sure," he said. "So, what happened to the wife and kids?"

The bartender took his glass. "No one really knows," he said. "He was supposedly kind of abusive, or so they say. All we know for sure is that they disappeared one night almost twenty years ago. Some say the wife ran off with the kids to escape her lunatic husband, hoping never to be found. Some say he killed them all in a fit of rage. Those who believe that story think he could have buried them anywhere on the grounds of the mansion. Their land extends far into the woods behind the house. Perhaps they're buried in the cellar. Or maybe in the cemetery nearby. One way or the other, there are a lot of Van Poucks in that cemetery."

"Didn't anyone investigate?"

"There was nothing to investigate," Deke answered. "No one saw or heard anything suspicious. There was no proof that any crime had been committed. The police talked briefly with the old man. He wasn't very cooperative. He told them she took the kids and ran away for no good reason. He was very surly. I think he may have cried at one point. They never pushed him because they had nothing to go on. Plus, some of the local authorities still fear the Van Pouck name. So, there was no formal investigation."

"That's quite a story," he said.

"It's local history and gossip," said Deke. "Don't put too much stock in it. It shouldn't have any impact on you."

"I guess you're right," he agreed. "Say, is it always this dead in here?"

"No," Deke replied. "It's usually hopping in here on a Saturday night. I suppose everyone's off somewhere celebrating the Labor Day weekend."

"You probably have a point there," he said. "I usually have plans for Labor Day myself. But this weekend, I'll be mostly unpacking and moving into my new house. I guess the thrill of starting a brand new life will have to sustain me."

"There's nothing wrong with that."

He stayed for one more drink. Then, he drove home. It was a slow drive under the brilliant finale of a Rhode Island sunset. Lavish layers of orange, yellows and reds bled from a tangerine sun. And stenciled with pink highlights, they spilled over the darkening skyline. Stars poked through the rich blackness like eyeholes in the wall of a nightmare fantasy. The street lamps, stores and taverns below sheltered the busy sidewalks and roads with safe, comforting light.

He took his time. He was in no hurry. He soaked in the mood and character of his new environment. It was full. It was simple. Eventually, it would belong to him.

Finally, he turned onto Agnes St. He drove up the hill to his house. Inside, everything still looked like a mess. Even with the clutter and countless boxes, it looked empty. He put a few things away. He fixed the place up a bit.

But, he couldn't focus.

Luckily, the television was plugged in. He watched from the sofa for a while. He grew bored. It was still too hot in that room. He thought about Kristina.

Now, there was a smile that could brighten any room.

So beautiful and caring. Such a tragedy!

He needed to take a walk. He grabbed his keys and headed out the door. It was much cooler outside. The fervent darkness was silent and soothing. He instinctively turned uphill and began to walk. His pace was slow and calming. Many of the homes on Agnes St. were bigger than his. They were attractive domiciles for families with money. It seemed strange that they would be so close to a cemetery.

He continued to walk at a leisurely pace. He passed one striking abode after another. Then, he saw an iron gate on the opposite side of the road. He stopped. He gazed at the big, gray mansion inside.

He didn't take his eyes off the structure as he crossed the street. He stood directly in front of the rusted iron gate while staring at the large building. The mansion was set farther back from the road than most of the houses on the street. It needed to be painted. The porch and one of the balconies were sagging. A few broken items littered the unkept lawn. It was very still and silent. There were a few lights on inside. The weathered mailbox just outside the gate read in faded lettering: "THE VAN POUCKS".

The gate was locked.

A quick breeze blew by. It rustled his dark hair. It felt a bit chilly.

After a minute or two, he turned and continued his walk. He passed more gorgeous homes.

Two blocks up the hill, he encountered another rusty iron gate. This one was made of chicken wire. This one was open like a gaping mouth. The wide, paved path stretched out from deep inside like an asphalt tongue....rolling outward and becoming Agnes St. Inside the gate, tombstones were lined in rows like concrete shark's teeth....hushed, motionless and waiting. The big, rusted, broken letters over the gate spelled out: "AUTUMN CEMETERY".

He stepped inside. He strolled past the first row of gravestones. He glanced up ahead. They seemed to stretch on for miles. He strode past the next row and the next. Old graves and new graves were lined up in neat organized queues as if awaiting Heavenly admission. Fresh monuments sat beside new monuments. All of them displayed names that longed in vain for eternal remembrance.

He read a few of the tombstones with casual interest. He wondered if anyone could still recall Sean Quimby who died in 1864, for instance. The stone was getting difficult to read.

The entire hilltop was quiet and incredibly dark. He walked for a long time, until he saw the opposite entrance in the gate. He had heard about this side of the hill. The big, lavish homes had been carved up into small apartments. People on this side of the hill rented their accommodations. They drank beer and drove delivery trucks for a living.

After a minute, he turned and walked back through the cemetery. He passed the same rows of stones as midnight approached. A bloated half moon rested in peace and innocence in a clear, black sky. And, he strolled between granite markers back to the gate, which had offered him access to the graveyard.

Then, when he was about ten rows from the entrance, he saw something. He hadn't noticed it on his way in. He went over for a closer inspection.

About fifteen feet in from the path, there was a brand new hole. It had been dug recently. There was a fresh mound of dirt beside it. The proportions were perfect for a grave. It appeared to be about six feet deep. It was a well-sculpted rectangular hole that seemed to exist for a rather obvious purpose. However, there was no stone. Nothing was inside. It was just an empty hole.

He watched it for a minute. Then, he left the cemetery. He strode past big houses and the Van Pouck mansion. He maintained a steady pace until he reached home.

He couldn't get to sleep that night. He tossed and turned for an hour or so. Suddenly, he sat up. He felt hungry. He ambled downstairs and into the kitchen.

He looked in the refrigerator. He regarded a tray with sleepy curiosity. He spooned some food into a bowl and heated it in the microwave. When the timer sounded, he took out the bowl. He stirred it as he sat. He took a bite and raised an eyebrow as he chewed.

"This isn't too bad," he commented with a mouthful of Meatball Surprise.

CHAPTER 2.....
FRAGILE_DARKNESS_____

He slept late that morning. It was nearly noon by the time he stumbled into the kitchen. His sleep had been light and restless. The bedroom furniture was set up. However, most of his clothes were still in boxes.

He had not yet showered when he had his coffee and Bundt cake breakfast. But by 4:00 P.M., he was clean and predominantly unpacked. "Nice job," he said to himself as he glanced about the living room. "It's not perfect, but it's respectable. Furniture's in place. The few remaining unpacked boxes are hidden and out of sight. I can deal with them when I need to. This really is a nice house. I'm going to like it here. All I have to do now is stop talking to myself. My nosy neighbors will think I'm crazy."

He allowed a quick chuckle.

He rested on the sofa. He had a can of cola on the coffee table. The television played as a peaceful distraction. After a minute or two, the phone rang. This time, it was hanging on the wall by a cabinet. He walked over and picked up the receiver. "Hello," he said.

The silence on the other end was steady and unyielding.

He repeated his greeting impatiently.

Still, no response was offered.

As soon as he hung up, he dialed a number. When someone answered, he said, "Hi, Steve. This is Russ."

"Hey, pal," said the voice on the other end. "How are you? Did you get to Rhode Island okay? Are you all moved in? I wasn't expecting to hear from you for at least a couple of weeks."

"Yes," he said. "I'm all moved in. Everything's fine. Actually, that's why I'm calling. I want to check my new phone. I may be having trouble with the connection. Could you call me right back, please? I'm at 401-582-5468."

"Sure," said Steve. "No problem."

"Thanks," he said. He hung up and waited for the call. A minute later, the phone rang. He answered it with an anxious, "Hello?"

"It's Steve," said the caller. "Can you hear me all right?"

"I hear you just fine," he said. "Thanks. I was a little worried. So far, the phone ringed a few times. But every time I answer it, nobody's on the line."

"That's weird," Steve said. "Must be kids playing pranks."

"Probably," he agreed. "I'm surprised they found me so quickly, though. The phone hasn't even been on for a full two days. I only have this phone for business, anyway. I usually give people my cell phone number."

"I understand," said Steve. "Well apparently, those kids with the prank calls really mean business."

"I guess so," he chuckled. "So, how are things out in Yonkers?"

"Fine," Steve replied. "Everything's the same. Believe it or not, Andy and Lisa got back together again."

"Again?" he said. "When will those two ever learn?"

"We'll all be dead first," Steve said. "How is your new place?"

"Not bad," he said. "I'm all moved in, mostly. It's a pretty house. You'll have to come out and see it sometime."

"I'd love to," Steve said. "I'll have to check with the wife and see when we can get a free weekend. We should probably give you a month or two to settle in first, though. I'm sure we can work something out. What do you have planned for the rest of the holiday weekend? It's a shame we won't see you at Henry's annual barbeque tomorrow."

"He certainly knows how to throw a party," he said. "I'm not sure what I'm doing yet. I don't know anyone in this town. I have to stock up on supplies for the house. I don't want to eat out all the time. I'll probably go to my new acquisition. I think I told you I bought a small place called The Golden Eagle General Store. I'll probably stop by there this evening. Then, I'll go out and let this town know that I have arrived."

"It'll do you good to get out," Steve said. "You haven't dated at all since Kristina died. I know you need some time. But, it's been five years, Russ. You have to move on."

"I know," he admitted. "That's one of the reasons I moved out here: To get away from things and move on. I just hope I'm ready."

"You'll do great, pal."

"Thanks," he said. "Listen, I'll let you go. Thanks for your help with the phone. Give Denise a kiss for me."

"Will do," Steve replied. "No problem. And, good luck. Don't worry about a thing, Russ. You'll be fine out there."

"Thanks again."

When he hung up the phone, he stood silently for a moment. Staring at the wall, he could almost see Kristina's beautiful smile. He could almost hear the music in her laughter.

He rubbed his eyes. He forced himself to grab his keys and head for the door.

Sunday rush hour traffic was infesting the streets of Autumn. Cars moved steadily along roadways that were saturated with family vehicles and vacationers with out-of-state license plates. A dense, gray mask of clouds had cloaked the sky. A light, refreshing rain soothed dry lawns and chased pedestrians inside.

He drove toward Thornton Ave. He knew the way. He had the route memorized. There was no reason to hurry. Traffic didn't bother him. Neither did the rain.

The Golden Eagle General Store was larger than a convenience store, but smaller than a supermarket. It employed about a dozen people or so in various capacities. The half-full parking lot was built to hold nearly thirty cars. He found a parking space near the entrance. He stepped out onto the wet, crumbling pavement. He went inside.

Bright lights illuminated the aisles. A radio gently aided shopping with an oldies station. There was a refrigerated produce aisle and a fully stocked deli counter in the back. Customers carrying handcarts inspected merchandise and checked prices. Two of the three available cash registers were manned.

The first cashier he encountered was a plump Japanese woman in her forties. She saw him approach as she bid farewell to a departing patron. Her smile was warm and genuine. "Hello, Mr. Wilburn," she said. "It's nice to see you again."

"Daisy Nakajima," he said. "It's a pleasure to see you, too. And, please call me Russell. How are things here at the store?"

"Okay, I guess," she said. "We still get paid every week. When are you taking over?"

"October 1," he said. "So, you only have to keep this place afloat for about a month. Do you think you can handle it?"

"We'll do our best," she teased. "By the way, have you met Heidi O'Dell? She's a cashier of ours, too. I think she was out the last time you were here. Heidi, this is the new owner, Mr. Wilburn. He'll be taking over next month."

She was busy with a customer. Even with her chestnut hair tied up, she looked beautiful behind her work smock. She glanced over with big, green eyes and an inviting smile. "Nice to meet you," she said. "Excuse me, okay?"

He watched her resume her duties. "Of course," he quietly replied.

"So, what brings you here today?" Daisy asked.

It took an effort to return his attention to the elder cashier. "Oh, I just moved into town," he said. "I need some groceries. And, I figured I might as well patronize my new establishment. If we're going to save this place, every dollar helps."

"Well," Daisy offered. "If you just moved into town, allow me to welcome you to Autumn."

"Thank you, dear," he said. "I might even take this opportunity to meet some of the staff while I'm here. If they're not too busy, that is. Is Bill Green here? I'm sure I have a few things to discuss with him before I take this place off his hands."

"Bill's out today," Daisy replied. "He doesn't seem to care as much about the store these days . . ." She hesitated before concluding, ". . .Now that he has a buyer."

A customer came to Daisy's register as Russell replied, "I see. Well, carry on. Don't let me keep you."

He watched Daisy greet her customer. As she began to ring up the girl's purchases, his gaze returned to the younger cashier. She was also serving a new patron. She was quick, though courteous and graceful. It was a pleasure to watch her.

After a few moments, he took a handcart and ventured down the canned goods aisle.

The store was busier than he had expected. He decided not to bother the staff. He picked up the necessary sundries and headed for the front of the store. There was one patron at each of the available cash registers. He chose a line. He waited his turn.

Finally, he stepped up and unloaded his basket onto the counter. He was met with surprise. It quickly turned to a gorgeous smile. "Welcome to The Golden Eagle," she said with dutiful courtesy.

"Hello, Heidi," he said. "I'm glad we actually get a moment to talk."

"Me too," she said. She was already ringing up the items before her. "So, you're the guy who bought this place, huh? I was expecting someone much older and . . ."

Her voice trailed off. He waited for her to finish. When it became apparent that she had nothing to add, he offered, "I hope you're not disappointed."

"Not at all," she said. "It doesn't matter to me who runs the place. I'm just worried about the rumors. Everybody says there are going to be lay-offs. Or we'll all get fired. Is it true? Should I be worried?"

"I wouldn't lose any sleep over it," he said. "I just moved to town. So, I don't have my own people to bring in here. From what I've seen, the place is not over-staffed. The books show a lot of poor management. I think Mr. Green has wanted to get out of this store for quite a while. That's why he let this place go to hell. He just doesn't care anymore. I think we can save this place without losing anybody."

"That's nice to hear," she said. "I need this job. I live alone."

"You do?"

"Yes," she said. "And, the landlord just raised the rent on me. We haven't had any raises in here in over three years. And, the cost of living is always going up. That'll be $43.78, please."

He regarded the number on the register with discontent. He reached for his wallet. "It's a shame we didn't get to talk longer," he said. "I know the store will be closing in a few hours. There's a good chance I'll be at Fehr's Steak and Ale on Marshall Ave. around that time. Do you know the place?"

"Yes," she said. She winced in a gesture of a polite decline. "I'm not really sure it's a good idea, though. We just met. All I did was ring up your groceries. And, I'm not the kind of girl who would sleep with the new boss just to keep her job."

"Nobody said anything about sleeping with anybody," he explained. "I already told you that no one's going to lose their job. I'm just going there for a quick drink or two. I just moved to town, and I don't know anyone. It would be nice to have some company for a few minutes before going back to my new empty house. If you would like to join me for one harmless drink, you're welcome to do so. I would consider it a favor. But, I promise there are absolutely no strings attached."

She accepted his payment with thanks.

"I know we just met," he continued. "And, I won't push you. I understand your skepticism. All I can do is promise you have nothing to worry about. We can talk about the store, tell me about yourself, or whatever. It would just be nice to have a pretty girl to talk to for a few minutes on my first weekend in a strange town."

She blushed slightly and glanced downward. Then, she handed him his change while hesitating to respond. "I don't know," she finally said. "I'll think about it."

"Fair enough," he said. "I hope to see you soon."

He took his bags and waved to Daisy on his way out of the store.

"Are you going to go?" Daisy asked her friend. "He is kind of cute."

"Maybe he is, a little," she said. "I probably shouldn't, though. I really don't know."

When he arrived home, he took his time preparing dinner. He ate slowly. He had all evening. He wasn't particularly hungry. Eating was just something to do.

Afterwards, he went upstairs to clean up before going out. Even though the sun was still out, the bedroom was a little dark as he approached. A few scant ribbons of light slipped through the windows between closed curtains. And in those ribbons of light, he saw a form. Perhaps, it was just a shape. It was a faint objection to the fragile darkness.

He stopped in his tracks. He stared.

It was merely light and shadow. It was the shape of a woman.

She stood still. She was facing him.

Then . . . in the flash of an instant, she was gone.

He couldn't move for a moment. He looked between the ribbons of light for a sign. He searched for a trace of reason in a vacant room.

He found nothing.

He flipped the light switch. Brightness instantly filled the room. All shadows were erased, along with his immediate fears. He shrugged off the experience with a laugh. "Steve was right," he told himself. "I've been alone too long."

He resumed the task of getting ready to go out.

The rain had stopped by the time he reached Fehr's Steak and Ale. The sun was sinking in an orange patch of sky. It tried to hide behind the zebra-striped cover of clouds.

There were only a few couples in the restaurant. There were only three customers at the bar. Deke smiled when he saw his new friend take a stool. "So, you came back already?" he asked. "I never would have pictured you as a regular. Not here, anyway."

"I haven't bothered to find anywhere else to go yet," he said. "I might as well take advantage of the quiet of a holiday weekend."

"I don't blame you," Deke said. "Gin and tonic?"

"Yes, please."

Deke began to make the drink. "I'm glad you're here," he said. "I could use the company on a lonely Sunday night."

"Actually, I may have a guest coming. That is, if she bothers to show up."

"You found yourself a girl, did you?" Deke grinned. "Good for you. It didn't take you too long, buddy."

"I wouldn't get excited yet," he said. "I'm not even sure if she's coming. And, it's just for a quick drink, if she does."

"An awful lot of wild adventures start off with a single drink," Deke prophesized.

"Just don't. Okay?"

Deke's smile vanished. "Sorry, Russell," he said. "I didn't mean anything by it."

"That's all right. I'm sorry, too."

"So, you really like this girl?" Deke asked.

"How can I?" he said. "I just met her. Apparently, she's one of my new employees at The Golden Eagle. I never thought I'd be the type of guy who would go chasing after the help. It's so cliché. It's just that it's been five years since my wife died. I'm alone in a new town. I thought it would just be nice to have a little female company for a few minutes."

"I understand," Deke said. He decided to watch his tongue as he rinsed out some glasses. "Are you sure you're okay, pal? You seem a bit out of sorts."

"I'm fine," he said. "But, just before I left the house, I thought I saw . . . I mean, do you believe in . . . I guess that story you told me about the Van Pouck family stirred my imagination. It's got me thinking that I see things."

"Like what?"

"Never mind," he said. "Listen, is there anything else you can tell me about that family?"

"Are you sure you want me to tell you?" Deke asked. "Especially if you're seeing things? Sounds like you have a vivid imagination already. Besides, why would you even care about the Van Poucks? Once the old man kicks off, they won't be causing any more trouble in this town."

"What makes you say that?" he asked. "Have they caused a lot of trouble?"

"Sure," Deke nodded. "Back when they practically ran Autumn, they caused plenty. That family had more than its

24

fair share of crazy people. But, that's all in the past. Since I've been alive, they've caused nothing but rumors and kids' stories."

He perked up. "Like what, for instance?" he asked.

"Listen," Deke scoffed. "There's nothing you need to take seriously. Like I said, once the old man dies, the Van Poucks will never harm anyone in Autumn ever again."

The bartender excused himself. He had to fill a few drink orders. By the time he came back, Russell needed a drink, as well. As Deke poured the gin, something caught his attention. He looked intently over his patron's shoulder. "Now, if I wanted some female company while I was in a strange town," he commented. "That's just the kind of female company I'd go looking for."

Russell turned toward the door. She caught him off guard. Even though she was dressed quite casually, he noticed how striking she looked with her hair down. The smile she offered doubled the effect.

"I'm glad you made it," he said as she approached.

"Thank you," she said. She placed her purse on the bar as she sat. "I hope I'm not too late. Frankly, I'm not sure why I came at all."

"It's just an innocent drink," he assured her. "There's nothing to worry about."

She said nothing. She looked at him with big, green eyes.

"Good evening, Miss," the bartender interjected as he assessed his new customer. "I'm Deke Danaher. I'll be serving you this evening."

Russell regarded the bartender's manner with mild annoyance. "This is Heidi," he introduced.

She greeted Deke with a polite nod. Then, she ordered a Sea Breeze.

There was an awkward moment of silence. She watched without interest as the bartender gladly set about the task of making her drink.

Russell was the first to speak. "So, was it really such a big decision to come out here tonight?" he asked.

"I don't know," she sighed. "Like anywhere else, that store is a rumor mill. I didn't even tell Daisy I was coming here. I'm sure she'll ask me tomorrow, though. God only knows what she'll tell everybody."

"Don't worry," he said. "I'll back you up. Nothing's going to happen tonight. I just wanted to talk to somebody. I just moved to town a few days ago. I don't know anyone here. I have to start my new life somehow. Having a quick drink with you seems like a pleasant way to begin."

She looked at him with uncertainty. "So, what brings you to a worthless town like this, anyway?" she asked.

He hesitated. He watched her eyes for a moment. In this low light, they were beautiful in their mistrust. The radio offered a gentle background to the mood. A Smokey Robinson song played as he slowly began to recount his recent past. She listened intently to his story. Her eyes softened. Her posture became less defensive.

"Well," he concluded. "That's about it. I haven't socialized much these past few years. I didn't feel like it. It didn't seem right. Plus, the trial monopolized most of my time. But, I'm human. I have to move on. I need to have a life."

"Everyone does," she offered. "It's a shame what happened to your wife. From your description, it seems like she was quite a woman."

"She was."

"By the way," she added. "Why does everyone always say you have to go up a hill to get to the cemetary? It's not really much of a hill."

"Well, it's a bit of an incline, anyway," he said. "It's almost a hill, sort of."

"Still, I hope things are more peaceful for you over here."

"Thanks," he said. "But, I've rattled on about my sad little life long enough. Tell me about you. Aren't you seeing anyone right now?"

She glanced down at her drink. Stirring it appeared to be a nervous habit. "No," she finally muttered. "I broke up with my last boyfriend over a year ago. His name was Charlie Putnam. He was always very jealous. After a while, he became physically abusive. I can't believe I stayed with that jerk for more than three years. I still have a restraining order out against him. I haven't seen much point in dating since then. Maybe I'm afraid of falling into that same situation all over again. Who knows? For the time being, however, I feel I'm doing fine on my own."

"You have friends, don't you? And, family?"

"Oh, sure," she said. "I go out with my friends on a regular basis. They're always trying to fix me up with someone. Even Daisy has tried her best. But . . . I just haven't been interested."

"You don't still love Charlie, do you?" he asked.

"God, no!" she scoffed. "I am so better off without him. It may sound evil for me to say this, but I look forward to dancing on his grave."

"No one could blame you for saying such a thing."

"I just don't need a man in my life right now," she commented.

27

"That's perfectly natural," he said. "There's no set schedule for a person's healing process. If you still need time to readjust, you should take it. Don't let anyone rush you into anything. You only have to answer to yourself. There's no reason to impress anybody. Only you will know when the time is right to jump back into the game. Believe me. I know about these things from personal experience."

"It sounds like you do."

The sincerity in her smile was refreshing. Neither one of them noticed the bar was beginning to fill with the slow trickle of new customers. Small talk allowed them to share another leisurely drink together. The store never became a topic of discussion.

Perhaps, a few boundaries fell away.

As she finished her drink, she said, "I really have to go."

"Must you?" he asked.

"I have to go to work tomorrow."

"I understand," he said. "Have you decided what you're going to tell Daisy tomorrow?"

"Who knows?" she shrugged. "I haven't even thought about it. I'm sure she'll ask. I guess there's no reason to lie. It's not as though this was a date or anything."

"That's true."

She stood quickly. She offered a smile and a brief hug of graditude. "Thanks for the drinks," she said. "I enjoyed this more than I was expecting."

"My pleasure," he said as he rose to his feet. "Good night, Heidi."

She said good-bye and beat a hasty retreat out the front door.

Deke managed to catch a glimpse of her as she left. "My hat's off to you, buddy," he told his patron. "That's quite a girl."

"Just give me one for the road."

"Sure thing," Deke said. He knew to let the subject drop. "But, I still have one thing I have to ask. You never told me before why you've developed such a sudden interest in the Van Poucks."

He considered how to respond. "Frankly," he said slowly. "I have no idea."

After a final drink, he drove the quiet, dark roads of Autumn back to Agnes St. The night boasted a warm, clean darkness. It was a fresh darkness, as if it had just come out of the dryer. Bright stars were spilled about the sky like crumbs from a big, half-eaten moon. The peaceful streets allowed the occasional signs of casual recreation. It was a town with no worries and nothing to fear.

He drove up the gradual incline of the Agnes St. hill. He navigated the subtle curves that led toward his home. However, he stopped dead in the streets when he saw his house. He watched the building for a minute. It looked beautiful between the trees, set back from the road in the mild affliction of night.

He listened to his motor running as he sat there.

Then, he suddenly felt the inexplicable urge to keep driving. He drove further up the hill. He knew where he was headed, but he didn't know why. There was purpose, but no reason. He rode past dim street lamps and impressive homes. He just drove onward.

Finally, he saw the open gate of Autumn Cemetery. He drew his car to a stop just outside. He put it in park, and opened the door. He stepped out onto the pavement. He stared up at the sign above the gate. The iron letters were rusted and worn. There was no breeze to invite or forbid passage. There was only a vast display of stone monuments spread out before him, like a huge granite banquet to honor centuries of death.

He carefully strolled into the cemetery. His path was predetermined. His course was set. He strode past the first few rows of tombstones. A map was clear in his mind. He recognized these markers. He was aware of his destination. He walked past the next few rows. He glanced in the right direction. Even in the darkness, something was amiss.

He approached that certain location. He wanted to see. He expected to find proof of what had been there the previous night.

He stopped. He stared in disbelief. "What?" he gasped. "There's nothing here!"

He dropped to his knees and checked the dirt and grass with his hands. "The ground hasn't even been broken!" he observed with curiosity. "This is the spot! Isn't it? There was a hole here last night! A grave! I know there was! How could this be?"

He tested the ground with his fingers. The earth was intact. The grass was undisturbed. He looked around. He tried to ascertain his precise position. He felt more certain than ever.

He stood.

The faint strains of music played off in the distance. It was accompanied by voices. He surmised it was neighborhood children. Teenagers were likely trolling through the far end of the graveyard. He decided to leave.

He walked casually back to his car. He got in and headed for home.

The drive back down the hill was marred by doubt and confusion. He considered the possibilities. He wondered if he could have been mistaken. His mind drifted as he descended the hill.

Then, he stepped on the brake. The car skidded to a stop. He sat and gazed out the side window. This iron gate also looked the same. The gray mansion still sat farther back from the road than the surrounding houses. He heard an occasional banging that seemed to come from the side of the house. A tired breeze came from nowhere and toyed with nearby tree limbs. He guessed the banging was a loose shutter against the wall of the mansion. The same few lights were on inside.

He watched silently for a minute. Nothing moved, except the banging shutter.

Finally, he took his foot off the brake. He drove home.

Back at his house, he decided to turn in earlier than he had the previous evening. He made a quick midnight snack of Meatball Surprise and Bundt cake. He thought back to the events of the day. Most of them were positive . . . but not all of them.

He was getting ready for bed when the phone rang. He wasn't in the mood. He stormed over to the phone and picked up the receiver. He was about to admonish the caller for the repeated pranks.

However, something immediately seemed different when he got the phone to his ear.

He could feel the presence of the person on the other end. There was something fearful and alarmed in that presence. There was terror and desperation. Reluctantly, he spoke into the phone. "Hello?" he said.

The response did not come right away. A fear grew more intense as the moments passed. He held his breath and waited. Then, he heard the timid, shaky voice of the caller. She simply said, "Help me . . .!"

Then, it was done.

"What?" he called into the phone. "Who is this?"

Another moment of dread went by. Then, he heard a click. The dial tone which followed carried the monotonous weight of reality.

It droned on as steady and uncompromised as the flat line of a heart monitor.

He was nearly trembling when he hung up the phone.

CHAPTER 3.....
WHAT_IS_OR_ISN'T_
THERE_____

The scream brought him out of a sound sleep. His eyes opened wide. He sat up and quickly surveyed the room around him. The bedroom was mostly burdened by darkness. Only those few familiar ribbons of light slipped between the curtains like bony fingers caught in the closing door of opportunity. However, nothing seemed out of place.

He was alone. Everything was still.

It was an early morning light that poked through the curtains. Its color and angle matched the alarm clock's digital declaration that it was 8:44 A.M. He figured that a bad dream must have been responsible for his wake-up call. Still, he knew he would feel better if he looked around a bit.

Of course, nothing turned up. "It was just a dream," he muttered to himself.

He wondered why this house had such an effect on him as he made a pot of coffee. He cleaned up and prepared for a fresh, new day. He even had a chance to drink a few hot cups before the doorbell rang.

A familiar face greeted him from the porch when he opened the door. "Hello, Mr. Burgdorf," he said. "How are you?"

"Just fine," his guest replied. "And, please call me Jerry."

"Come on in," he invited. "Can I offer you a cup of coffee?"

"I wouldn't want to trouble you," his guest said, as he stepped through the doorway.

"It's no trouble at all," he said. "It's already made. I was having some myself."

"Then, thank you," Jerry said. "A small cup with just a hint of sugar would be wonderful. I hope I haven't bothered you too early. I know that some people don't rise as early as Maria and I. We're morning people. That's one of the main things we have in common."

"Is it?" he called from the kitchen. He was stirring sugar in a steaming cup for his company.

He brought the cup out as Jerry replied, "Oh, yes. It's made for a happy marriage that has lasted 31 years so far . . . knock on wood."

"Congratulations," he said while handing over the cup. "Not many marriages last that long these days."

Jerry thanked him as he took a sip. Then, he said, "The secret is communication. Of course, honesty and fidelity don't hurt either."

"That sounds like a faultless plan."

"Say, Russell," Jerry said as he glanced around the room. "This place is really beginning to shape up. It looks much better than the last time I was here."

"Thank you."

"Of course," Jerry added. "No one could blame you for how this place looked a couple hours after you moved in.

34

But, you've really pulled this together. It looks marvelous. I can't wait to tell Maria. She'll be so pleased. She really likes you."

"Well, I like her, too."

"We're both hoping you'll work out keeping this house," Jerry said. "It would be nice to have someone decent in here. And, someone who might stick around for a while."

"Why?" he asked. "Have you had some bad neighbors in the past?"

"Most of the folks who buy this place aren't quite equipped to handle it," Jerry said.

"What do you mean?"

"Oh, nothing," Jerry assured him. It only took a moment to come up with an answer. "This house takes a lot of love to run it. That's all."

"I see," he replied. "I gather from what you've been saying that this house changes hands too often. Is that what you're inferring?"

Jerry cleared his throat. His sharp, brown eyes betrayed his disapproval of the path this discussion had taken. "Why are we even talking about such things?" he quickly impeded with a smile. "The past is the past. There's no reason to concern yourself with what anyone did before you arrived. I'm sure you'll do fine here. That's not why I came over this morning."

"Then, what can I do for you?"

"It's Labor Day," Jerry cheerfully reminded. "It promises to be a gorgeous day out there. We figured since you're new in this town, you won't have any plans. And, we always have a big barbeque to celebrate the end of summer."

"What a coincidence," he imparted. "I usually attend a friend's barbeque back in Yonkers every Labor Day. I was just discussing it with someone yesterday. We were saying what a shame it was that I would miss it this year."

"You don't have to miss anything, my boy," Jerry said. "You're cordially invited to attend our big bash this afternoon. It starts at 1:00, if you're interested."

"That sounds great," he accepted. "Thanks. I'd love to."

"Glad to hear it," Jerry said. "It will be a wonderful chance for you to meet some of your new neighbors. Of course, they're dying to meet you, too."

"I'm looking forward to it."

"Sorry for the short notice," Jerry offered. "We didn't even know anyone bought this place until we saw the moving van the other day. And, it didn't even occur to me when we came over to introduce ourselves. If Maria hadn't mentioned it this morning, it probably wouldn't have even entered my mind. Am I an awful neighbor, or what?"

"You're nothing of the kind," he assured. "There's no reason why you would have thought of me. We just met. I find your invitation most gracious. Can I help? Would you like me to bring anything?"

"Don't even think of it," Jerry replied with a gesture of his hand. "You just moved into town. You're not even set up yet. And, you had no warning about this shindig. It's not necessary. Everything's under control."

"Okay," he said. "Thanks for the invitation. And, extend my appreciation to your lovely wife. Tell her I'll be there at 1:00 sharp."

"Maria will be so pleased," Jerry said as he stood. "Thanks for the coffee. I must be going. I have a grill to prepare."

"You're welcome to stay a while," he said as he walked Jerry to the door.

"Thank you just the same," said Jerry as he stepped out to the porch. "But, I have a lot to do. And, it looks as though we're having one more guest at our little celebration."

"I'll see you then," the host called after his departing company. "Thanks again."

"Don't mention it."

* * * * * *

She took her seat. She didn't look her friend in the eye. She recognized that look. She didn't want to do this now. She immediately began to count her money.

"Good morning, honey," her friend said with an expectant tone.

"Good morning," she muttered. She focused on her task.

"How was your evening?" she asked with that same tone.

"It was okay, I guess."

"You're not going to leave me hanging, are you?" she prodded. "You have to tell me. Did you do it? Did you meet Mr. Wilburn like he asked?"

She sighed. "Damn it, Daisy," she complained. "Can we not do this now? I lost count. I have to start all over again."

"I knew it!" her friend beamed. "I knew you'd go! Tell me everything."

"There's nothing to tell," she said. "We had a couple of drinks. We talked."

"So, what's he like?"

"I don't know," she said. "He's a widower. His wife died a few years ago. He moved out here to get away from everything. Just like me, he doesn't seem to be looking for anything serious right now."

"You can't fool me, Heidi," poked Daisy. "I recognized the look on his face when he first saw you yesterday. And, I recognize the blush in your cheeks right now. Plus, you can't even look me in the eye. You two are headed somewhere."

"We are not!"

"If you say so, Heidi."

"God damn it, Daisy!" she snipped. "Cut it out! I lost count again. Believe me. When I need a man, or when I find one, you'll be the first to know. Until then, just mind your own business. Okay?"

"Well, what are you waiting for?" Daisy asked. "Mr. Wilburn is the perfect age for you. You told me yourself that you think he's cute. He smart, and he's got money. And, the fact that he's going to be your new boss couldn't hurt either. You could be going places, girlfriend."

"You just let me decide where I'm going," she averred. "And, don't you dare spread any rumors in this cesspool. If you breathe a word of this to anyone, I'll make you pay!"

"Don't worry, honey," Daisy assured her. "You can trust me. My lips are sealed."

"They'd better be," she warned. "Now, let me finish. We'll be getting customers in here soon."

* * * * * *

The sky was bright blue. A strong, watchful sun stood guard and kept the clouds away. Only an occasional harmless, puffy cloud was allowed to slip by. However, it was a hot afternoon, even for those who were not standing over a grill.

The host greeted all his guests with a smile on his face and a spatula in his hand. A chef's hat hid the bad comb-over. His apron had seen a lot of barbeques. Burgers, sausages and chicken breasts sizzled as they spat smoke into the air. Folding tables held bowls of various salads, side dishes, chips and dips. People were spread out across the spacious backyard. They were talking, laughing and playing games over the background music coming from an unseen radio. It was a perfect portrait of the holiday.

He smiled when he saw his latest arrival. "Russell, my boy," he beamed. "It's great to see you. I was afraid you wouldn't show up."

"Sorry I'm a little late, Jerry," he said. "I had a few things to do around the house. I did manage to bring a few big bottles of soda for the occasion, though."

"Oh, thank you," said Jerry. "That really wasn't necessary."

"It's the least I could do."

"Bring them over to Maria, will you?" Jerry said. "She's over by the house. She'll be delighted to see you. And, grab a burger or a chicken breast. Or if you like, my friend Alan Cox is working the other grill. He's got steaks, franks and some sort of pork slop. I don't know what it is, but it's a big hit every year. The man's a wizard. Help yourself. There's food everywhere."

"Thanks," he said. "It looks like you've got quite a turnout."

"That's why I have to keep flipping these burgers," Jerry said with a wink.

He allowed a quick laugh. Then, he worked his way through the crowd to the house. Maria smiled when she noticed his approach. "Oh, Russell dear," she said. "I'm so glad you could make it. I feel terrible for not inviting you sooner."

"Believe me," he said. "It was wonderful of you to invite me at all. I wasn't sure what to bring. But, I managed to wrangle up some soda."

"Thank you, dear," she said. "You didn't need to do that. We know you have a lot of unpacking to do. You haven't even settled in your new place. Grab a paper plate and a fork. Help yourself. There's plenty of food."

When he had filled a plate, Maria sat him at a table with a young couple. They didn't appear to be much older than he. "Russell Wilburn," she introduced. "This is Clayton Spencer and his wife Janelle. They live across the street a few houses down. Russell just moved a few doors up at 857 Agnes. I'll leave you to get acquainted."

He watched her disappear into the crowd. He felt a bit self-conscious.

Clayton offered his hand. "It's nice to meet you, Russell," he said.

"You, too."

They shook hands.

"What line of work are you in?" Clayton asked.

"I just bought The Golden Eagle General Store down on Thornton," he said. "I'm going to try to build it back up to a thriving business."

"Good for you," Clayton said. "That was a nice little store once. I thought that place was doomed."

"Not if I can help it."

"Good attitude," Clayton chuckled. "I'm a plumber. I own Drain Right Plumbing and Heating. Let me give you my card. If you ever have any problems with that new place of yours, I'm the man to call."

"I'll remember that," he said as he took the card. "What about you, Janelle? What do you do for a living?"

"I'm a clerk down at City Hall," she said. "It's not much of a job, but it brings money into the house. Do you have any family, Russell?"

"I'm alone now," he said. "My wife was killed a few years ago by a drunken driver."

The couple offered their condolences.

He thanked them. Then, he added, "You learn to move on. How about you? Do you have any children?"

"Our Kyle just turned eight," Janelle said. "He's our only child, but he's a handful. He's over there. Kyle! Don't run with food in your mouth!"

"So," Clayton said with a change in tone. "You're the one who bought the old Beckenbauer house, huh? I've got to give you credit. That's a hell of a place."

"Beckenbauer?" he asked. "Was that the name of the last owner?"

"Oh, no." Clayton shook his head with a strange look in his eye. Then, he explained, "That's a name that's a bit infamous in this town. That name has some history behind it."

"You've captured my interest," he said. "Please go on."

"Don't, Clayton," Janelle urged.

"Edgar Beckenbauer bought your house in the fall of 1928," her husband expounded. "That was about a year before the big stock market crash. It was also shortly after Edgar went into business with Gordon Van Pouck. He was a very rich and powerful man in this town back then."

Russell raised an eyebrow. "Gordon Van Pouck?" he asked. "I suppose he's an ancestor of Elliott's. That's the only surviving member of the family, isn't he?"

"Have people already been talking to you about this?" Janelle asked. "Elliott is Gordon's youngest grandson. And as far as we know, he's the last Van Pouck in this area."

"I've only heard a few bits and pieces of the story so far," Russell said. "But, I'd love to hear more."

"Then, you're in for a treat, pal," Clayton announced.

"You're only going to stir him up with your fairy tails," Janelle protested.

Her husband ignored her. He continued, "I'm not sure exactly what agreement they entered into, but I think Edgar wanted to import something illegal. Maybe poached animal pelts or guns or something. Gordon was intrigued by the fiscal possibilities. And, he had the resources to get the project started."

"Will you please stop?" Janelle persisted.

"Things started out well enough," her husband continued. "But, something went terribly wrong."

"And, what was that?" he asked.

"No one knows for sure," Clayton began.

Before he could go on, however, Maria interrupted with a cheerful smile. "How is everyone getting along?" she asked.

"Just fine," Russell answered.

"You're plate is empty, dear," she observed. "Why don't you get another burger or some chicken? Mrs. Waters makes an extraordinary potato salad. You have to try some. Follow me. I simply must introduce you to the Glickmans. You'll love them."

She kept chatting as she ushered him quickly away from the table. He was mildly irratated about not having the chance to finish his conversation. However, he politely appeased his hostess.

The Spencers gave each other a glance as they watched.

A minute later, Maria returned to them. "You weren't talking to Russell about his house, were you, Clayton?" she questioned.

"Yes, he was," Janelle answered.

"Why would you want to get him all worked up with local legends and gossip?" Maria asked. "The poor dear has been through quite enough with the death of his wife."

"I just want him to know what he's getting himself into," Clayton said.

"He's getting into a nice, cozy house," Maria said. "And that's all."

"I'm telling you, Maria," Clayton stated. "There's something wrong with that place."

"The only problem with that house," she insisted. "Is that innocent people listen to upstarts like you."

"There's a reason why nobody will stay in that house for more than a few months," Clayton averred. "All those families can't be crazy."

"Well, it doesn't help matters," Maria argued. "Having people like you filling their heads with childish stories and superstitions. Sharon Kellerman has been trying forever to unload that property once and for all. Let's give her a fighting chance, okay?"

The Spencers watched her walk away. She quickly disappeared into the crowd.

By 6:00, the gathering began to thin out. Everyone had eaten their fill. Families needed to get small children home. People realized they'd be returning to work the following day. The festivities were gradually winding down.

The yard was still packed with party-goers when he left, however. He thanked his hosts for the wonderful food and the great time. He bid farewell to some new acquaintances. He walked back up to his house.

It didn't take him long to spruce himself up a bit and throw on a clean shirt. He had every intention of heading straight into town when he got into his car. However, he turned the wheel in the other direction. He drove uphill.

Without knowing why, he parked by the front gate of the cemetery. He felt a strange compulsion to stroll inside. He knew where he was going. But, he still didn't have a reason. If nothing else, idle curiosity drew him to the familiar spot. He wandered back about ten rows. He wanted to see if it had been his imagination. He found the exact location. He could tell the ground was still untouched as he approached. He was disappointed, but not surprised. Once again, he dropped to his knees. He tested the earth with his fingers. Once again, it was undeniable that no dirt or grass had been disturbed at this site.

Then, something caught his attention. He slowly turned his head to the right. The gravestone directly beside the plot on which he knelt. The very next plot over sent a chill up his spine. Carved in marble, it read:

EDGAR BECKENBAUER

BORN: DIED:

May 12, 1898   April 3, 1929

R.I.P.

* * * * * *

"It's almost 7:30," she announced. "We'll be closing up soon."

"So?"

"Aren't you disappointed that he didn't show up?" she asked.

"I wasn't expecting him."

"Come on, Heidi," she said. "This is me. I know you were hoping to see him today. You've been climbing the walls since you came in here this morning."

"I have not!"

"Maybe he'll call you tonight," she suggested. "You did give him your number, didn't you?"

"Why would I?"

"I see," she nodded. "You didn't want to seem too anxious. Good thinking."

"I swear, Daisy," Heidi warned. "If you say one more word about Russell Wilburn, I'm going to lock you up in your own cash register and leave you there overnight."

Daisy perked up as she glanced over her friend's shoulder. "That's going to be a little difficult. He just walked through the door."

She swallowed hard. She took a deep breath.

"Don't you dare embarrass me, Daisy!" she threatened.

"Don't worry about a thing," Daisy said without taking her eyes off her new boss. She displayed a big smile as she greeted, "Hello, Mr. Wilburn. It's nice to see you. Some of us were afraid we weren't going to see you today."

"That's sweet, Daisy," he said. "But really, you can call me Russell."

He tried to ignore the glower Heidi was giving the other cashier. "And, how are you this evening?" he asked.

She forced herself to look him in the eye. "Okay, I guess," she said.

"I just came in to pick up a few items," he said. "But while I'm here, it would seem a shame to pass up a chance to ask you if you would like to get a bite to eat. It's almost

45

closing time in here. And, we had a good time together last night. I just figured . . ."

"Well," she replied with great effort. "I'm not really hungry. And, I thought we agreed that neither one of us are ready to date yet."

"Fine," he said. "I'm still not going to push you. Besides, I'm not hungry either. I've been at a barbeque all day. I'll just pick up a few things, and I'll get out of your way."

Both cashiers watched in silence as he disappeared into the aisles of the store.

"Listen, Heidi," her friend imparted. "Playing hard to get has its advantages and everything. But, that guy's not going to wait for you forever. Don't let him get away."

"I'm not playing hard to get," she said. "I'm just not ready."

"How long are you going to wait, Heidi?" Daisy asked. "It's been over a year. You can't keep hanging on to your past disasters. You have to let go of the time you wasted with Charlie. This guy is no Charlie, and he could be a good catch for you. Maybe he isn't, but you'll never know unless you go for it."

"I don't know," she said. "I'll think about it."

"Well, don't think too long," Daisy said. "You're window of opportunity could close at any second without warning."

Neither girl spoke much after that. They were almost ready to begin closing the store. Many of the staff had the holiday off. The only customer in the building was their new boss. Plus, they had worked a long day.

When their only patron unloaded his basket on Heidi's counter, he said, "I'm sorry if it seemed like I was pressuring you. I understand your concerns about being with your boss. I am interested in you, and I think something may be developing between us. At least, I got that impression last night. If you disagree, that's your decision. If you would like to at least discuss it, you can meet me for a drink . . . you know where."

She didn't say a word as the money changed hands. But, he saw a look in her big, green eyes that made him smile to himself as he carried his bags to the car.

Daisy knew to let the subject go with a grin. She had a feeling that words would only complicate her friend's choice.

The sun was setting. The clouds were growing thicker in a darkening sky. The official holiday celebration was drawing to a close. There was no cause to hold back the oncoming rain.

Once again, there were only a few patrons in the bar. A familiar face smiled at him from behind the tap as he entered. "Hey, Russell," said the bartender. "How was your Labor Day?"

"Not too bad," he said. "My neighbors invited me to a barbeque. They did a nice job. They may be nosy old coots, but they throw a good neighborhood party."

"Great."

"I still get the impression they're trying to hide something from me, though," he said. "About the house, about the area, or the town in general. I'm not sure what they're up to, but it makes me a little nervous."

"I wouldn't worry about it," said the bartender. He placed a gin and tonic on a coaster. "Old folks are unpredictable no matter where you go. There's no escaping that sort of thing."

"I guess you're right," he said. "So, how was your Labor Day, Deke?"

"Okay," the bartender said. "I took my wife out for a private celebration. By the way, will your lady friend be joining you this evening?"

"It's possible," he said.

"Hang on to that girl, my friend," Deke smiled. "I can already tell she's something special."

He walked off to tend to some new customers who had just entered.

Russell stirred his drink. He took a sip. There were plenty of things to think about.

Deke spent some time talking with his new patrons. Then, he came back. "You look a bit troubled," he observed. "What's the matter, buddy?"

"Nothing," he said. "A few strange things happened today. I was talking to some people at the picnic, and . . ."

He stopped. He didn't know how to proceed. Then, he said, "Never mind. It's not important. Everything should work out."

Deke perked up as he glanced over Russell's shoulder. "I suppose it will," he said. "It looks like things are looking up for you already."

He spun around to see what his friend had in mind. The girl with a beautiful smile stood in the doorway. He rose to his feet as she approached. "I'm glad you decided to come," he said.

"Thanks," she said. She placed her purse on the bar as she sat. "Me, too."

"It's nice to see you here again," Deke added. "Did you want a Sea Breeze?"

"Hi, Deke," she said politely. "Yes, please."

Russell sat as he told her, "This is a good sign. We just might be able to break you out of your shell."

"Don't get too excited," she said. "I'm just here to talk. I understand what you said to me back at the store. Last night left me feeling that there may be a slight possibility . . ."

She stopped. She didn't want to continue. She wished she could retract her last sentence. Russell watched her eyes as he waited.

Finally, she repeated, "I'm just here to talk."

"That's perfectly fine, Heidi," he replied with quiet assurance.

She began to get comfortable as they shared a drink. His attentive attitiude and soothing tone put her at ease.

They hadn't been there long. They were ordering another drink when two men walked into the building. They had been drinking. They laughed as they walked up to the bar.

The thinner man had dark hair. He poked his friend with an elbow as he said, "Hey, Jack. Look who's here."

Jack rolled his eyes when he saw. "Oh no, Charlie," he suggested. "Let's just get out of here, okay?"

"What are you worried about?" Charlie asked with a tone. "I'm not going to start nothing. Hi, Heidi. How are you, baby? Long time, no see."

She grew tense in her seat. She pulled away when she felt his hand on her back. "Get out of here, Charlie. You're violating your restraining order."

"I'm not violating nothing," he said. "I just walked into a bar. I didn't know you were here. But since you are . . ."

"Just go, Charlie," she ordered.

"What's the matter, baby?" he said while grabbing her upper arm.

Russell jumped to his feet as Heidi pulled away with an angry squeal. "The lady told you she's not interested, pal," he averred. "Keep your hands off her."

"Let's go, Charlie," Jack recommended. "We can find another bar."

Charlie had a threatening look in his eye as he adressed Russell. "What business is it of yours, boy?" he asked. "Hey, Heidi. Is this your new boyfriend? Is this what you left me for, baby?"

"I'm the guy who's going to take your head off if you don't leave her alone," Russell informed him.

"Is that right?"

"Hey!" Deke shouted. He was holding a baseball bat in his hand. "If I have to come over this bar, I ain't going to stop swinging this thing 'til your head is nothing more than a stain on the floor! Now, get out of here and don't come back! You're not welcome here!"

Everyone was still. Only the radio in the background broke the silence. The tension grew heavier with each passing moment. Charlie glanced at Heidi . . . and then at Russell . . . and then at Deke.

"Come on, Charlie," Jack coaxed. "Let's go. You don't need any more jail time. I'll buy you a drink at The Scathing Cauldron."

"I'd listen to your friend," Deke sternly advised.

Charlie glanced around at the three anxious faces again. He considered his options. Then, he said, "Let's get out of here."

He stormed off toward the exit. Jack quickly followed behind him. Everyone breathed a sigh of relief when the door closed behind them.

"Are you all right, Heidi?" Russell asked.

"I'm fine," she said. "All he did was grab my arm."

"Is that the asshole you were talking about last night?" Deke asked. "No wonder you dumped him. He's been in here before. He tends to be trouble."

"I don't know what I ever saw in him," Heidi said.

"Don't worry about it," Deke said. "We all make mistakes. But, I can promise you that jerk won't be coming back here anymore."

"I'm glad to hear it," she said.

"I could've handled him, Deke," Russell said with mild irratation.

"I know you could have, buddy," he replied. "But, I can't have that shit in my bar. Guys like that need to know I'm in charge here. Tell you what? Why don't I get you two a drink on the house?"

"I don't know," Heidi said. "I just want to get out of here."

"Are you sure?" Russell asked.

"Don't let that ass run you out of here," Deke said. "He's gone now. And, this is the one place in this town where you know that you're not going to run into him again."

She fidgeted a bit in her seat. "I just don't want to be here," she said.

"Would you like to at least finish the drink you already have?" Russell asked.

She stared at the bar as she considered his request. Then, she acquiesced with a sigh. "Well, okay," she said.

"I'm glad," Russell smiled. "And, if you want to get out of here afterwards, we can still grab a bite to eat somewhere, if you'd like."

"Maybe."

She watched her drink as she stirred it. He watched Deke run off to serve some patrons at the other end of the bar.

"I hope this won't turn into a reason to not give us a chance," he said.

"I doubt that it will," she said. "Daisy told me I can never really be free of Charlie if I don't move on. This incident reminded me of what I wanted to escape in the first place. Maybe Daisy was right. I have to move on."

"We both have reasons to let go of our pasts," he said. "I haven't allowed myself to move beyond my own tragedies."

"That's why you came to Autumn," she reminded. "But, I'm not going to just fly into your arms. And, you shouldn't just fly into mine. I'm going to take it slow this time. And, don't worry. If something is there, we'll find it."

"I'm looking forward to the journey," he said.

"I think I am, too."

No one planned the kiss. It just happened. Nobody knew what it meant. Nobody knew where it came from. And, no one could guess where it would lead.

When they finished their drinks, she said, "I really have to get out of here."

"Would you like to get a bite to eat somewhere?" he asked.

"I do feel a bit hungry," she said.

"I wish I was more familiar with this town," he said. "I can't even recommend a good place to go."

"I know a place," she said. "You can follow me in your car."

"Sounds great."

As they stood, Deke asked, "So, you're leaving?"

"I'm sorry," Heidi said. "I just can't stay here right now."

"I understand," Deke said. "It was a pleasure to see you again, my dear. Please come back. I promise that jerk won't set foot in this building again. And, I still owe you two a drink on the house."

They thanked him as Russell threw a tip on the bar.

The sun had disappeared by the time they stepped outside. The sky was a dingy tarp of dismal cloud cover. A light, steady rain gently showered the pavement. They ran to their cars beneath the playful drizzle.

She led him down Marshall Ave. heading toward his Agnes St. home. About a mile or so from their starting point, she pulled into a parking lot. The sign overhead read, "The Turtle's Nest".

The atmosphere inside was elegant and nearly romantic. A single candle encased in glass adorned each table. The lighting matched the delicate music which sounded softly in the background. The booths were private and discreet.

The woman who escorted them to their table had once been quite striking. However, even a heavy coat of make-up could not mask what time had stolen. She handed them each a menu with a smile. Then, she disappeared like an unnecessary memory.

"I'm surprised you chose a place like this," he said.

"Why?"

"You seem to be afraid of what this place represents," he said.

"To me, it represents food," she told him. "I haven't eaten much today."

"Were you working all day?"

"Yes," she said. "From opening 'til closing. All three days this weekend. I need the overtime."

"When's your next day off?"

"Wednesday," she said. "And Thursday. I plan on catching up on my sleep."

"Haven't you been sleeping well?"

"Not lately," she replied. "I'm not sure why. I've been pretty happy. My job and my friends keep me busy. I don't really miss . . ."

Her voice trailed off. She didn't want to finish. The expression on her face betrayed her mistake. Her hesitation was captured beautifully in the artistic, fickle shades of candlelight.

"What don't you miss?" he pressed gently.

She glanced down at her hands on the table. "Oh, nothing," she mumbled.

"You've been pouring yourself into your work lately, haven't you?" he continued.

"As I said," she reminded. "I need the money. I live alone, and I have bills."

Despite her efforts, her eyes appeared vulnerable in this light. It would be wrong to press any further.

"So, what do you do when you're not working?" he asked.

"My friends take good care of me," she replied. "We're always going to bars, clubs, parties, the movies . . . you name it, we do it."

"Sounds like you're the right person to show me around this town," he said. "Being new here, I'm going to need someone to introduce me to everything Autumn has to offer."

That smile looked even sweeter than before. The candle flickered again as she spoke. "Maybe I am the right person," she allowed. "Just maybe."

Dinner went well. Conversation drifted softly in the proper direction. Defenses continued to crumble. Horizons began to expand.

Afterwards, she said she had to leave. She had to go to work in the morning. Of course, he understood. She intentionally spared him the task of looking up her phone number in the personnel records at the store.

She even made a joke of it.

Their kiss was more certain this time. They knew where it came from. They knew why. It lasted through layers of doubt. There were implications of future possibilities. It inferred that old baggage on both sides was expendable.

She left with a smile that tempted the beginning of a voyage.

The rain was more pervasive on his drive back to Agnes St. It slapped at his windshield like watery little hands. It was obnoxious and cumbersome. It tainted visibility and soaked the streets with the carelessness of mischievous children.

He didn't care. He enjoyed the ride home.

He didn't even mind entering the house in wet clothes. It had been a pleasant day in this new town. It was starting to feel like home.

He decided to wind down with a glass of juice before bed. He only left a few dim lights on in the living room as he sat before the television. It didn't matter what show was on. He watched with mild interest. He allowed a natural lethargy to settle in.

The hour grew late. He began to nod off. Then, he perked up. Had he heard something? Had he caught a glimpse of something out of the corner of his eye?

He glanced over at the dark hallway. He stared with wide eyes.

There was a shape in the darkness. Glowing shades of light filtered through the black background like an opaque stain on reality. He almost recognized the face. It looked like the same woman he had seen before in his bedroom. However, her presence was more pronounced this time.

He could detect definition in her slender form. Her long, flowing dress draped casually from her hips to the floor. Pale cheeks accented a lifeless expression. And, vacant eyes studied the frightened man on the sofa.

He couldn't move. He couldn't speak. All he could do was stare at the incredible sight as his muscles tensed.

He shivered against the chill of fear and uncertainty.

She almost seemed to be looking right through him. It wasn't clear if she knew he was there. However, he had no doubt about this glowing vision. Its presence held him captive in its forbidding ambiguity.

She stood there for a minute. He wanted to speak. He didn't dare!

Finally, she turned away from him. She moved toward the stairwell. It seemed to take no effort on her part. She just glided smoothly across the hardwood floor. She moved at a slow, even pace toward the stairs.

Without hesitation, she then began her ascent. The apparition's movement continued in a smooth, unfaltering progression. She appeared to be nearly floating up to the second floor.

He jumped off the sofa. He rushed quietly over to the stairwell. He didn't want to call undue attention to himself. Still, he had to see where this specter was headed.

She continued her silent ascent. Her fluid motion mesmerized the anxious witness at the foot of the stairs.

Then . . . as she reached the top step, she vanished.

The sudden departure caused Russell to let out a scream. His terrified gaze met only undisturbed, inky blackness.

He ran upstairs. He quickly surveyed his dismal surroundings with wild eyes. Nothing broke the belittling, pitch black silence around him.

He stood alone in the unforgiving darkness.

CHAPTER 4.....
NOBODY'S_GRAVE_____

It was still dark when the phone rang. It woke him from his restless sleep. The digital clock on his nightstand read 2:58. Rain still tapped gently against the windows. He didn't want to get out of bed. However, the phone kept ringing. It rang again and again. With a certain sense of dread, he dragged himself to his feet.

The phone nagged him with its incessant, grating call for attention. With his eyes half open, he turned lights on to guide his way down the hall. The stairwell remained veiled in shadows. However, he managed to carefully make his way down to the first floor.

Still, the phone continued to ring, and ring again as he turned on a light near the main room. Fear overpowered his exhaustion as he reached for the phone. He knew the voice he would hear. He wondered why he had been chosen.

The phone rang one last time before he lifted the receiver. He was trembling when he put it to his ear. "Hello?" he answered. His voice was tired and meek.

He felt the presence of the person on the other end. He knew it was her. It was the woman who had called before. Moments past, and his fear grew.

Finally, she spoke. Her voice sounded shaky and frightened. "Help me!" she begged. "Please! Help me!"

"Who is this?" he called into the phone. "How can I help you if . . ."

It was too late. He heard the click. The steady hum of the dial tone dismissed his question before he could finish. He placed the receiver back in its cradle. He looked at the phone for a minute with a disquieting concern. Then, he unplugged the instrument from the wall with an impatient yank.

"There!" he declared. "That should put an end to this crap."

He stood in the short hall that led from the living room to the kitchen. The only lamp he had turned on downstairs offered limited visibility. He desperately wanted to go back to sleep. He knew it would be impossible.

He threw on some shoes. He grabbed his car keys and an umbrella. He stepped out into the bothersome rain. The umbrella stayed closed as he approached the car door. He let the mild showers cool his face and run through his hair as he fumbled with his keys. However, he was glad to be inside when he started the engine.

Street lamps sparsely dotted the route uphill, as the rain grew heavier. Larger drops seemed to beat against the windshield with a temper. He didn't know why he felt compelled to drive there. Still, he knew where he was going.

He drove past beautiful, sleeping houses, and lush trees which rattled their leaves against the breeze. The road was dark and deserted. He just drove, without cause.

Suddenly, he stopped. The large, gray mansion was across the road. Rain drummed against the metal mailbox that announced the family name. He couldn't stop staring at this mysterious abode. Something was oddly different. The iron gate was open. The breeze toyed with it. It squeaked as it rocked back and forth beneath the mischievous showers. Plus, the walls were littered with the intrusion of multiple bright lights. It appeared as though every light in the house was on. He continued to stare because something else seemed to be amiss. The front door of the house was also open. It banged against the house as a bright light from the hallway inside seemed to beckon.

He sat in the safety of his car and watched. He watched the iron gate and the wooden door flail about as rain and wind batted them around like a cruel children's game. And between the breeze and the showers, a voice seemed to whisper, "Come in."

He couldn't believe his ears. His motor was running. He could feel his car beneath him. He could see the raindrops pelting his windows. He could see the lights shining from inside the mansion. He watched the iron gate and the wooden door swaying unchecked as a rebellious gust swept by.

And, again the voice coaxed, "Come in. Join us."

He felt a fearful chill beneath his skin. He stepped on the gas and continued his journey uphill. He didn't stop until he reached the cemetery. The rain was cumbersome and unremitting. He opened his umbrella as he stepped out onto the puddled pavement.

The rain bounced loudly off his protective cover as he strode through the rusted entrance. The compulsion to return to that spot grew stronger. He didn't know why, but he was certain it would be there this time. Walking became imperative.

The rows of tombstones moved quickly behind him as he neared his destination. He could see his destination getting closer. He smiled as the rain soaked the cracked asphalt beneath his feet. He could see the hole in the ground. He could see the fresh mound of dirt turning to mud beside the fresh grave. "I knew it!" he said to himself.

He stepped off the path. He strolled through the muddy grass to the hole he was meant to find. "He peered into its depth as he proclaimed, "I knew it was here all along."

He leaned over and looked deeper into the opening. However, he was not prepare to see a human skeleton lying in the dirt at the bottom. There was no casket. There was no protection. There was only a skeleton resting in the grave and getting filthy in the rain.

He was startled by the unexpected sight. He lost his footing in the slippery grass. He fell into the six-foot gap. He fell face first onto the skeleton.

He screamed as he jumped to his feet. He was wet and dirty as he glanced down at the skeleton. It just lay there. His breathing was anxious. He didn't seem to realize he had dropped his umbrella out at ground level when he slipped. The rain poured over him as he stared at the lifeless collection of bones at his feet.

It was almost silly that the skull appeared to be staring back at him. He knew the thing was harmless.

Then, it moved. He screamed again as the grave's occupant slowly raised its bony arm. He was petrified. The skeleton pointed its bony finger toward the interloper. Then, it stretched its arm toward the side of the hole. It dug its finger into the dirt wall of the grave. With a bony, thin index finger, the skeleton wrote the letter "K" in the dirt wall beside him. Then, the arm dropped back to its original position.

He didn't have time to scream again.

The floor dropped out from under him. He fell deep into the earth.

He fell quickly and silently through a narrow aperture that seemed endless. There was no way to stop himself. There was no way to scream. There was nothing to do but fall.

Suddenly, he was standing on a street corner. He recognized this place. It was the corner of Fifth and Lark. He knew the fried chicken place by the newsstand. This was only three blocks away from his old home in Yonkers. He glanced around in awe. Everything was just as he remembered. These were the right stores. The buildings and faces all looked so familiar. He was back in his old neighborhood!

He laughed as he spun around. He wanted to take in everything. He watched, laughed and spun around, until . . .

She stood right in front of him. She was close enough to touch. He could see her. He could smell the sweet hint of her perfume. Her auburn hair blew delicately in the gentle breeze. Those enchanting blue eyes could still break a heart with a glance. But, her smile could heal any pain.

"Kristina!" he gasped. "It can't be! You're . . . You're dead!"

"That's right, Russell," she softly replied. "I'm deceased."

"What? Then, how . . .?"

"I will always love you," she said. "And, I know that in your own way, you will always love me. But, I'm gone and you're not. You have to move on, honey. You have to leave this town behind. You have to live again. You have to love again. You must live on. You must."

"I have," he stammered. "I mean, I want to. I mean, I have . . ."

Her face began to melt. Flesh dripped off her like hot candle wax in fast-forward.

"Kristina!" he shouted. "What's happening?"

He could see her vacant eye sockets. Her bare cheek bones were visible beneath chunks of falling skin. "Move on, Russell," she advised. "Let me go and move on."

"Kristina!" he called. "Don't leave me!"

"It's too late," her naked skeleton said. "Let me go, Russell. Move on."

He watched in silent horror as the skeleton quickly crumbled to dust. It tumbled to the ground before him. It fell at his feet like a pile of ashes. He stared in dismay at the pile of insignificant gray dirt at his feet. He stared for a long time.

Then, he glanced up. He gasped as he saw her again. She was in the driver's seat. He recognized the car. It was a red Ford Taurus. It was the last car she ever drove. It was the last car they owned before . . .

She waved and smiled at him as she pulled away from the curb. The car seemed to move so slowly. Still, she smiled and waved.

She didn't see the Global Freight Express truck as it barreled toward her from the left. She just smiled and waved.

"Kristina!" he called out. "Watch out! Look to your left! There's a truck coming!"

She didn't hear him. She just smiled and waved. The car moved so slowly. The truck was coming too fast. It was aimed right at the driver's side door.

"Kristina!" he yelled. "Look out for that truck!"

She still didn't hear him. She smiled and waved. The car seemed to move too slowly. The truck was coming on way too fast. It was about to plow into the driver's side door.

"Kristina!" he called. "KRISTINA!"

He sat up in bed. The room was dark. He was desperately gasping for air. He was sweating profusely. He glanced around as he tried to catch his breath. He recognized the room. It was the main bedroom in his new house in Autumn. He kept looking around to be sure. His breathing stabilized.

As soon as he was able, he put his face in his hands.

He began to cry.

* * * * * *

The center cash register was unoccupied. The women at the other two registers were giggling when she took her seat. "Good morning, Heidi," they chorused.

Hi," she said. "God, Tamara. Look at you. You've only been gone three days. How did you get so tanned?"

"We were at the beach."

"And, I've never seen hair that blonde in my life," Heidi continued.

"So, I wanted a change," Tamara said. "But, enough about me. Tell me what's happening with you. Daisy tells me you finally found a man."

"Daisy!" she snipped. "You promised to keep your mouth shut!"

"It's only Tamara," she said. "What's the harm?"

"You're kidding me," Heidi shot back. "You might as well have plastered the headline on the front page of The Autumn Chronicle!"

Donald Gorman

"What's your problem, Heidi," Tamara retorted. "You should be proud. This is the biggest scoop to hit this town in five years. Now, tell me all about him. Is he cute?"

"Yes," Daisy answered quickly. "He's about thirty . . ."

"Great age for you, Heidi," Tamara commented. "You're going to turn 28 next month, aren't you?"

"Don't rub it in, Tamara," she said. "You're only seven months younger than I am."

"And, get this," Daisy added. "He's rich, and he just bought this store."

Tamara pretended to gasp in shock. "Let me get this straight," she teased. "Our little Heidi, the girl who's avoided all male contact for the last twelve months . . . she just landed our new boss?"

"I didn't 'land' anybody," she denied. "We're not even going out, really. We just had a few drinks. . . ."

She paused while her face grew a few shades pinker. "And, last night," she added. "He offered to take me to dinner. But, it was all very innocent."

"So, where'd he take you?" Daisy asked first.

"Well, he's new in town," she explained. "He doesn't really know his way around, so I suggested The Turtle's Nest."

"Wow, honey," Tamara snickered. "You're digging your claws in deep nice and early, aren't you?"

"It's no big deal," she defended. "I like their eggplant parmesan."

"Eggplant, huh?" Tamara teased.

"I think our little Heidi is smitten," Daisy alleged.

"I am not!"

"Did you sleep with him?" Tamara asked.

"No!"

"But, you kissed him," Tamara observed. "I can tell. How was it?"

Her friends giggled as her face turned beet red.

"Kinda nice," she finally admitted.

"I think you're right, Daisy," Tamara poked. "Our little Heidi *is* smitten."

"Quit it, you guys!"

"Okay," Daisy said. "Let's leave her alone. It's almost time to open."

"That's right," Heidi said. "Let me count my money so I can open my drawer. And, I swear, Tamara. If you tell Marilyn or Stacy about this, I'll kill you!"

"Don't worry, babe. Your secret's safe with me."

* * * * * *

The clouds had all but departed. A strong, proud sun dried the pavement. An occasional breeze fanned rainwater from tree branches. Air conditioners could be heard from neighboring houses. The late morning air smelled of freshly-bathed, wet grass.

He sat barefoot on the cement steps which began the walkway leading to his front porch. He picked a few dandelions and threw them out into the road. He sipped coffee in the shade of a row of birch trees that lined the narrow street. He felt more relaxed. The unpleasant dream from the previous night was fading from memory.

He still missed her. He would always love her. But, the dream was his own way of accepting a valuable message. He knew it. That's why he moved to Autumn.

A young teenager strolled slowly up the hill. The bag slung over his shoulder made him look like a newspaper delivery boy. He watched the youngster's approach. The kid didn't seem to notice him at first. He readjusted his canvass bag. He checked the baseball cap which sat snug and backwards on his head. He looked down at his sneakers as he walked.

Then, the boy looked up. He noticed the man with a coffee cup sitting on the steps. "Hey, Mister," he said. "I don't remember seeing you around here. Are you new in the neighborhood?"

"Yes."

"Do you get a daily paper?" the kid asked.

"No."

"Would you like to subscribe to . . .?" the kid began. Then, he stopped. He looked beyond the man on the steps. Then, he said, "Never mind."

He sat up straight and studied the kid. "Why did you stop your sales pitch?" he asked.

"No reason," the kid shrugged.

"I'm really curious," he persisted. "I was thinking of getting a paper."

The kid hesitated for a moment. Then, he pointed as he asked, "Is this your house?"

"That's right."

"Well . . ." the kid struggled for a proper response.

"What's wrong with my house?"

"People don't tend to stay there very long," the kid reluctantly replied.

"They don't?"

"As a matter of fact," the kid explained, "People tend to leave real sudden. The last family still owed me money."

"Is that so?"

"Yup," the kid nodded. "It hardly seems worth the hassle of even starting you on my route."

"And, you think the problem comes from my house?"

"I'm almost sure of it," the kid announced. "That's the Beckenbauer house. Didn't they tell you? Everybody around here knows about the Beckenbauer house."

"What about it?"

"It's haunted," the kid explained with a fascinated look in his eye. "I don't blame people for leaving there real sudden. I wouldn't spend a night in that house for all the money in the world."

"It's just a house," he stated.

"I don't think so, Mister," the kid argued while shaking his head. "People have died there. And, not just a long time ago. Recently, too. They say Mr. Pratt and his wife were stabbed to death four years ago in the summer of '98."

"And, you think the house is to blame?"

"Well," the kid explained. "Things haven't been right in that house since Old Man Beckenbauer and his wife got killed by Gordon Van Pouck back in 1929."

"Gordon Van Pouck killed the Beckenbauers?" he asked.

"Everybody thinks so, anyway," the kid said. "I don't think it was ever proven. They never even found the wife's body. They figure that's why they both haunt the place. Mr. and Mrs. Beckenbauer are searching for each other 'til the end of time. Or at least until they find her body so they can bury her next to her husband in Nobody's Grave."

"Nobody's Grave?"

"That's what they call the plot next to Mr. Beckenbauer's grave," the kid explained. "They call it that because nobody can be buried there . . . well, nobody except the old guy's wife."

"Why can't anyone else be buried there?" he asked.

"They've tried," said the kid. "Since they've given up on finding Mrs. Beckenbauer, they've tried to bury a few people in that spot. But, they can't break ground."

"They can't?"

"They've tried shovels, jackhammers," said the kid. "Even a backhoe. Nothing works. Some people say Beckenbaur's spirit is reserving it for his wife. Some people even say that if you go there late at night, you can see the grave dug up and waiting for her."

His eyes grew wide. He felt a chill as he listened to the kid's tale.

"Have you ever seen that?" he asked.

"No," said the kid. "But, I know people who have. My friend Ryan Anderson told me he saw someone get swallowed up in that thing."

"Do you believe him?"

"He tells stories sometimes," the kid shrugged. "But, I believe him about that, though. I would never go in Nobody's Grave if I saw it. Some say that if you go in it, you can see answers to your own deepest fears and issues. Others say you can see the truth about what happened to Mrs. Beckenbauer . . . maybe even where to find her body, so she can be reunited with her husband."

"Really?"

"Some people think that's the only thing that'll bring your house to rest," the kid said. "If Mrs Beckenbauer is buried beside her husband, then their spirits will stop searching for each other. They'll finally be at peace. They'll stop chasing away or killing intruders. And, I even heard that the wife calls your house on the phone . . . looking for her husband and begging him to help her escape Gordon Van Pouck. What's the matter, Mister? You're as white as a sheet. Are you okay?"

"I'm fine," he muttered.

"Well, listen," said the kid. "If I'm not home in time for lunch, my mom will kill me. Take it easy, Mister."

"Hey, kid," he said. "What's your name?"

"Mitchell. Why?"

"Well, why are you delivering papers this late in the morning?" he asked.

"School doesn't start again until tomorrow," Mitchell explained. "I'm in no hurry until then. Last day of summer vacation. Good luck with that house, Mister. You're going to need it."

"Thanks, Mitchell."

He watched the boy stroll slowly up the hill.

* * * * * *

The morning rush was over. They knew to expect a lull before the midday rush. She toyed with her long, very blonde ponytail as she asked, "What's the matter, Heidi? You should be excited. You know, dating the new boss and everything."

"That's part of the problem right there," she pointed out. "You guys are talking like I'm going after the boss just because he's the boss."

"I'm sorry," she said. "I didn't mean it like that. I was just kidding."

"You're always kidding, Tamara," she complained. "It's hard moving on after Charlie. Every time I even want to like somebody, I'm afraid he's going to turn into another Charlie. I don't need that shit anymore."

"I know, honey," she said. "That's why we keep pushing you, or setting up dates for you. We want you to move on. We want you to be happy."

69

"Sometimes, I think I'm better off by myself," she muttered.

"No," Daisy interjected. "It's better to be alone than to be with someone like Charlie. And, it's good to take time to heal. But, you don't want to curl up inside yourself and die, either. You can't be afraid to love forever."

"She's right, Heidi."

She was quiet for a moment. She stared at the keys on her cash register. "You know, I saw him last night," she mumbled.

"What?" Tamara gasped. "Who?"

"Charlie," she said. "He came into the bar I was in with Russell. I didn't even know he hung out in that place."

"What happened?" Daisy asked in shock.

"Not much," she explained. "He was drunk. But, Russell and the bartender ran him off before anything really happened. Luckily, Jack was there to drag him out of there, too. That helped. The bartender said he'd bar Charlie from the place. He offered us a free round of drinks, also. But, I just had to get out of there. The whole thing made me wonder if it's the right time to start something new."

"Listen, Heidi," Daisy advised. "Don't you dare let Charlie run the rest of your life! You're through with him. He's gone, and you have to live again. From what little I know about Russell Wilburn, he's a good, smart, sensitive man. He's definitely not another Charlie. He's a nice looking guy, and I can see why you like him. And, you do like him. I can tell."

"You guys always think you know me so well," she complained. "I'm not even dating Russell officially. Sure, we had dinner after we got rid of Charlie. And a kiss . . . or two. And, I gave him my number, but . . ."

"Well, what do you call that, Heidi?" Tamara asked.

"I don't know."

"You obviously like this guy," Tamara insisted. "Even I can see that, and I haven't even met him yet. You could use a good break right now. Plus, this guy's going to be your new boss in a few weeks. This could be just what you need, Heidi. You can't run away and hide inside yourself forever. Give yourself a chance to be happy, babe. You deserve it."

"You're right," she said. "But, still . . ."

"Don't second guess yourself on this," Daisy urged. "Don't drag your feet or play with his head. Russell's not going to wait around for you forever. I'm not saying you have to jump into bed with him. But, don't keep pushing him away. Russell could be the best thing to happen to you in a long, long time. Don't let Charlie take that away from you."

She thought for a moment. Then, she said, "Okay. You both made your point. I do deserve this. But, I'm still going to take it slow."

"That's my girl," Tamara beamed. "Now, hang on. We have a few customers coming."

* * * * * *

There was a sign over the aisle that read, "Bathroom Fixtures". He walked over to the display of shower heads. He inspected the merchandise. He didn't notice the older man with a bad comb-over walk past.

The man's face wrinkled with a big, friendly smile when he caught a glimpse of a familiar face. "Russell?" he said. "Is that you?"

He looked up with a startled expression. "Oh," he said. "Jerry Burgdorf? How are you today?"

The old man's tone was cordial and sincere as they shook hands. "It's nice to see you, my boy," he said. "I wasn't expecting to run into you here in the hardware store."

"Yes," he agreed. "This is a pleasant surprise. I'm just picking up a few things. You know, a brand new homeowner. There's a few odds and ends to fix up. The upstairs bathroom's going to need some work. I think I'm going to have to regrout the whole thing. But, it could be worse."

"Ah, yes," Jerry nodded. "The trials and tribulations of ownership. I understand."

"By the way," he added. "I wanted to thank you and your wife again for inviting me to your party yesterday. I had a great time."

"Think nothing of it, Russell," Jerry said. "You're more than welcome. We were both so glad you could make it. We wanted to help you meet your neighbors, so you can fit in better on our cozy little street."

"That's very kind of you."

"So," Jerry said. "You're having some problems in the bathroom, are you? How does the rest of the house look? As I recall, the last time I was in there, the place was in good shape overall."

"Yes," he agreed. "It's a good, sound building. But, there are a couple of troubles I could mention."

"Like what?"

"Why don't you tell me?" he asked. "I got the impression that you were hiding something from me the first day we met."

Jerry found it difficult to look him in the eye. "What do you mean?" he asked.

"Things have happened in my house the past few days," he said politely. "Strange things. I doubt that I have to explain them to you. I get the feeling that you're well aware of a certain situation involving that house."

"What could I possibly know?" Jerry asked. He began to fidget. "Listen. If you think something strange happened, it's probably your imagination. You're alone in a new town, with a new house and new responsibilities. It's bound to put you on edge."

"Something is definitely going on here," he pressed. He maintained an even tone as he continued, "The whole town knows about it. I've heard stories from more than one source. I'm sure you and Maria know about this, but for some reason, you keep trying to hide the truth from me."

Jerry gave in with a sigh. "It's not that we're hiding the truth," he defended. "We just don't want to cause you any unnecessary stress. Sure, we know the legends and fairy tales that have been floating around this town longer than we've been alive. But, that's all they are. Fairy tales. Almost every town in the world has had some rich, powerful family with a checkered past. And, those families probably all get away with stuff that they shouldn't have done. Tall tales and legends always circulate around such people. And over time, those stories get embellished. We just wanted to protect you from those stories as long as possible."

"Did you think you could keep this town's history a secret forever?" he asked.

"Of course not," Jerry admitted. "Every resident of Autumn knows the legends. Children are raised on them, for Pete's sake! But, there's nothing to be afraid of. And, there's nothing wrong with your house! Maria and I have watched poor Mrs. Kellerman try to sell that place ten times in the past twenty years. And every time we think we have a new neighbor, they go screaming out of there before the first mortgage payment comes due. And, it's all because they listen to stupid fabrications from dim-witted locals with nothing better to do than stir up trouble."

"You think the locals are trying to start trouble?" he asked.

"Not all of them, obviously," Jerry said. "And, they may not mean anything intentionally. It depends on who you're talking to."

"Clayton Spencer told me a few things at your party yesterday," he said.

"The plumber?" Jerry mocked. "Now, he's a troublemaker."

"And, I was talking to a paperboy named Mitchell this morning," he added.

"Mitchell Lorenzo?" Jerry scoffed. "He delivers our paper. The boy's thirteen years old. He's a typical kid. He's not a bad boy, but he's been late with our Chronicle every day these last couple of months. They all tell stories. I suppose he told you the one about some magical grave that only appears in the cemetery at midnight. And, it's only visible to certain people. The kids all live for that nonsense. Of course, no one believes it except for the local kids. And, nobody has seen that grave except for children who are trying to impress their silly friends."

"I'm telling you," he insisted. "I've seen things."

"Listen, Russell," Jerry said. "Maria and I both like you. You seem to be a smart man with a lot of good qualities. Don't let blow-hards and little kids fill your head with childish twaddle. You have a mind. Use it. Surely, you see how ridiculous this is."

He closed his eyes and took a deep breath. "Maybe you're right," he finally agreed. "What could I have been thinking? Things like this just don't happen. I moved here to get a fresh start in life. Why am I listening to paperboys?"

"That's the spirit, Russell," Jerry grinned and gave him a pat on the back. "There's nothing to fear. And, I promise there's nothing wrong with your house."

"I'm sorry, Jerry," he said. "I guess it's harder than I thought to start life all over. I'll probably be okay once I settle in."

"I'm sure you will," Jerry nodded. "Nobody can blame you for needing time to adjust. I'd hate to think how I would handle beginning again in brand new surroundings after losing my wife. I just hope you find the strength to keep moving forward."

"I will," he said. "Thanks again. And, tell Maria I'll return her pans soon, too."

"Take your time, son," Jerry said. "There's no rush. You have all the time in the world."

When he was finished at the hardware store, he took a drive through downtown Autumn. The sky was a firm, unadulterated blue. A few small, white clouds floated by like puffy cartoon fish without purpose. The sun burdened the streets below with an oppressive heat. Swimming pools and fans worked to ease the pain of summer's final showdown.

His pleasant drive eventually brought him back to a familiar parking lot. There were a few cars parked in various spaces near the brick building's entrance. Still, he had plenty of room for his vehicle. He made his way quickly from his car to the nearest sliding door in the front of the store. He wanted to avoid the outside heat.

Inside was cool and comfortable. Soft rock music played quietly in the background. A few customers could be seen shopping in the aisles. All three cash registers were attended. Two of the cashiers were finishing with their last patron each as he approached their area.

"Good afternoon, ladies," he said.

They all said hello.

"You're looking lovely today, Daisy," he said.

"Thank you, Russell."

"It's especially nice to see you, Heidi," he said.

"You too," she replied. "Russell Wilburn, this is Tamara Rosenthal. She's one of our best cashiers. Russell just bought this store. He'll be taking it over next month."

"It's a pleasure to meet you, Tamara," he said. "Did you say Rosenthal? Are you related to the man who runs the deli counter?"

"He's my uncle," she replied while trying to control her smile. "He got me this job, but I didn't want to work directly under him."

"I understand," he said. He ignored her obvious visual inspection. "Well, I look forward to seeing you here again."

"Me, too," she said. "It's great to meet you, sir."

"Is Bill Green here today?" he asked. "He's the main reason I'm here. We really do have to go over the books again before the end of the month."

"He's in the back," Daisy said. "In his . . . I mean, *your* office."

"Thank you," he said. "Heidi, may I call you later?"

"Sure," she said. "I get out at 5:00 today."

"Great," he said. "Do you have plans for dinner?"

She glanced back and forth at her friends. "No," she replied with a beautiful, timid smile.

"Maybe we can rectify that, if I call around 6:00?" he inquired.

"That would be nice," she said.

"Wonderful," he said. "I'll let you girls get back to work, then. Daisy, it's always a pleasure to see you. Tamara, it was delightful to meet you. And Heidi, we'll talk in a little while."

They all said good-bye as he turned and walked toward the back of the store. They watched silently until he was gone.

Then, Tamara turned to her friend with a gleam in her eye. "Oh my God, Heidi," she practically squealed. "He's gorgeous! I'd dump Josh for him in a second! I swear, if you don't scarf him up immediately, I'm never speaking to you again!"

"Tamara!" she whined as her cheeks reddened.

"I told you so," Daisy reminded playfully.

"I mean it," Tamara insisted. "You're just lucky you saw him first. He's perfect for you. This is exactly what you need right now, honey. If you let him get away, I'm going to lose all respect for you."

"Isn't that a little drastic?" Heidi asked.

"Not in the least," Tamara replied firmly.

She was rushing around her apartment and getting dressed at 6:10. She still had so much to do. She was checking herself in the mirror when the phone rang. She gave him her address. She told him that he could pick her up at 7:00.

He did his research. He knew the perfect place to take her to dinner. He was only a few minutes late when he arrived on her doorstep. He waited patiently on the sofa for her to finish getting ready for their date. He commented on how beautiful she looked.

She thanked him. She told him the flowers were lovely. She put them in water before they left.

They drove to a wooded area near the eastern edge of Autumn. It was a peaceful, leisurely ride. The sun was still a bit too warm. It had begun to sink into a billowy cushion of passing clouds. Traffic was moderate and steady. The heavy air had changed somewhat in its sticky sweetness. It was almost as if the unofficial end of summer had been duly notarized.

Nicole's Secret Retreat was a beautiful little restaurant. It was tucked far enough away from the main road to be discreet. Inside, the atmosphere was elegant, yet informal. The intimate ambiance was not as pronounced as it had been in the place they'd attended the night before. Still, it offered an appropriate mood for the evening.

They were seated at a cozy little table near the picture window.

"This is a nice place," she said. "I've never even heard of it. I thought you didn't know this town. How did you ever find it?"

"It wasn't hard," he said. "You just have to be willing to put some effort into looking. Of course, I'm not sure what to do after dinner. I checked a newspaper for theaters. We could always see a movie. What do you like? Action? Comedy?"

"I don't care," she said. "You decide."

"Comedy it is, then," he said without hesitation.

She allowed a quick laugh while saying, "Fine. Oh, look. The sun is starting to set. You can almost catch a glimpse of it between the trees. It's beautiful tonight."

"It certainly is," he agreed. He wasn't looking out the window.

She glanced down at her drink with a shy smile.

"Would you call this our first date, or our second?" he asked.

"I'm not sure," she said. "I guess you could call it our second. It's more like one and a half, really."

"That sounds reasonable."

"I just hope Charlie doesn't come along and ruin this one," she added.

"I'll make a deal with you," he said. "I promise not to mention my late wife, if you promise not to mention Charlie. I want us both to enjoy this evening."

"You're right," she agreed. "Daisy and Tamara told me to move on and leave that jerk behind me already. Of course, they're right. They practically pushed me into this date. God, I hope I don't mess this up. They'd never forgive me."

"You can't possibly mess this up," he assured her. "All you have to do is be yourself. Let everything flow naturally. I like you. And, I think you like me. Everything should come together like a puzzle that solves itself."

"Is there such a thing?" she inquired.

"We're about to find out, I suppose."

Her big, green eyes spoke with a greater ability than words.

"By the way," he added. "I hope it's all right that I asked you out in front of your friends. I usually prefer to exercise a bit more discretion. But, I got the strong impression that if I didn't ask you out right then and there, Tamara was going to handcuff us together anyway."

"You picked up on that, too?" she giggled. "I have to admit, Tamara is a very opinionated girl. She always knows exactly what everyone should be doing at all times."

"She obviously cares about you, though," he said. "I think she's just trying to look out for you. I have friends telling me that I have to let go of my past, too. It makes sense. The future won't happen unless you make it happen."

"Well, then," she said while raising her glass. "Here's to 'making it happen'."

He raised an eyebrow. "Making it happen," he agreed.

They clinked their glasses together. They each took a sip.

After a fine dinner and a movie, he drove her home. By then, it had cooled a little. The darkness had cloaked the town with the enticing splendor of mystery. The moon was slowly vanishing. Still, it was bright and boastful. The stars seemed dim and meek. Evidently, they hadn't learned that there was safety in their numbers.

The question grew stronger in her mind as they neared her home. However, she did not allow it to interfere with their conversation. When they reached her building, she invited him in for coffee.

Her apartment was small, but clean and tasteful. They sat together on the sofa with two steaming mugs on the coffee table. They assessed each other as a puzzle neared its resolution.

"I had a wonderful time tonight," she said. "I'm glad the girls pushed me into this."

"Did they really have to push you into anything?"

"Not really," she confessed. "I probably would have gone even without their help. But, a little nudging did make the decision easier."

"Well, I'm glad you came, too," he said. "Maybe your friend Tamara knows what she's doing, after all."

"Maybe," she agreed with a smile. "She's a bright girl."

"She doesn't have your eyes, though."

"Is that your standard line, cowboy?" she questioned with mock disapproval.

"No," he grinned. "I reserve it for very special occasions."

She giggled for a moment before their kiss. It drew them closer together. It beckoned them to approach the fire at the heart of the puzzle.

"If I remember correctly," he pointed out. "Isn't tomorrow your day off?"

"Yes," she said. "I wanted to catch up on some sleep. And, I have some errands to run. Why?"

"No reason in particular," he said.

She knew what he meant. She was tempted.

"I really am very tired," she said. "I've worked a lot of hours this week."

"I understand."

The brief pause was just a little uncomfortable.

"Do you think this could be a mistake?" she asked. "After all, you're going to be my boss soon. Don't you think it'll be a bit awkward?"

"It shouldn't have to be," he said. "I won't be spending much time anywhere at work that would require much contact at the store. I probably won't even be there every day. Besides, we're both reasonably mature adults. There's no need for problems."

"I'm not looking forward to the gossip and the funny looks," she said. "The people I work with can be rather juvenile."

"Just ignore the people at work," he said. "And if anyone gives you a hard time, remember I can fire them."

She giggled again before their next kiss. This one was longer. It was calling them even closer to the flame at the heart of their puzzle. Perhaps, the flame itself was growing larger and warmer.

They looked at each other afterward. And, another kiss was necessary. This kiss became a warm cushion against the cold, hard emptiness. It was a pillow that was no longer out of reach. It was wrapped in the silken comfort of a long-forgotten willfulness.

Then, she said, "You really have to go."

"Are you sure?" he asked.

"Yes," she said. "I had a great time. Thanks for everything. But, I have to get some sleep."

"Okay," he said. "I'll call you tomorrow. I'd really like to spend some time with you. We should get to know each other a little better. At least, for the sake of harmony in the workplace."

"That's true," she agreed softly. "We really should."

They said their final good-bye with a kiss. It told of each other's pain at parting. It spelled out forthcoming wishes. And, this moment was not all they shared.

He drove home in the muggy darkness of Autumn. Traffic was light. Labor Day was long over for most people. The sweet air of nighttime lingered like a hint of perfume. The waning moon watched over the sleepy town. And, stars rested like weary travelers across the blackened sky.

Somehow, he felt happy as he drove through the quiet streets. The evening replayed in his mind as he neared his home. He drove casually with one hand on the wheel. With his other hand, he raised an imaginary glass.

"Here's to 'making it happen'," he whispered.

CHAPTER 5.....
THE_GRAY_MANSION_____

He drove up Agnes St. His mood was relaxed and pleasant. Beautiful houses lined the dark road behind tall, stately trees. Most of the houses had a few lights on, but not many. One by one, the residents of Autumn were turning in for the night.

The air was warm and calm. His radio played quietly. He drove up the gentle slope of the hill. He continued driving past his home. He didn't realize he was doing it. He just kept driving at an easy pace.

Suddenly, he began to wonder what he was doing. He glanced around as he recognized the block he was passing. An S.U.V. passed him heading downhill. He kept his foot on the gas pedal. He steered straight toward the cemetery.

A disturbing sensation came over him as he entered a familiar block. Once again, he felt compelled to park by the big, gray mansion that was set back from the road. He grew nervous as he studied the ominous building from his car seat. Once again, all the lights were on in the house. Once again, the iron gate was wide open. The front door was agape as well. It seemed as though the house itself was inviting him to enter.

He began to tremble as he stared at the enormous structure. The urge to accept the mansion's invitation was becoming stronger. His curiosity toward this house was becoming a fascination. He didn't want the fascination to turn into an obsession. He wanted to drive away, but he didn't.

A sudden breeze blew by. Perhaps it was more of a gusty wind. It knocked the iron gate back with an eerie squeaking sound. It banged noisily against itself two or three times. The metallic clanking seemed hollow and mysterious. In addition, he heard a voice amid the windy gusts whisper, "Come in."

He sat frozen and quivering as he stared at the mansion. The open gate squeaked again. And, he stared.

Finally, he turned away. He wanted to go home. However, he drove uphill. He continued his journey to the cemetery. His compulsion made him feel uneasy. He feared Nobody's Grave. Still, he knew it beckoned his return.

He parked by the cemetery gate. He hurried through the opening. Although, his pace grew slower after entering. He became cautious. He wanted to turn back, but his feet carried him forward. The knot in his stomach tightened as he neared the point of his apprehension. Tombstones were lined up like motionless toy soldiers awaiting battle instructions. He was still a few rows away in the dismal darkness. However, he could see the fresh hole in the ground. He could see the pile of dirt which held the filthy shovel upright. He swallowed hard with the realization that he must continue.

His steps were quiet and measured. His heartbeat quickened. He proceeded with care and vigilance. Something drew him nearer, but he did not want to obey. Still, his feet followed one after the other. Anxiety and curiosity fought for control of his thoughts, as he stepped up to the well-manicured, gaping fissure in the earth. He planted his feet near its treacherous edge. He was mindful not to get too close. He strongly wished to avoid any repeats of his last adventure at this site.

Slowly, he leaned forward. He needed to know why he had been summoned. It was imperative that he discover his intended purpose.

His gaze fell deeper into the pit as he leaned over its edge. A sweat broke out on his forehead as goosebumps plagued his flesh. It was almost as if he knew.

Then, he saw it lying without fanfare on the dirt floor of the grave. It rested motionless, casually outstretched in the mud. It appeared to be the same filthy skeleton that had occupied this space earlier. It startled him. He pulled back with a gasp.

After the initial shock however, he felt the strong urge to look back into the hole. He remained brutally cautious. He slowly leaned forward again. He knew the human skeleton would be there. He knew it would look identical to the one he had encountered before. But, something was different this time. One detail caught his attention.

As he gazed down at the fetid human remains, he noticed something that had escaped his watchful eye before. He stared at it from his lofty vantage point. The skeleton stayed still and lifeless as he focused. "Is that a gold chain around its neck?" he finally muttered to himself. "With a locket? Was she wearing that last time? Kristina never wore anything like that."

Then, the skull moved. It turned slightly. It gave the impression that its eye holes were staring at the intruder above. The man jumped with a start. However, he could not look away from the intimidating collection of bones in his sight.

Suddenly, its lower jaw dropped open as it emitted a menacing hiss. He cried out in alarm. Still, he couldn't move from the spot where he stood. He felt compelled to watch as a bony arm slowly reached up from the bottom of the grave. The skeleton pointed a long, slender finger at the intruder. Then, it turned its hand around. He could hear the clacking of bone against bone as the hand curled into a loose fist . . . all except for the skinless index finger. It used that finger to beckon the man into the hole.

"Oh no!" he insisted while shaking his head. "I'm not going back in there!"

The skinless finger continued to beckon, silent except for the scraping together of naked bones.

"No!" he repeated. "I won't! You can't force me!"

Then, he felt a hand on his back. He didn't see who pushed him from behind. All he saw was the skeleton growing closer as he plummeted into the grave. He screamed as he fell helplessly onto the waiting human remains.

It sickened him to once again have this contact with the grime and rot of death. The bones made it difficult to brace himself in the dirt. However, he managed to leap off the skeleton as quickly as possible.

The skull was still staring at him. The bony arm was still raised. The index finger still pointed outward as the arm fell against the filthy wall of the grave. Again, it carved the letter "K" into the dirt.

"No," he begged. "Not again. Please don't make me watch that again."

He could only watch as the bony finger traced a second letter into the wall.

He was still frightened. However, he observed, "K-A? What does that mean?"

There was no time to wonder. The floor dropped out beneath him, as it had before. He screamed as he fell into the deep chasm of fear and despair.

He tumbled downward through the open abyss. He saw nothing around him. It was impossible to tell which way was up. He just kept falling . . .

Then, he was in a huge, spectacular room. It was decorated in an old-style fashion. The furniture must have been chic at one time. Everything was bright and festive. A crackling flame blazed in the fireplace.

Four women sat in various outmoded chairs. Their long, elegant dresses were buttoned all the way up to their necks. They each had their hair tied neatly in a bun which rested just below their elegant hats.

He thought it looked like an old Cagney movie.

The white-haired woman spoke first. "Katalina?" she asked. "When do you suppose dinner will be ready? Any proper hostess knows a Christmas goose should be served promptly at 7:00."

"I know, Mother," Katalina replied. "Good help is so hard to find."

She rang a little bell while calling (in a civilized tone), "Lillian! Lillian!"

A short, squat woman in a maid's uniform quickly emerged from a side room. "Yes, ma'am?" she answered.

"Lillian," Katalina adressed. "What time shall we expect dinner? Will the Christmas goose be ready at 7:00 as instructed? We have guests, you know."

"Yes, ma'am. Preciesely at 7:00, ma'am."

"Thank you," Katalina nodded. "That will be all."

"Yes, ma'am," said Lillian. She scurried out of the room.

"If we had agreed to dinner at our house," the blonde interjected. "We wouldn't have to worry about such things. Our Rachel is a marvel."

"Yes, Barbara," Katalina politely admitted. "But, you only have the one maid, dear."

"Girls, girls," Mother interrupted with a raised hand. "There is no need for such petty displays. That is no way for a lady to behave."

"I'm sorry, Mother," Barbara said. She changed the subject. "I have so enjoyed this Christmas. And, I look forward to the coming year. Each year seems lovelier than the last. What do you think, Mother? Will the coming year be as lovely as this one has been?"

Mother cleared her throat as she considered her response. "That's difficult to say," she finally commented. "I think 1929 holds a lot of promise, financially."

"I agree," Katalina added. "My Gordon says that business is booming. Our stocks are up, and The Market is sound . . ."

"Your Gordon!" Mother scoffed. "I have no interest in the opinions of such a wretched little man. I don't know why you would ever defy me and marry a Van Pouck, Katalina. There is something wrong with that entire family. Besides, Gordon is a widower."

"He's one of the richest men in Rhode Island," Katalina defended. "And, he can hardly be blamed for the fact that his first wife died while giving birth to his second son."

"Both of his sons are spoiled little monsters," the forth woman said.

"Vivian!" Katalina gasped. "What a thing to say in my own home! And, on Christmas day!"

"She's right, Vivian," said Mother. "You should watch what you say to your sister. Still in all, Katalina, marrying Gordon Van Pouck was an atrocious mistake."

"He treated me like a queen in the beginning," Katalina muttered as she gazed at the floor. "Everything was so perfect."

"And now?" Vivian gently prodded.

Mother frowned at Katalina's failure to respond. Finally, she spoke for her daughter. "Have you nothing to say, Katalina? There is nothing to hide in this room. Certainly, not about your husband. Gordon Van Pouck's indiscretions are legendary. I told you that he would hurt you with his infidelity."

"He was tactful with the first few," Katalina explained. "He kept them quiet and private. However, he's been flaunting his latest dalliance all over town. Everyone in Autumn knows about it, with the exception of the poor tart's husband, of course."

"It's a disgrace!" Barbara declared.

"It's difficult to feel any sympathy for a common smuggler like Edgar Beckenbauer," Mother said.

"He's not a smuggler," Vivian said. "He's a merchant with foreign connections."

"African diamond mines?" Mother scoffed. "Smuggling and hording like common beggars? Gordon is rich enough that he should be above such dealings with a man like Edgar. And, he should definitely be above toying with that man's wife! I tell you, Ingrid Beckenbauer is a woman of loose virtue! If she were here, I would give her a piece of my mind!"

"Don't get excited, Mother," said Katalina. "Remember your heart. Anyway, I'm not worried. He got over his past affairs. He'll get over this one. And, if he doesn't . . . I've been considering getting a divorce."

"Divorce?" Mother scolded. "This family will not suffer the humiliation of a divorce! You have shamed us enough by marrying that philandering smuggler, Gordon Van Pouck! You will not add divorce to the list of your scandalous insults to this family! You made your mistake, against my wishes. So, live with the consequences of your actions! You'll have to find another way to deal with your misfortune."

Katalina and Barbara glanced at each other.

"Don't get upset, Mother," Vivian advised. "Let me take you out for some fresh air. I'm sure dinner will be ready soon."

"That's a good idea, Vivian," Mother said. "Wheel me out of this room. I have had quite enough of your sister's company."

"Yes, Mother," Vivian said as she stood. As she wheeled her mother's chair out of the room, she added, "I'm sorry, girls. I must attend to Mother. I'll see you at dinner."

Katalina and Barbara said their good-byes. Then, they turned to face each other.

"Mother has gotten worse in so many ways these past few years," Barbara observed.

"Yes," Katalina nodded. "It's really quite a pity. Still, I'm glad we have this chance to talk alone. Have you spoken with your friend? The one we discussed?"

"I saw her the other day, as a matter of fact," Barbara said. "She told me that she would be delighted to meet with you."

"Splendid," Katalina smiled. "I'm so excited. The whole thing sounds so deliciously sinister and taboo. Gypsy spells, witches' beads and the like? How ever did you meet with such an unseemly character?"

"I'll make a deal with you, Sister dear," Barbara offered. "You don't meddle in my affairs, and I won't ask what you plan to do about your wretched husband."

"I've hardly slept a wink in days," Katalina said. "I'm almost giddy with anticipation. Are you sure she knows what she's doing?"

"I've heard stories from reliable sources," Barbara confided. "Name dropping would be indiscreet, of course. But, trust me. I'm sure she can deliver the results you require."

"Wonderful, darling!" Katalina beamed. "I can hardly wait. Gordon will suffer interminably for his appalling disrespect for me and our marriage. That scoundrel! He and both his sons will feel my wrath before I'm through!"

"Katalina!" her sister gasped. "You would victimize the children?"

"Why not?" she grinned. "They're not mine. It's not as though I could bear his demon spawn even if the notion appealed to me. They are all Van Poucks, and all Van Poucks are a scourge on our great society. I would like to see anyone who bears that name rue the day my husband dragged me into his world of indignity and degradation!"

"At this rate," Barbara pointed out. "You'll wind up like Mother in a few years. Be careful, won't you?"

"You let me do the worrying, my dear sister," she said. "Make the arrangements, and I'll handle the rest. I might even have a few surprises for our friends the Beckenbauers. Both of them. The insipid little fools! They have been a blemish on my marriage and family long enough!"

The sunlight awakened him. He was lying on his back. He wiped his eyes so he could stare up at a clear blue sky.

The sun was bright and amiable. He could feel and smell the grass all around him. He glanced around. Tombstones were everywhere. The marble marker beside him belonged to Edgar Beckenbauer. Still, it took him a few seconds to work out where he was.

He sat up. His neck and shoulders were a little stiff. He rubbed them to work out the kinks. He stood and brushed the dirt from his clothes. "Great," he muttered to himself. "This is my good shirt."

He looked around again and checked his watch. It was 8:33. He frowned. "I knew I shouldn't have listened to Jerry Burgdorf," he considered. "Something is very definitely wrong here. And, I refuse to lose my house!"

He walked quickly out of the cemetery. His car was waiting for him just outside the gate. He drove down the hill toward home. He slowed to a stop when he approached the big, gray mansion. He didn't expect to see anything out of the ordinary. The mailbox still announced the family name. It was hard to see if any lights were on inside. The front gate was locked shut. The front door seemed to be closed.

He expressed his disappointment with a sigh. He checked his rear view mirror. He checked for traffic. There was none. No one was anywhere in sight. The street was utterly vacant. He prepared to pull away from the curb.

Then, he heard a loud clank. It was followed by a long, creepy squeaking sound. He turned his head. The iron gate had mysteriously opened. There was still no one in sight. However, the rusted door was noticably agape, in the quiet warmth of the morning.

On closer inspection, it appeared as though the door of the mansion was also wide open. He couldn't help staring at the unsettling sight.

"Weren't they both closed a moment ago?" he wondered to himself.

With all that had happened recently, his curiosity got the better of him. The open doors stood before him like a personal invitation. It seemed obvious that he was somehow linked to this family through his house. And, he wanted answers.

He steered his car over to the waiting iron gate. He drove down the long, crumbling driveway which led to the mansion. It stood like a withering monument to pomposity as he drew near.

He parked the car in a convenient spot. He cautiously stepped out onto the cracked pavement. He took a breath for courage as he approached the mansion. Then, he slowly ascended the once beautiful staircase that led to the front door. The building had fallen into a conspicuous state of disrepair. The bannisters were leaning and useless. The steps were warped and sagging. The ouside of the house had not been painted in eons. Window shutters needed to be nailed back in place. The door knocker was rusted and tarnished. His trepidation grew as he stood on the decayed landing.

He rang the doorbell. He could hear it echo through the empty halls inside.

"Hello?" he called in. "Is anybody home?"

There was no response. He could see the lavish main room from his spot on the landing. It had once been a grand reception area. Beneath the cobwebs and layers of dust and debris stood an elegant main hall.

He rang the bell again. He used the door knocker. "Hello?" he repeated. "Were you expecting company? Mr. Van Pouck?"

Still, there was no reply.

Reluctantly, he stepped into the main hall. "Is anyone home?" he called. "I don't wish to intrude. My name is Russell Wilburn. I assume you wanted to see me?"

He listened to the echo of his voice bounce eerily through the house. It was indeed a glorious dwelling inside. Only a few lights were on. It accented the room's need of a good cleaning. The furniture must have been quite stylish once. It was tastefully decorated with original oil paintings that were obscured by years of sediment.

He took a few more steps and called out again. There appeared to be no sign of life in the house. The silence felt discomforting after the echo of his voice died out. He took a few steps toward a once magnificent staircase. It was filthy and in need of repair. At the bottom, an old man lay sprawled over the last two steps. He was nearly seated on the carpet at the foot of the stairs. Dried blood caked the front of his shirt all around the knife which was buried in his chest up to the hilt.

The visitor nearly screamed at the ghastly sight. His entire body suddenly felt cold. He shivered as he stared at the motionless spectacle before him. He took a wary step toward the body. He wanted to call out. The notion seemed futile.

He took another step.

Then, the body vanished before his eyes.

He jumped back with fright. He stared in disbelief at the blank, empty stairwell.

Then, a heard a bang and a clang behind him. Nobody was there. However, the front door of the house had closed and locked . . . apparently, without anyone's help.

He looked in awe at his blocked exit. His eyes grew wide. Had he seen a face in the door? It seemed to be a human face emanating from the dirt and wood grain in the door's surface. However, it disappeared before he could bring it into focus.

He wiped his eyes. He glanced around the room. Aside from the dust and cobwebs, everything seemed normal. "Ridiculous," he laughed at himself. "Bodies on the stairs? Faces in the door? I've got to get a hold of myself."

Still, he found the locked door a little unsettling. He decided to go further into the house. He stayed watchful. He glanced around as he slowly crossed the room.

He called out again as he entered a smaller room. This appeared to be a dining area. He still heard no response as he surveyed the dust-covered furniture and cabinets around him. There were still no signs of human activity as he ventured with caution over the creaking, dirty floor.

He neared the next doorway. He saw a flash of light out of the corner of his eye. He spun around. He caught a faint glimpse of a woman crossing the far entrance. He gasped as he recognized her face from a recent dream.

"Katalina!" he whispered in shock.

Then, she was gone. He was the only person in the room.

A chill went up his spine as he stood frozen with fear.

It took a few moments to compose himself. He needed another deep breath for courage. He was determined to continue on. He stepped with silent care through the next door.

He had entered what appeared to be a spacious study. Shelves were lined with books of all sizes. There was a beautiful, dusty antique writing desk. A few comfortable chairs were strategically placed about. There even seemed to be a small conference table. Wooden chairs lined around the table. The chair on the far side faced away from the door.

Protruding over the back of the chair, he saw a white-haired, balding head.

The unexpected sight caught him off guard. He wanted to speak. He hoped the motionless head would not vanish. He took a silent step forward as he watched with distrust. The back of the old man's head remained stationary.

The old man seemed real enough. However, he still didn't move.

"Hello?" he called.

The old man did not reply. He didn't even flinch.

"Hello?" he repeated. "Sir?"

The old man still didn't make a sound. He didn't move a muscle.

"Hello?" he called a bit louder, as he took a step closer. "Are you alive?"

The sudden response from the old man made him jump with a start.

"Certainly, I'm alive," barked a gruff voice from the chair. "Would you expect anything less?"

"I'm sorry," he said with reticence. "When you didn't answer me, I . . ."

He ran out of words. He waited for a moment. He hoped the old man would speak, or at least move.

After an uncomfortable pause, he continued, "I'm sorry to disturb you. My name is Russell Wilburn. I don't know why, but I get the impression you were expecting me."

"Perhaps I was."

"Am I addressing Elliott Van Pouck?" he asked.

"Of course not!"

The old man suddenly spun his chair around to face his guest. He quickly stood with an angry expression on his round, wrinkled face. He glared at Russell as he lept to his feet. Russell gasped and took a step backward in surprise.

What shocked him the most was that the old man was wearing a long, pink bathrobe with white fur trim.

"Do I look like Elliott to you?" snarled the old man. "I may have been married to the man for what seems an eternity, but we are hardly identical! Are you inferring that I even look mannish in any way?"

He was astounded. He could only stammer, "W-well, I . . ."

"That no good husband of mine!" complained the old man. "What has he done now? Is he in some sort of trouble?"

"N-not that I'm aware of," he replied. "Did you say that Elliott Van Pouck is your husband?"

"Yes," the old man proclaimed. "My name is Penelope. You may call me Penny."

"Penny?" he asked with alarm. "But, you're . . ."

"Pardon me?" the old man said expectantly. "Have you got something to say?"

"Uh, no," he said. He felt his skin crawl. He took a defensive stance. He was prepared to run on a moment's notice. Out of necessity, he continued, "If you're Penny, then where is your husband?"

"He's supposed to be downstairs," the old man explained. "With the children. That's where I left them last. If he's escaped, I'll be ever so annoyed."

"Escaped?"

"Oh, excuse me," Penny said. "Poor choice of words. It's not as though I'm holding him against his will. He was going to leave me once, a long time ago. But we sat down and really hashed things out. I think he's seen the error of his ways. He's usually quite docile, lately. However, he occasionally feels the need to rebel. He's like a child, sometimes. Still, he's good with the kids. He should be watching them now."

"I see." His tension was building.

"It's nearly time to feed them their breakfast," the old man informed. "Would you like to come along and meet them? We rarely get company. The children will be delighted."

"I don't want to intrude on your meal."

"Nonsense," Penny said. He walked around the table. His guest took a step backward as the old man approached. "We have plenty of food. You're welcome to join us. I did have something I wanted to tell you, my dear boy. Walk with me to the kitchen, won't you? We'll talk along the way."

"All right," he said reluctantly. He stayed behind the old man as they walked through the house. He tried to keep at a safe distance. He loosely inspected the various dusty lavish rooms as they walked.

"Do you like the house?" Penny asked. "We had it remodeled just last year. I think the decorator did a marvelous job. Don't you?"

"Yes. It looks . . . wonderful."

"The den is my favorite," Penny continued. "Elliott can't stop raving about it. Remind me to show you after breakfast."

"Okay."

They finally reached the kitchen. He was astounded. It had been a grand kitchen long ago. However, it was filthy as Russell glanced about. More than one sink was filled with dirty dishes. Floor and ceiling tiles were chipped and cracked. He hoped the stains on the wall were catsup. Plus, the counters were covered with canned food stacked in large piles. Even the floor was littered with stacks of canned groceries.

"Grab a few cans of tuna, will you please?" Penny requested. "The children like tuna. And, I think there's some sweet potatoes over on the counter. You don't mind carrying a few items, I presume."

"I, uh, I guess not," he stammered. He was feeling a bit shaky as he picked up a few cans from various piles.

"Please be careful not to spill anything," Penny said. "Elliott simply hates it when anyone leaves a mess. Oh, and can you handle that can of creamed corn? That would be lovely."

He held the items in his arms. He figured he was safe because the old man was carrying an even greater armload of cans.

Off the side of the kitchen was a large door. The old man opened the door and flipped a switch. A light immediately illuminated a dank stairway which appeared to lead to some sort of cellar.

"Follow me, please," the old man instructed.

Russell halfheartedly stayed a few steps behind Penny as they descended the stairs. Knotted wood creaked and sagged beneath his feet as he slowly traversed the ancient steps to the cellar. The light grew more dim as they neared the bottom. Odors and cobwebs grew more dense.

"Is there another light down here, Penny?" he asked anxiously.

"Of course."

He already began to regret his decision to follow the old man. It seemed to easy to get trapped in such a place. He had no idea what could be waiting down here. Not a sound could be heard. The silence was intimidating.

"Maybe I shouldn't stay," he said. "I don't wish to impose."

"Don't be ridiculous," Penny replied. He flipped another light switch. The cellar brightened somewhat. It was still a bit dismal and forlorn. "You're not an imposition. You're already here. You might as well meet the family."

The cellar was a dreary, gloomy chamber. Brick walls were cracked and weathered. Wooden rafters were warped and moldy. The old cement floor was beset with more stacks of canned goods. Cans were piled on work benches, chairs and even an unused pool table.

"Elliott!" called Penny. "Children! It's time for breakfast!"

He glanced around. He saw no one. The silence was getting rather creepy.

He waited a few extra seconds. The old man didn't move.

He felt the need to say something just to break the eerie silence. "Shouldn't we have taken a can opener down here with us?" he finally asked.

"That's not necessary," Penny explained while pointing. "There's an axe leaning against that far wall. And, a sledge hammer. Elliott will be able to manage. Just put those cans on the floor."

He watched the old man. Penny was placing the cans on the dirty cement floor. He stacked them very neatly in a brand new pile. Russell was not as demanding with his stack. He began to fidget as he waited.

It was still too quiet.

"So, where is your family?" he needed to ask.

"Down there," Penny said as if it had been a stupid question.

He began to quiver as he watched. The old man was pointing directly at the floor.

"Y-your family is under the floor?" he asked with wide eyes.

"Yes," Penny said indifferently. "I told you Elliot can be a bit rebellious. He threatened to leave. He wanted to take my children away from me. He doesn't say things like that anymore. And, the children are as good as gold."

Russell found it difficult to contain the terror that was mounting in his heart.

"Perhaps they eat too much," the old man calmly continued. "Children love their snacks. I worry about their weight, but what mother doesn't? Aside from that, the children are very well-behaved. They lie very still in a nice, neat pile . . . and hardly make a sound."

"I r-really have to go," he declared while slowly backing away.

"But, what about your breakfast?" asked the old man.

"I'm n-not hungry anymore," he stuttered. He took another step backward.

"We still haven't discussed the message I have for you," Penny reminded. "That's the reason you were invited here in the first place."

"Message?" he asked with anxious curiosity. "What message?"

"I have a message for you from Ingrid," the old man explained. "I believe you know her. Apparently, you've been staying at her house the past few days."

"Ingrid Beckenbauer?" he asked with growing concern.

"Yes," Penny nodded. "That's the woman. She wanted me to tell you something."

"And, what might that be?"

He was not entirely sure he wanted to hear the answer.

"She asked me to tell you," the old man imparted. "That she was happy to put you up for a couple of days. But, now it's time for you to leave."

"Ingrid told you this?" he asked as he took another step backward.

"That's right," said Penny. "You see, she's trying to find her husband. She thinks your presence there might interfere."

The old man stood still as he spoke. However, Russell felt an increasing urge to escape. He took another step backward. He was nearly at the foot of the musty wooden stairwell.

"I really need to leave, Penny," he announced timidly.

"Take my advice, Russell," Penny conveyed. "Don't overstay your welcome. Ingrid is a fine woman, but she does have a bit of a temper. And, her husband's even worse."

"I'll keep that in mind," he replied with one foot on the warped bottom stair. "Good-bye, Penny. It was nice to have met you."

He quickly made his way up the stairs. Boards creaked and sagged beneath his feet as he rapidly moved toward the ground floor.

"Would you like me to show you out?" the old man offered. He was walking toward the stairs.

"No, thanks," he called back. "I can find the way."

"Good-bye then, Russell."

He hurried through the kitchen. However, he was careful not to knock over any of the stacks of canned food. He kept a constant eye on his surroundings as he rushed through the rooms. Each room remained still and motionless as he passed. The waning grandeur in each area of the house eluded him at this point. Escape was his only concern. One room after another loomed up before him as a potential threat. Then, it fell behind him like an obstacle that had been beaten.

Finally, he entered the great hall at the front of the house. The front door was in view. It was closed. The grand stairwell could be seen off to the side. A shadowy figure walked slowly down the steps. He refused to look at it. He only hoped the door wasn't locked as he raced toward it.

He grabbed the doorknob. He tried to turn it. It wouldn't budge.

He tried again. It still didn't move.

"Come on!" he cried. He looked behind him. The figure on the stairs was utterly silent. It was at the foot of the stairs. It turned toward him.

He grabbed the doorknob with both hands. He jiggled the handle and tried again.

The knob turned with a clunk. The door opened.

He ran outside into the sunshine. The morning was warm and inviting. He didn't care. He darted down the large, decaying outside stairwell. His car was still beside the mansion. He unlocked his door and jumped in. The engine didn't turn until his third try. He was growing frantic. He looked up at the front door of the mansion. It was closed. Nobody appeared to be following him.

He spun the car around. He sped out of the driveway. Luckily, the front gate was still wide open. Even as he passed through the gate, he didn't feel safe.

He drove the car quickly toward home.

CHAPTER 6.....
UNSEEN_TRAPS_____

It was nearly noon. The curtains were drawn. Her bedroom remained unsoiled by light. She rolled over and searched for comfort on the pillow. Her eyes opened to meager sleepy slits. She could almost make out a few shapes in the surrounding darkness. She let out a tired sigh before closing her eyes again.

She lay motionless for a minute. However, hope was failing. Despite all wishes and efforts, consciousness was returning. She rolled over again. Her eyes opened, and she looked around. Everything was peaceful.

She smiled when she saw the time on her alarm clock. It seemed nice to have kept that thing quiet this one morning. She stayed under her covers. There seemed to be more than one reason to smile. She counted them.

Finally, she gave in to consciousness. She sat up and got out of bed.

She made some coffee. She needed a cup before taking a shower. There were a few errands to run. Still, she was in no immediate hurry. She had a little time to relax in front of the television before running out of the house.

The phone rang. Her voice was calm and pleasant as she answered, "Hello?"

"Good morning, Heidi," said the caller. "This is Russell."

"Hi, Russ," she replied. "You've got great timing. I just woke up about twenty minutes ago."

"Really?" he commented. "It's just about noon. I guess you really were tired."

"I told you I've been working a lot of overtime this past week or so," she reminded. "I needed this day of rest."

"Are you all caught up yet?" he asked. "I was hoping we could get together later. Maybe we can have dinner or something."

"That would be nice," she smiled. "I'd like that. I have some things to do this afternoon. You know, pick up some dry cleaning and such. But, I should be free by 5:00 or so. You can call me then."

"Great."

There was an awkward pause.

"Heidi?"

"Yes?"

"I had a wonderful time last night," he said. "I'm glad we're getting to know each other a little better."

"Me, too," she said. "And . . . Russ? Are you all right, honey? You sound a little strange. Is anything wrong?"

"No," he said. "I'm fine. I've just had . . . a rather hectic morning. That's all."

"But, you're okay?"

"Believe me," he said. "There's nothing to worry about. So, I'll call you around 5:00, then?"

"That would be perfect," she said. She paused. Then, she added, "I'm glad you called, Russ."

"I am, too. Talk to you later."

"'Bye," she concluded.

She felt warm and happy. Still, there was a nagging hint of doubt. "He did sound a bit off," she thought. "I hope nothing's wrong."

She cleared all uncertainty from her mind. She finished her coffee and prepared to hop into the shower. The water was running when the phone rang again.

She rolled her eyes. She quickly answered it with an impatient tone.

"Heidi?" said the caller. "It's me. I'm on my lunch break, and I just had to call."

"What do you want, Tamara?" she asked. "I'm just about to take a shower."

"You have to be kidding me," Tamara prodded. "You know I couldn't get any sleep last night. I was up all night wondering about how your date with your hot new boyfriend went. I want details."

"Nothing happened," she informed her. "We had a good time, and that was it."

"Nothing happened?"

"Cut it out, Tamara," she asserted. "Everything went well. He seems like a great guy. I love his car. He drives a black 2002 Monte Carlo. He called this morning, and we're going out again, probably tonight."

"Monte Carlo, huh?" Tamara commented. "Nice ride."

"And, it's in excellent condition."

"So, he called you back?" Tamara pressed. "You're seeing him again tonight?"

"Yes," she replied impatiently. "Now, let me go. I've got the water running."

"Okay," Tamara said. "Good girl, Heidi. Keep me informed, honey. 'Bye."

"Good-bye."

She shook her head with a bit of a chuckle as she hung up the phone. Then, she hopped into the shower.

* * * * * *

"Are you feeling all right, sir?"

"I'm okay, I guess."

"You look a bit haggard," she said. "Would you like some more coffee? Maybe something to eat?"

"That's not a bad idea," he said. "I haven't eaten anything all day."

"It's almost 12:45," she observed. "You must be famished."

"Not really," he said. "I've had a bad morning. Could I order some breakfast, or is it too late for that sort of thing?"

"We don't serve breakfast here," she informed him. "This is more of a steakhouse."

"If I order a sandwich," he said. "Could I eat it here at the bar, or do I have to go to the dining area?"

"Here would be fine," she said. "Do you need a menu?"

"Could I just get roast beef on wheat with lettuce and Russian dressing?" he asked.

"Sure," she said while writing on her pad. "Anything else? Fries? Chips?"

"No, thanks."

"I'll put your order in," she said.

He watched her disappear into the kitchen. Her sandy blonde ponytail bounced upon her slender shoulders as she walked. The place was fairly quiet. He was the only person at the bar. The dining area was half full.

She was smiling when she came back out. He thought she still looked pretty, despite her deepening crow's feet. The beginning onslaught of age had not yet caused too much damage to her beauty. "It should be about fifteen minutes," she informed him.

"All right."

"In the meantime," she offered. "Would you like to talk about it? You know, whatever's bothering you?"

"I don't know," he muttered. "It's pointless to talk about it. There's nothing you can do. It's just . . ."

He hesitated.

"What is it?" she asked. "Sometimes, it helps to talk."

"You'll think I'm crazy," he said. "Anybody would. It *is* crazy. This town is crazy. I just moved here a few days ago. Autumn seems like a nice town on the surface. But, anytime you mention the Van Pouck family, people go nuts."

Surprise showed deep in her pleasant blue eyes. "Did you say 'the Van Pouck family'?" she asked. "You're new in this town, and you already know about the Van Poucks? How is that even possible?"

"I met one of them this morning."

"You must be joking," she said with a gasp. "Everybody knows that there's only one member of that family left in this town. The old man. I think his name is Elliott. He almost never comes out of that mansion. He never talks to anyone. He's always been a raving lunatic. People say he's even worse, since his wife and kids disappeared."

"It's the truth," he said. "He's completely insane. And, I . . ."

He couldn't bring himself to continue.

"Go on," she urged.

"I can't," he said. "It's too awful to even think about. I don't know what to do. I only came here because I just moved here and I don't know anywhere else to go. I'd love to tell somebody, but I don't even know you. Maybe it's better to talk to a stranger."

She held out a dainty hand. "You don't need a stranger," she said. "I'm here. My name is Amy Tolakis. I'm the day bartender. I'm kind of watching this place this week while the owners are out of town."

He shook her hand. "I'm Russell Wilburn," he said. "Nice to meet you. But, I was sort of under the impression that Deke owned this place."

"Deke Danaher?" she scoffed. "Are you kidding? He's just the night bartender. He's not a bad guy, but he gets a little carried away sometimes. Tom and Helen Fehr own this place. That's why it's called Fehr's Steak and Ale."

"That makes sense."

"So," she said, returning to the original subject. "How did you come to meet Elliot Van Pouck?"

"He sort of invited me."

"He invited you?" she asked guardedly.

"That's not important," he expounded. "The point is . . . I know what happened to his wife and kids. I know where they are."

"If you know that," she noted. "You'd have the answer to a mystery that has plagued this town for twenty years."

He took his time. He glanced at his coffee cup while gathering his courage. Then, he looked her in the eye and said, "He killed them."

She gasped. She was still a bit scared when she replied, "That's not a big surprise. Most people assume that's what happened."

"But, do most people know that the bodies are buried under the floor in the cellar of the mansion?" he asked.

"Not for an absolute fact," she replied with wide eyes. "Some people have guessed, but . . . Are you sure? How do you know?"

"He wanted me to help feed them," he said.

"Feed them?"

"I'm telling you," he averred. "The man's gone completely off his rocker! He was dressed in a pink bathrobe. He wanted me to call him Penny."

"Penny?"

"That was his wife's name," he explained. "He thinks he *is* his wife. I don't know what to make of it all. I'm not a psychiatrist. All I can think is that he couldn't deal with the fact that he killed his wife and kids. He buried them in the cellar, and he's talked himself into believing they're still alive. Taking on his wife's identity must be his way of convincing himself that his family is still alive."

She hesitated before responding. "That's an awful lot to swallow," she finally said.

"I don't know how much is true," he continued. "I'm not sure what to believe. I want to go to the cops, but I don't know what to say. Everyone I've talked to so far tells me the cops are afraid of the Van Poucks. That may have made sense a long time ago, but why now? There's only one of them left. And, he's a crazy old man."

"You have to remember," she said. "That family is a major part of Autumn's history. They used to live all over in this town. They practically ran this town at one point. They either were politicians or owned politicians at every stage of Autumn's existence. Sure, everyone in this town will be happy when the old man dies. It'll be the end of a tragic era. There will probably be a big party in the streets. But until someone can prove that Elliott is dead, it's going to be useless to expect the cops to help."

"Somehow, I just knew you were going to say that."

"The first question they would ask," she explained. "Is why did Elliott choose to talk to you if you just moved to town?"

He took a moment to answer. Then, he said, "Apparently, I own what is known as the Beckenbauer house."

"You bought the Beckenbauer house?" she gasped. "Well, in that case, the cops definitely won't talk to you. Everybody who buys that house runs to the police. Nothing ever happens, and nobody stays in that building long enough for it to matter. I just hope you don't leave town before you pay for your sandwich."

He gave her a look. She apologized.

"If they need proof," he suggested. "All they need to do is dig up the cellar at the mansion."

"They'll want proof beforehand," she explained. "The police are not going to take your word for it. And, they're not going to cross a Van Pouck. That's just the way it is. Until you have Elliott's cold, dead body, the police are just going to ignore you."

He sighed. "I was afraid of that," he muttered. "The worse thing is I just found a great girl. We've only dated once or twice, but she seems real nice."

"You have a girlfriend, already?"

"Sort of," he said. "Well, yes. Her name is Heidi O'Dell. She's a cashier. How do I tell her about any of this?"

"It sounds like you really like her."

"Well, it's still too early to tell," he said. "But, so far she's been wonderful. How do I tell her about Elliott? How do I break the news that I live in the Beckenbauer house?"

"If she's a local girl," she said. "You don't want to tell her any more than you have to. There's a real stigma attached to this whole story. Of course, you can't keep her away from your house forever, either. She's bound to get suspicious."

"So, what do I do?" he asked. "Eventually, I'll have to say something. She seems like a sweetheart. I don't want to chase her away. And, I definitely don't want her to get involved in this whole mess. I don't want her to think I'm crazy. But, I've seen some weird things."

"I don't know what to tell you, Russell."

"I'd like to see our situation turn into something special," he explained. "She deserves it. And, so do I. We both have had some bad luck in the recent past. We both need a break right now. I'd like to see things work out between us. I just hope we get the chance to find out. That's what bothers me more than anything else."

"Well," she said. "I wish you all the luck in the world. Let me go check on your sandwich. I'll be right back."

He watched her disappear into the kitchen again. He rubbed his throbbing temple. He took a sip of coffee, and made a face.

It was ice cold.

* * * * * *

She sat at her desk. She poured over some overdue paperwork. Phones were ringing. People were talking. She adjusted her glasses and brushed a long, curly strand of black hair from her face. These were standard forms. They were not difficult. There were just too many of them. She sighed and resumed her reading.

Suddenly, she perked up. She thought she heard something in a muffled phone conversation at the next desk. She looked over at the woman seated beside her. She watched the hefty woman with streaked hair speak quietly into the phone. She waited patiently for the call to end. She did not act until the hefty woman hung up.

Then, she asked, "Celia? What was that all about?"

"Nothing," the woman replied with a guilty expression. "I was talking to a client about a house on Ohio St."

"That's not what it sounded like," she charged. "Tell me the truth. Are you people running some kind of office pool to see when Mr. Wilburn bails on the Beckenbauer house? Is that what you're doing?"

Celia hung her head. "Maybe," she muttered.

"That's about the cruelest thing I've ever heard in my life," she snipped. "It's not my fault Colby dumped that property in my lap. I do my best with what I have. I've sold that dump ten times. How can I help it if every buyer I run into turns out to be a flake?"

"Nobody's blaming you, Sharon," Celia explained. "We all know you're one of the best real estate brokers we have. That's why Colby gave you the Beckenbauer house in the first place. But, let's face it. No matter who anyone sells it to, it just doesn't stay sold. That's just the facts. You have to have a sense of humor about it, or you'll go nuts."

"Who's responsible for this atrociousness?" she asked.

Celia hesitated.

"Come on," Sharon insisted. "Who was it?"

"Doug Pickering."

"Doug started this?" Sharon asked. "I should have known. He always has to be the class clown. That's it! I'm really going to let him have it! Then, I'm taking this all the way up to Richard!"

"Don't take it so personally, honey," Celia consoled. "It's not a reflection on your abilities. No one's trying to insult you. It's just . . . funny. That's all."

"Is that right?" she argued. "Well, we'll see how funny it is when I tell Richard!"

"Well, you can tell Richard, if you want," Celia replied. "But, I think he already put $30.00 down on September 21."

"What?" she fumed. "Richard Colby's in on this, too? Unbelievable!"

She quickly stood. She stormed off in the direction of Richard's office.

Celia shook her head as she watched. "I knew phone calls were a mistake," she mumbled to herself. "We should have stuck to emails. I'd better warn Doug."

* * * * * *

He was nearly ready to leave the house. He was almost on time. He was nicely dressed. A wallet full of credit cards and cash were at his disposal. His mood was one of pleasant anticipation.

He walked cheerfully down the stairs to the ground floor. He turned in the direction of the kitchen. Then, he saw it. It was lying on the floor just inside the main room.

The body of a man was curled near the door. He was motionless and silent. The body was facing inside the room. And, it was bleeding on the carpet.

He gasped as he stared at it. He wasn't sure what to do. The stranger obviously did not belong in this house. Still, he was hurt . . . if not dead.

He rushed over to check on the man. "Hey, pal," he said. "Are you all right? What are you doing in my house?"

The body didn't move.

He knealt beside it. The man's face seemed pale and lifeless. His bloody suit was outmoded. The body seemed limp and unresponsive.

He reached out to touch it. However, it disappeared.

His hand passed through thin air. There was no sign of a body. There was no blood on the carpet.

He gasped as he jumped to his feet. He gawked at the empty space on the floor.

"Aw, crap," he muttered. "What the hell? I don't have time for this."

He glanced around the room. Everything seemed to be in order. He needed to communicate. Even as he shouted out, he didn't know to whom he was shouting. Maybe it was the Beckenbauers. Perhaps, it was to the house itself.

"I'm not going to let you ruin my date!" he demanded.

He ran into the kitchen. He got what he needed. Then, he ran out of the house. He did not check the main room when he left.

His mood had stabilized by the time they got to the restaurant. They chose to return to The Turtle's Nest. It didn't take much effort to concentrate on his date. She looked 'exquisite' that evening. That was the word he'd used when she opened her door. But in the candlelight at their booth, that word seemed grossly inadequate.

Still, she seemed to be a little preoccupied at first. He asked her what was wrong.

"I don't know," she said. "I was so happy when I woke up this morning. And, it was nice when you called. I was looking forward to a nice day."

"And, what happened?"

"I think I told you I had some errands today," she reminded. "Today cost me a lot of money. Prices on everything keep going up, and . . . Russ? Do you really think you can save the store? I know you said not to worry, but I can't help it. Business has been declining lately. The store's not getting as many customers as it used to."

He sighed. "This was not the sort of subject matter I was expecting this evening," he divulged. "But if you really must know, I am a little concerned. But, I think things will be fine. The books are a mess, but I'll be working on them this month before I take over. Bill Green has obviously given up on the place."

"So, what are you going to do?" she asked.

"Well, to start with," he said. "Everybody I talk to seems to think the place has already closed down. And if you look at the store from the outside, you can see why. It looks like a dump. It looks abandoned. We have to fix the building up. Do some refurbishing. Hopefully, without closing it. Throw a grand re-opening sale. Do some advertising. Let everyone know we're still here, and we're not going anywhere."

"Do you think that will work?" she asked.

"It should," he said. "I can put together the money for whatever we need. Everyone seems to have 'fond memories' of this place, and would like to come back here. Once we put the word out, things should come together for us. Then, the money should start rolling in, and we'll all be rich. Or at least I will be, anyway."

"And, what about the rest of us?" she asked.

"You people can live in squalor, for all I care," he teased.

"And, here I thought you were our knight in shining armor," she poked back.

"Well, my armor may not shine," he admitted. "But, I can kick booty when I have to."

"That's nice to know."

He allowed a brief pause. Then he added, "So, is that all that's troubling you?"

"I guess so," she said.

"You don't sound too sure."

"Well," she began. "I suppose I'm worried about the future . . . you know, of everything. Sometimes, it seems like life is a sort of minefield full of traps. Of course, you never see any of them. They're always hidden out of sight. You always have to be so careful where you step, or what you do. Because if you make one wrong move, something will snap down on you without warning."

"I see," he said knowingly. "And, do you feel trapped right now, Heidi?"

"No," she said. "But, you never do beforehand."

"Well, if it helps any," he offered. "I promise not to spring any traps on you without warning."

"So, you thought I was talking about you?" she asked.

"Either way," he said. "I'd like to think I've covered myself."

In the dancing glow of the candle, her smile displayed its own mystical elegance. Innocence and shadow intermingled. Soft, gentle traps were set without even trying.

Later that evening, they were sitting on her sofa.

"So, how did you like Sky Shards?" she asked.

"It was a nice little club," he admitted. "I don't believe you talked me into going to that kind of place. I haven't danced like that in years."

"You're pretty good at it, Russ," she said. "I'm almost surprised."

"Thank you," he said. "It was fun. We got to see a few interesting places tonight. I'm glad you decided to show me around. Is that what passes for culture in this town?"

"Those were some of my favorite places," she confided. "It's what *I* call culture, at any rate. Some people prefer museums or the theater. But for me, paintings and sculptures are okay, but they have no rhythm. You can't dance to them."

"No one can argue with that sort of logic."

She took a moment to sip her coffee. He watched her with a grin.

"It's no wonder you have no sense of culture," he poked. "You slurp when you drink."

"No, I don't," she said. "You're making that up. Besides, I have plenty of culture."

"You do?"

"I have scads of culture," she insisted. "I'm stuffed full of it."

"I can't argue with you there," he agreed. "You're full of it, all right."

They shared a laugh before the kiss. It was merely an opening. The second kiss was immediate. It was longer. It was more sincere. It intimated a source of being.

They were still holding each other on the sofa when they finished. She inquired, "So, if I have no class, why are you kissing me?"

"I didn't say you had no class," he enlightened her. "I suggested that you may be lacking a certain amount of culture."

"What's the difference?"

"Well," he said while leaning forward. "This is class."

Their kiss grew slowly involved in the tangling of answers that bore no connection to any doubt. Oceans were becoming civilized. And, skies boldly erased their tears. They were finding each other in what had been lost in themselves.

Afterward, she looked at him with sweetness in her big, green eyes. And, he continued, "And, this is culture."

She expected this kiss. She wanted it. Liquids of comfort poured through chasms that had been left dry and empty for too long. They showered through valleys, and ran like wild rivers to a waterfall of delight.

She looked up at him when they were done. She held him as he lay on top of her. With a pleasant smile, she said, "I still don't see a difference."

"Well," he replied playfully. "That's because you have no class."

She giggled before they kissed again. They began with a few short kisses that grew longer as they progressed.

Finally, she stopped. She said, "I'm not sure if I'm ready for any more lessons on class or culture."

"Are you sure?" he asked.

"Yes."

"Well, how about if I just kiss you?" he gently persisted.

She said nothing. Her beautiful eyes were smiling as she looked up at him.

So, he kissed her again. It moved closer to where they both wished they could be.

Then, she commented, "Wow! You were right. That wasn't classy at all."

They kissed again. And, the warm, angelic embrace enveloped them. It brought them even closer than it had before. The soft velvet traps that ensnared them could not have gone unseen. Their allure was powerful and sensitive. They fell willingly into the need that became both of them. They drifted in the abyss they created together.

Together, they would create again what had never been lost.

CHAPTER 7.....
BEYOND_RATIONALITY____

The curtains were parted. Sunlight drifted through the windows like silent, lazy streams of contentment. She was the first to open her eyes. She could see his bare chest beneath her arm. It rose and fell calmly to the slow breathing rhythm of his sleep. She felt his loose embrace behind her back, with his hand on her flesh. Her head felt comfortable on his shoulder. She closed her eyes. She had no wish to move.

After fifteen minutes or so, she had to get up. She kissed his cheek. She delicately wiggled out from his resting grip without waking him. She was out of the shower and in the kitchen before he came to life.

The sounds and smells of something sizzling in the other room carried him peacefully back to consciousness. He glanced about the small, somewhat cramped bedroom. It was tidy and unfamiliar. It took a moment to remember where he was. The past few days had left him wary of waking up in strange places.

Still, he allowed a relaxed smile as he lay in the safety of this bed. With eyes closed, he drank in the soothing noises and aromas wafting in from the kitchen. After a minute, he decided to rise. He dressed and walked out to greet his hostess.

The sizzling grew louder as he stepped into the tiny kitchen. "Good morning," he said.

She turned her attention from the pan with a smile. "Hi, Russ," she said. "How did you sleep?"

"Quite nicely," he announced with a kiss. "That's probably the best sleep I've had since I came to this town."

"Really?" she asked. "I would have thought that with your own big house, you would have better accommodations than I can offer."

"It's not big by any means," he said. "It's fairly spacious in its own way, I guess. But, it's far from big. Still, your little apartment has something that my empty house could never provide."

She laughed and gave him another quick kiss.

"If my house could provide that sort of thing," he continued. "I would have paid double the price for it."

"You're terrible!" she pretended to complain. "Would you like some scrambled eggs? I made enough for two. And, the coffee's made. Help yourself to a clean cup in the dish rack."

"Thanks," he said. "I wouldn't mind a few eggs."

He poured a cup of coffee and sat at the small table. "I really had a great time last night," he said.

"So did I," she said. "Thanks for everything."

He watched her dish some eggs onto a plate before him with a spatula. Her hair looked darker as she regarded him with cheery green eyes. Daylight leaked subtly through windows and traced playful highlights in the curly, wet locks that rested against her old blue bathrobe. Even in these circumstances, she looked radiant.

"Well, thank you for showing me around town," he replied. "Autumn may turn out to be a decent place to live, after all."

"I've always liked it."

"So, you've lived here your entire life?" he asked.

"Not really," she said. "We moved here from Buffalo when I was ten. My father got transferred by his company. They just moved him back to Buffalo again last year. He doesn't care. He likes Buffalo, and he'll be retiring soon. I stayed here, because I have a life in Autumn. My friends and everything I know is out here."

There was a pause as she sat by her guest with her own plate of eggs. "These are very good," he said. "Thank you."

"You're welcome," she said. "I don't have breakfast very often. But, I just felt like it today."

He watched her sip her coffee. "Heidi?" he asked cautiously. "Do you have any regrets about last night? I know you wanted to wait and take things slowly."

"Not at all," she readily replied. "If I didn't want to, I wouldn't have done it. I always stand by my decisions. Although, whether I regret this in the long run is up to you."

The look in her eye was lighthearted. But, he knew she meant it.

She smiled at him as she chewed her food.

On the drive home, he wondered. He worried about what might be waiting for him at the house. He thought about how to resolve the issues at hand. After all, he still wasn't too sure what was happening. He wondered how he could keep Heidi away from it.

He didn't want her to get involved in this mess. He didn't want her to get hurt. He didn't want to lose her this early, either. He figured nothing would keep her from leaving if she even knew where he lived.

The sun ruled over a cloudless sky with a brutal heat. The noon hour traffic rush had begun. Air conditioned cars were filling the streets. He was in no hurry to get home. He considered telling the police about the crazy old man in the Van Pouck mansion. Everyone seemed to think the cops wouldn't listen. Even if they would listen, what could he actually tell them?

He just kept driving toward Agnes St.

* * * * * *

She sat at her desk. She had more tedious paperwork to get through. She adjusted her glasses. She sighed as she began to read.

The phone rang. She picked up the receiver and answered, "Colby Real Estate. May I help you?"

The male voice on the other end sounded courteous and cordial. "Hello," he said. "Is this Mrs. Sharon Kellerman?"

"Yes."

"I was hoping you could help me," he said. "I have a large house that I want to sell. I want to unload it as quickly as possible. I've heard good things about you. I was wondering if you could come take a look at it today."

"Of course, sir," she said. "May I have your name, please?"

"Uh, Gordon Elliott," he said.

"Okay," she said while writing on a pad of paper. "And, what's the address?"

"1110 Agnes St."

She raised an eyebrow. That neighborhood was familiar. "Fine," she said.

"Can you hurry, please?" he asked. "I would really like to move on this house. That's why I specifically asked for you. I've heard you're the best."

"Thank you," she said. She glanced at the papers on her desk. Then, she checked her watch. She shuffled things around in her mind as she offered, "I can probably tear myself away now, if you're honestly in that much of a rush. It's difficult to guarantee an immediate buyer, but I'll certainly do what I can. Of course, I'll know more once I see the house."

"I understand," he said. "When can I expect you?"

"If I leave now," she said while glancing at her watch again. "I can probably be there in less than half an hour. Shall we say 11:00?"

"That would be fine."

She hung up the phone and grabbed a folder. "Celia," she said to the woman at the next desk. "I have a lead on a new house for sale. I'll be back as soon as I can."

"Okay," Celia said. "Good luck."

She rushed out the door. She got in her new foreign car and sped away.

The relentless sun made for a hot, sticky day. The morning traffic was moderate. She made decent time driving across town. She kept her car moving at a brisk, though prudent speed. She couldn't afford another mark on her license.

She slowed a bit as she ascended the Agnes St. hill. She didn't check house numbers right away. She knew the 1100 block would be up closer to the cemetery. She only encountered a few cars while negotiating the road that took her past the old Beckenbauer house. There was no car in that driveway. She hoped Mr. Wilburn was all right.

She began to check house numbers a block or so further up the hill. She grew a bit anxious as she neared her destination. This was getting too close to a house with an unsavory past. She knew she was approaching a mansion with a notorious reputation.

A lump stuck in her throat. She slowed her Toyota down to a crawl. Her skin began to feel a bit itchy as it seemed harder to escape the probability that . . .

Her eyes grew wide as she stepped firmly on her brake pedal. She gasped with surprise and apprehension as she stared at the large gray mansion. The rusty gate was wide open. The mailbox was worn. Its paint had faded and chipped over the years. It had once proudly announced the name of the Van Pouck family. Currently, the words seemed like a paled, shameful proclamation. The address "1110 Agnes St." was displayed in much smaller letters beneath, almost as an afterthought.

A sense of dread began to build in her. She cleared her throat. She took a breath for courage. So many thoughts ran through her mind. The name Gordon Elliott must have been a combination of the first names of the existing owner and his infamous grandfather.

"Elliott is selling the Van Pouck mansion?" she whispered to herself. "Why did he lie about his name? Maybe he thought I'd be afraid to come out here."

She sat and stared as questions raged through her troubled mind. Perhaps she would have been scared to come over if she had known. Why had he chosen her? Why was he moving so suddenly? Would it be possible to sell a house that still received such negative publicity? Would all the legends, gossip and problems stop in Autumn if he were gone? Of what she had heard about this place, how much was true?

She watched the place with consternation. It didn't appear to be well kept. Still, it must be worth a fortune. The possible commission made it worth further investigation.

She took another deep breath. She pulled the car around and drove slowly through the gate. She led the Toyota cautiously down the long driveway. She regarded the carriage house behind the mansion with anxiety. It also appeared to be in a state of disrepair. Still, it would add to the property value.

She parked as close to the mansion as possible. She felt nervous as she stepped out onto the crumbling pavement. From her vantage point, the building looked like a huge, intimidating structure. Its past grandeur had withered and eroded.

With trepidation, she climbed the once impressive stairwell to the main entrance. She clutched the unstable, ornate banister for balance. It creaked as loudly as the stairs, as she set one foot after another up one step at a time . . . nearing the front door with mounting fear.

Reaching the landing did nothing to calm her nerves. In all her fifty years of existence, she had heard of this house. However, she had never really seen it. She certainly had never been inside the gate. And here she was face to face with the entrance. The door was slightly ajar. Beyond it lie a world that every resident of Autumn had dreamt of seeing . . . but, so few had actually seen.

Curiosity gave her the strength to continue. The thought of a large commission also made it easier to set aside her growing anxiety. She rang the doorbell. She could hear it echo inside. The door was not open enough that she could see in. She waited a few seconds, then tried again. She listened to the echo of the bell.

Still, she got no answer.

When she used the door knocker, the door squeaked open a bit. She didn't want to be impolite. But, she had dropped everything and rushed over here. She deserved a reply.

She pushed the door open. "Hello?" she called. She rang the bell again.

She stepped warily through the door. She glanced around as she called, "Hello? This is Sharon Kellerman. I believe you sent for me."

There was still no response. She took a few more anxious steps into the house. She grimaced as she saw the filthy condition of the opulent main room. "My God," she muttered to herself. "This is disgusting!"

She glanced over at the fireplace. Then, she looked over at the great staircase. It appeared to be rickety and covered in grime. "Hello?" she called again. "This is Sharon Kellerman. Mr. Van Pouck?"

She took a few more steps into the room. She was becoming a little more fearful. She wasn't sure which name to call for. Cooperation and delicacy were necessary. She tried, "Mr. Van Pouck? Mr. Elliott? Is anyone home?"

She took another cautious step inside.

Then, she heard the door slam shut behind her. It was followed by a click, as if the door had locked. She gasped as she leapt in fright. She spun around. The door had definitely been closed. However, no one was in sight.

She wanted to escape. Suddenly, a figure appeared out of nowhere. It was the shadowy shape of a man. However, half of his head seemed to be missing.

She screamed in terror.

Without thinking, she turned and ran deeper into the mansion. As she entered the next room, she spun around. She slammed the door closed. She leaned against it as she frantically looked around for a barricade. Nothing was available.

So, she turned and ran further into the house. Her eyes were wide with horror and confusion. Her heart beat with a thunderous fear. She already had no idea where she was. An instinctive panic motivated her to bolt across the room. She didn't take the time to glance around. She just ran.

However, she was brought to a sudden halt. A woman stepped into the doorway just fifteen feet in front of her. It was a glowing specter of a beautiful young lady. She wore a decorative, old fashion hat. Her pretty face bore a pained expression. The dagger in her chest dripped blood down the front of her long, flowing dress.

Sharon shrieked with absolute horror.

She turned to run.

However, a balding, white-haired old man stood just inches in front of her. He glared at her with an intense anger. He wore a pink bathrobe with white fur trim.

She had no time to react to the shock of his sudden appearance. He raised a long, solid gold candlestick over his head. In less time than she could gather the breath to scream, he brought the blunt object down on the top of her head with brutal force.

She collapsed beneath the weight of the powerful blow. She tumbled to the ground like a sack of broken toys. She lie motionless on the floor, as a trickle of blood oozed from her scalp.

The old man looked down at the unconscious woman at his feet. His gaze softened only a bit as he regarded his prey.

Then, he dropped the blood-stained candlestick on the dirty carpet beside her.

* * * * * *

Thick clouds took advantage of the heavy darkness. They used its cover to converge and plan a late summer storm.

He held the door for her as they entered the building. Most of the tables in the dining area were occupied with couples. There was even a family or two. The bar area still had a number of empty stools. The radio played. The friendly chatter was not too loud. It was a reasonably amicable atmosphere for a Thursday evening.

They sat beside each other at the bar. The bartender offered a big smile as he greeted them. "Russell and Heidi," he beamed. "It's great to see you two back in here. I missed you last night."

"Hi, Deke," he said. "We had other plans."

"You're looking fabulous tonight, Heidi," the bartender observed.

"Thank you, Deke," she said with a polite smile. "It's nice to see you."

"Hey, I still owe you crazy kids a free drink from the other night," the bartender offered. "Don't think I've forgotten. The first round is on me. A gin and tonic and a Sea Breeze, right?"

"Thanks, Deke," he said. "That's really not necessary."

"I insist," he said as he began to make the drinks. "It's the least I can do. I'm glad that ass didn't scare you away from here for good, Heidi. Believe me. He's never setting foot in this place again. I'll make sure of it."

"That's sweet," she said. "But, don't worry. It takes more than that to scare me off."

"Good for you, honey," Deke grinned. "I like you two. You make a sweet couple. I hope to see you both in here on a regular basis."

"We like you too, pal," he said. "Especially if you keep up with the free drinks."

The bartender laughed as he set their glasses down on coasters. "If there's anything you need," he offered. "Just ask."

They thanked him as he went off to attend the other patrons.

"We can just have a few quick drinks," he told her. "And, then we can go, if you'd like. We should probably stay for at least one more round. After what Deke just did, I ought to spend a little money here."

"You're right," she agreed. "That was very kind of him to remember."

"Don't worry, though," he added. "I'll get you home nice and early."

"Thanks for understanding," she said. "I enjoyed last night very much. I really did. But, I have to turn in early tonight. I have to work a full day tomorrow. I can't invite you in, or I know what will happen. And, I still want to keep a handle on things."

"That's perfectly reasonable," he said. "It's okay. At least, I got to see you tonight for a nice dinner and a quick nightcap. I don't blame you for wanting to get home early. Or, for wanting to take your time. I have no problem whatsoever. We have plenty of time."

"We certainly do," she agreed. "So, what will you be doing tomorrow while I'm hard at work? Will you be stopping by the store?"

"Probably not," he said. "I have some things to do at the house. Being a new homeowner has its disadvantages. I have to regrout the upstairs bathroom. I bought everything I need. I just have to take the time to do it."

"It sounds like an awfully big house for just one guy," she said. "I can't wait to see it. When do you think I can come over and check it out?"

He hesitated for a moment. "Well," he fumbled. "I'd really like to fix it up a bit first. It's not in bad shape, but it needs some work."

"I don't mind that," she said. "Every house has its flaws. I still want to see where you live."

"I'll have you over soon," he said. "I promise."

"Great," she smiled. "I'm looking forward to it. I'm sort of glad you won't be at the store tomorrow, though."

"Why is that?"

"The girls are going to be all over me about what we've been doing these past few days," she explained. "I'm not sure I want to admit anything. But, I have a feeling Tamara's going to figure it out . . . or smell it on me or something. She may not be able to calculate a 7% sales tax, but she's a genius when it comes to detecting who had sex."

He chuckled. "I have a feeling Daisy's no slouch, either," he said.

"You're right," she nodded. "She's pretty slick, too. And they're both going to torture me all day tomorrow."

"I'm sure they are," he agreed. "They seem like good friends, though. I think they're just looking out for you."

"I know," she admitted. "But, they can both be a royal pain in my ass."

"That's what friends are for, I suppose."

"Perhaps."

He kissed her.

"What was that for?" she asked.

"Just because you look beautiful tonight," he replied.

"Oh, cut it out."

"He's right," Deke nodded. "I'd kiss you myself, but Russ would probably slug me."

"Plus, your wife would hand you your head on a stick," he added.

She laughed.

"Actually, she probably wouldn't bother with the stick," Deke corrected. "Are you two ready for another drink?"

"Sure," he said. "Why not?"

"Russ?" she said shyly. "Thanks for tonight. Thanks for understanding. Thanks for everything these past few days."

"Believe me," he said. "The pleasure was all mine."

Deke continued making their drinks. However, he had to smile as he watched them kiss again.

After another drink or two, he drove her home. They rode casually through the dense, unfriendly darkness. Storm clouds were preparing to strike. They were in no hurry to unleash the inevitable downpour. They knew it would happen soon enough. They also knew that when they let loose, the town of Autumn would have no escape.

He threw the car into Park, as they sat outside her apartment building. "Should I call you tomorrow night?" he asked.

"If you think of it," she said. "Don't feel obligated."

"All right," he said.

They kissed for a while in the front seat. A subtle hum could be felt beneath them from the running motor.

"I wish I didn't have to go."

"Me too."

They kissed a while longer. She finally pulled away. She said her final good-bye. She hopped out of the car. As soon as she was inside the building, he drove off. The storm clouds were almost ready to unleash their fury. He hoped he could get home before they did. He sped off at a brisk pace in the direction of Agnes St.

Besides the impending weather threat, he felt pleased as he rode through the dark, empty streets.

* * * * * *

Her head felt as if someone had been chipping away at it with an ice pick. She felt as if she were upright and leaning forward. She opened her eyes after a great deal of painful effort. Everything was still a bit blurry.

She lifted her head. The throbbing pain just inside her skull made her wince. She tried to move. It didn't work. Her arms were stuck in their present position. Finally, her vision returned. She could see.

She gasped in fear and awe, as she glanced about the room. Apparently, she was in a very large kitchen. There were a few ovens and stoves. She noticed counters, cupboards and pantries. Everything looked filthy. The sinks were all filled with dirty dishes. Gruesome stains maligned the walls and other surfaces. Canned food was piled in tall stacks everywhere she looked.

It was disgraceful. It was shocking . . . and quite frightening!

She tried to move again. It seemed impossible. Her arms wouldn't budge. She was sitting down. And she wasn't moving.

She glanced down. It terrified her to learn that she was tied rather tightly to a chair. The perpetrator had used a thick, strong length of rope to bind her helplessly to a wooden chair. Her repeated terrified struggle for freedom had no effect.

She grew more frightened as her desperate exertion only made her tired and sore. Her head kept feeling worse. Tears filled her eyes as she grunted and whimpered. Still, she could not get free of those heavy ropes.

The calm male voice startled her. "I see you're finally awake," he said.

She glanced to her side. Her jaw dropped as her eyes went wild. The balding, white-haired man was standing only a few feet from her. She recognized him. He was the last thing she saw before passing out.

What really sparked her memory was his pink bathrobe. The look in his eye was determined. Maybe he looked angry. However, the thing that terrified her the most was the long, sharp knife in his hand.

"What's going on?" she begged. "What do you want from me?"

"Don't you know who I am, Mrs. Kellerman?" he asked. "I've seen you many times before. You spend way too much time in my house."

"I don't know what you're talking about," she said. "I've never been here before. I can only guess that you're Mr. Elliott Van Pouck."

"Certainly not!" he bellowed. "How is that even possible? Do you feel the need to add to the insults you have already cast upon me?"

"What insults?" she asked in a scared, timid voice. "I don't know who you are. Isn't this the Van Pouck mansion? I was asked to come here."

"That's right," he admitted. "I called you. I invited you here. Sorry to have deceived you over the phone. My real name is Ingrid Beckenbauer."

Tears formed again in her frightened eyes. "Ingrid Beckenbauer?" she stuttered in disbelief. "B-but, everybody knows she d-died in 1929."

"That's preposterous!" he shouted. "Do I look dead to you?"

"Please," she implored. "Please untie me. I haven't done anything. I still don't know what you want from me."

"I want you to stop walking into my house whenever you feel like it," he demanded curtly. "As if you own the place! It's not your house. It's *my* house! My husband bought and paid for it!"

"That's not possible," she claimed. "Your husband . . . I mean, Edgar . . ."

"What are you talking about, Mrs. Kellerman," he pressed. "Spit it out."

"Listen," she tried to explain as tears ran down her cheeks. "I didn't know. I was only doing what I was told."

"Doing as you were told?" he questioned. "Who would tell you to sell my house right out from under me?"

"My boss," she proclaimed. "Richard Colby of Colby Real Estate. He's the one who told me. I had no idea . . ."

"Don't blame this on someone else," he interrupted. "For years I've watched you saunter into my home. You bring parades of uninvited strangers into my house, and you accept money to let them live in the dwelling that my husband bought for us! For years I've watched! And, I said nothing! I won't be silent anymore! Stop trying to sell my house!"

He was waving the knife in her face. She was openly sobbing. She had given up trying to free herself from the chair. She was too petrified.

"Please, Mr. Van Pouck," she wept. "Please let me go!"

"My name is Ingrid Beckenbauer!" he averred with insane fury. He slapped her hard across the face. She was crying hysterically as he added, "I won't tell you again!"

"Please don't," she begged through a fresh wave of tears. "Please don't hurt me! I'll do anything! Just please let me go!"

"All I want you to do, my dear," he informed her. "Is stop trying to sell my house. Just because my husband is away, and I'm trapped in this hell hole . . . that doesn't give you the right to take over my place of residence. Don't sell it anymore. And whoever is in there now, tell them to leave."

"You mean, Russell Wilburn?" she asked. "I can't tell him to leave. He bought that house. He signed a mortgage."

"You had no right to sell it to him!" he yelled.

"I'm begging you to stop," she sobbed. "I can't talk like this! I'm in pain, and I'm scared! Please untie me! I can call my boss! We can discuss this! We'll do whatever you want! Just please stop!"

"I don't need to call anyone," he insisted. "Nobody is going to take my home! My husband will be back soon. He won't stand for any of this!"

"You have to face facts, sir," she contested through panicked tears. "Ingrid is dead!"

"I'm not dead!"

"I'm sorry, Mr. Van Pouck," she cried. "I can't! I just can't . . ."

Rage became visible in his wild eyes. "My name is Ingrid Beckenbauer!" he roared. And as he did so, he plunged the sharp blade of the knife deep into her chest.

She screamed with a mixture of horror and agony.

The old man was overtaken by his insane anger. Each time he repeated his strange assertion, he sank the knife forcefully into the woman's chest.

"My name is Ingrid Beckenbauer!" he hollered. "My name is Ingrid Beckenbauer! My name is Ingrid Beckenbauer . . .!"

She shrieked amid the vicious attack.

However, after seven or eight stabs, the woman fell eerily silent. She wasn't screaming or crying anymore. The old man stopped his ferocious rampage. He stepped back away from the motionless woman. His eyes slowly calmed as he observed the blood pouring over the ligature that held her securely in the chair. He watched the rope change colors as the crimson cascade spilled down her blouse.

Then, he turned and left the room. He left her in the chair with her head tilted back. He left her with her eyes and mouth wide open. He left her with a long knife buried deep in her chest.

CHAPTER 8.....
SHAKING_HANDS WITH A DEAD MAN_____

An intimidating darkness still hunched over the area. He began to speed up a bit as he approached Agnes St. He wanted to get home before the impending storm struck. He drove up the hill at a prudent rate. He saw a streak of lightning rip across the sky to the south. A few seconds later, a thunder clap sounded in the distance. He was glad he was nearly home.

His house was on the next block. No one else seemed to be on the road. There was no need to hurry anymore. He would be home momentarily. Another lightning streak shot through the air over by the woods. Then, the thunder sounded just a little closer.

Somehow, he had missed his house. He was still driving up the hill. He thought about how ridiculous he felt. He considered turning the car around. However, the Monte Carlo kept moving forward. He made no effort to turn the steering wheel. He just continued to drive.

He slowed a bit as he rode past the gray mansion. But, there was no reason to stop. His curiosity had been temporarily abated. He regarded it with a fleeting sense of dread as he headed for the cemetery.

A bright light sheeted the sky. The thunder followed a little sooner, and a bit louder.

"I want to go home," he said as he parked the car.

A few large raindrops splattered against his windshield, as he looked up at the sign over the cemetery entrance. "I don't want to do this," he told nobody in particular. "Please not now."

He stepped out of the car. The raindrops were large and heavy. But, they were still spaced widely apart. He knew what he had to do. He hurried through the gate. He jogged up the path to where he knew he would find the freshly dug grave.

The rain was just teasing him. Another flash of lightning preceeded a closer crash of thunder. He saw Nobody's Grave directly ahead of him. He wanted to turn back as the clouds taunted him with a few more pellets of water.

He stood at the rim of the hole. He glanced down at the skeleton which rested six feet down on the earthen floor. It still wore the gold chain with a locket. He was still afraid of this grave . . . and its occupant. Even though neither one seemed to mean him any immediate harm, they still gave him the creeps.

The skeleton turned its head to face the visitor standing in the grass above.

"You want me to go down there again," he spoke down into the grave. "Don't you?"

The skeleton didn't respond. The rain was gradually growing heavier. Another splash of lightning was followed by a boom of thunder.

He jumped down into Nobody's Grave. It didn't seem to be raining down here. His bony host seemed to be watching him. He wasn't sure what to expect.

Then, the skeleton raised a thin, squalid arm.

He jumped with a start. He took a step back. He watched his reclining host point a long, lanky finger at him. He felt the knot tightening in his stomach. He almost knew what would happen next. Still, he wasn't looking forward to seeing what was to come.

Once again, the bony arm of the host fell against the dirt wall of the grave. He watched as the slender finger wrote three letters in the fresh soil.

This time, it traced the letters K-A-T.

The darkness overhead was briefly interrupted by a blinking wall of light. Then, the thunder sounded like a shrill explosion going off in slow motion. The rain was pouring outside the grave. However, everything in the hole remained unchanged.

Suddenly, the ground dropped out from under him.

He hated this part. There was nothing around him as he fell. It seemed black and empty. Everything seemed lifeless and soundless as he tumbled downward again through the bleak chasm of fear and suspicion which gladly engulfed his vulnerable form. He fell as he tried to scream. He couldn't make any noise. He couldn't stop falling.

He couldn't stop falling . . .

Then, he found himself in a room he had seen before. However, it looked younger, newer and much cleaner. In fact, everything was polished and immaculate. Its magnificence was better displayed. The fireplace and the grand staircase . . . everything looked dazzling and spectacular.

The woman in the hat looked familiar. However, the well-dressed man beside her was unknown. He seemed quite dashing, though. The smile beneath his dark mustache made his face look to be around forty. The couple didn't appear as though they could see him. Still, he hid behind a huge, heavy curtain as he watched.

"You were very cordial this evening, my dear," the man said. "It's nice to see you put those sordid misgivings of yours behind you."

"I have put nothing behind me, Gordon," she said. "Etiquette dictates that a lady should conduct herself properly at all times. I would never dream of humiliating you the way you have humiliated me. It would be unbecoming, to say the least."

"For pity's sake, Katalina," he said impatiently. "How long do you intend to drag out this episode of yours?"

"How long do you intend to keep the company of that trollop?" she retorted.

"How dare you refer to Ingrid in such an unseemly way?" he argued. "She has done nothing to incur such a slanderous fabrication."

"Do you take me for a fool, Gordon?" she pressed. "My sister saw you alone with that woman in a public place! A restaurant, of all things!"

"That was months ago, darling," he answered. "And, I've explained all that to you. Edgar was out of town . . . putting food on your table, I might add. I was spending time with her, merely comforting the poor woman in her husband's absence. It was all very innocent."

"Innocent indeed!" she snipped. "This is not the first time you have disgraced me and our marriage. At least those other women had some standing in the community. Until now, you have only troubled yourself with the wives of your more refined friends. This harlot is . . . is a common smuggler's wife!"

He went to dry the tears that began to stream down her face. "Don't cry, Katalina dear," he said as he took her in his arms. "And, you mustn't say such things. You mustn't even think them. Edgar is not a smuggler. And, Ingrid is a fine, upstanding woman."

"Then, how could she allow herself to be seen in public with you behind my back?" she pressed.

"I would hardly call it 'behind your back'."

"You didn't tell me about it," she insisted. "I had to hear about it from my sister."

"Oh, Barbara is a meddlesome busybody," he protested. "She blows everything out of proportion. She saw me once in a restaurant with Ingrid Beckenbauer. And, now I suppose she's telling anyone who will listen that I'm flaunting some illicit affair all over town. You mustn't let her upset you like that, dear."

"It's not the first time you have cheated, Gordon."

"I made a few mistakes in the past," he confessed. "I've admitted that to you. But, those days are over. I am devoted to you, my love. I am completely committed to making our marriage last a lifetime."

"You had better be," she muttered under her breath.

"What did you say?" he asked.

"Nothing, dear."

"You know, you worry me sometimes, Katalina," he announced. "For instance, you have a look in your eye right now that perplexes me."

"Whatever do you mean, Gordon?" she asked nonchalantly. "What could I possibly be thinking that would concern you?"

He regarded her with consternation. "What are you up to, Katalina?" he asked.

"I'm sure I have no idea to what you are referring, darling," she reiterated. "It's like you're always saying: Edgar is a simple merchant with connections to diamond mines in Africa, and you're an importer. Ingrid is a fine woman. And, I am an ordinary housewife. What could possibly be wrong?"

He continued to watch her. "You had better not cross me, my dear," he stated.

"Why?" she asked. "What will you do, Gordon? Make me disappear? The way you did your own brother . . . and City Councilman Saunders?"

"Watch what you say, Katalina," he warned.

"How could I possibly be a threat to you?"

"Now I know you're up to something," he said. "What is it? Come to think of it, you were a little too nice to Ingrid at dinner this evening. I invited the Beckenbauers here to smooth a few things over. I was surprised by your civility. Especially when you took such an interest in Ingrid's jewelry. The gold chain with the locket. The one with Edgar's picture in it. Ingrid thought you were whispering something while you were admiring it. What were you whispering?"

"I'll tell you the same thing I told her," she reminded. "I was merely remarking to myself what a charming piece it was."

He watched her for a moment. He studied the innocence and purity in her dark eyes.

"You're right, my love," he chuckled. "I'm sorry. What could I have been thinking? What could you say to a gold chain? How silly of me."

"You've been working too hard, dear," she said. "I think we've all been a little on edge. Perhaps we should get away for a few days."

143

"Perhaps," he said. "It would do us both some good. Where is Davis? I could use a brandy. Would you care to join me, darling?"

"That sounds lovely, dear."

The sunlight brought him out of a deep sleep. He was looking up at a beautiful blue sky. He could smell the wet grass under his head. His clothes were soaked.

He was surrounded by puddles and tombstones. He sat up with a groan. His back and neck were sore. He rubbed a few aching muscles while considering going home to clean up. His wristwatch said 6:24. He stood and brushed as much moisture as he could from his tired body.

On the way to his car, he wondered what this latest vision could have meant. He walked out of the gate. The Monte Carlo was right where he had left it. He took out his key, and unlocked the door.

Then, he saw a boy trudging slowly by with a large canvass bag. "Mitchell?" he called to the boy. "Mitchell Lorenzo? Is that you?"

The kid looked up with wonder and suspicion. Then, he said, "Hey, Mister. I remember you. You're that guy who bought the Beckenbauer house."

"That's right."

"What are you doing in the graveyard this early in the morning?" Mitchell asked. "You look like hell."

"Thanks a lot."

"Oh my God," Mitchell gasped. "The Beckenbauer house! Did you spend last night in Nobody's Grave? I bet you did! Didn't you?"

"Don't get carried away, kid."

"What was it like?" asked Mitchell. "Is it true what they say? Did you have to face your troubled past? Did you see the Van Poucks? Was it scary? Are you going insane yet?"

"Calm down, Mitchell," he said. "I'm not sure what happened to me last night. I'd love to find out, though. Can I ask you a few questions?"

"Well, I don't know," Mitchell said. "I have to get home so I can go to school. And, I probably shouldn't even talk to you if you're going crazy."

"I'm not going crazy," he said. "I only want to ask what you know about that grave. You just mentioned my troubled past and the Van Poucks. What's the connection? What's really going on with that grave?"

"So, you *were* in Nobody's Grave last night," the kid observed with a gasp. "I knew it! Listen, Mister. I don't know if I should even talk to you . . . since you're on the edge of going crazy and all. Besides, I don't even know your name."

"I told you," he reminded. "I'm not going crazy. And, my name is Mr. Wilburn."

He offered his hand to the boy for a handshake.

"Listen, Mr. Wilburn," Mitchell said as he shook his head. "I'll talk to you for a minute. But, then I've got to go home. And, I ain't shaking your hand. Nothing personal. But, I never shook hands with a dead man before, and I ain't about to start now."

"What are you talking about?" he asked. "I'm not dead."

"You will be if you stay in that house," the kid informed. "Or crazy. Either way, I ain't touching you."

"Have it your way," he said while putting his hand down.

"I'm sorry, Mr. Wilburn," Mitchell said. "No disrespect, sir. I know you'll probably leave that place long before you die or go nuts. But, I'm not taking any chances."

"So, what can you tell me about Nobody's Grave?" he asked. "What's the connection between my past and the people in this town?"

"I can only go by what I've heard," Mitchell admitted. "But as I understand it, Nobody's Grave is what they call a fissure in the ground."

"A fissure?"

"It's like a fracture," Mitchell explained. "It's a gateway into the weaknesses we all have that makes us human. They say Gordon Van Pouck's wife used some gypsy curse to bring it about. Nobody knows exactly what it was. But, the Beckenbauers' need to find each other is the weakness that Mrs. Van Pouck was abusing."

"You mean, Edgar and Ingrid's love for each other?" he asked.

"Yup," Mitchell nodded. "Mrs. Van Pouck haunted her husband after she died. She drove him nuts, and convinced him to hide the body . . . knowing that the Beckenbauers would never rest if they weren't together through eternity. I don't think Gordon's wife knew the full power of the curse she used, or that it would mirror the weakness of anyone who entered the grave. She only wanted to torture the Beckenbauers. But, no one really knows why."

"So, the imperfection and fragility in the human mind is the key?" he asked.

"Pretty much," Mitchell said. "Nobody's perfect. We all have something we won't let go of. That's why the gypsy curse was so easy to find and use. That's why the curse worked even better than Gordon's wife wanted. All she had to do was curse some object that connected Mrs. Beckenbauer to her husband."

His eyes grew wide. "You mean like a gold chain with a locket?" he asked.

"What?"

"If Mrs. Beckenbauer wore a gold chain with a locket," he suggested. "And the locket had a picture of her husband in it . . . could Mrs. Van Pouck have cursed such an item to activate Nobody's Grave?"

"I guess," the kid shrugged. "Provided the chain stayed with Mrs. Beckenbauer and away from her husband. But like I told you, it's all legend. Can I go now? I'm late for school. My mom's definitely going to kill me."

"Sure," he said. He was staring off into space. "Thanks, Mitchell. You've helped me more than you know. Do you need a ride somewhere?"

"No thanks."

He watched Mitchell for a minute. He studied the kid who rushed down the hill. Then, he got in his car and drove home.

* * * * * *

She kept her gaze down. She refused to look up at eye level. She walked nonchalantly toward her destination. There was nothing unusual to tell. There was nothing to discuss.

She took her place at the center cash register, as two other cashiers regarded her with expectation. For a moment, the background music of a radio was the only thing that broke the silence.

Then, in the spirit of the charade, she spoke. "Good morning, girls," she said.

"Good morning, Heidi," they chorused.

"How did you like your days off," the younger girl asked. "Did you do anything exciting?"

"Not really."

She concentrated on the money she was counting. The other two girls glanced at each other.

"Tamara told me you had another date with Russell," the elder girl pointed out. "How did it go?"

"It went great," she said. She was still counting. "But, Tamara should learn to keep her mouth shut."

"I only told Daisy," she defended. "It's not as if she doesn't know already. You can't expect me to keep her in the dark."

"Why is my life such an obsession with you two?"

"Because we're your friends," Daisy replied. "And we care about you."

"I'm sorry," she sighed. "Listen. Everything went great with Russ these past few days. You have nothing to worry about. Okay? I'm really starting to like him, and I hope things keep going the way they're going."

"How much are you really starting to like him?" Tamara pressed.

"What does that mean?"

"Oh, nothing," Tamara fumbled. "I just . . ."

"Look," she insisted. "Everything is wonderful. There's no big news to report. We're not engaged or anything yet. Believe me. If there's something you need to know, I'll tell you. All right? Now, please let me count my cash drawer."

"Okay, Heidi," said Daisy. She watched as her friend counted her money with a familiar blush in her cheeks. "We'll leave you alone."

Then, she glanced over at Tamara.

Daisy and Tamara grinned as they nodded to each other. They each had a happy gleam in their eye.

Their friend finished counting in silence. Then, she closed her drawer.

* * * * * *

After a shower, he sat down to a cup of coffee. He had a lot to do. Still, he had time to relax in front of the television before getting started. He rubbed his sore neck as he watched the morning news.

One story in particular caught his attention. He sat up straight as he listened.

"Autumn Police are currently looking," the announcer said. "For a woman who has been missing since yesterday. Sharon Kellerman, who works as a broker for The Colby Realty Group on Sixth Ave., disappeared from her office around 10:30 yesterday morning. Celia Johnson, a coworker, said that Kellerman was going to look at a new house that someone wanted to put on the market. However, in her hurry, she never told anyone the address."

He watched the story with growing interest.

"She never returned to her office," the announcer continued. "And her husband, Bernard, said she never came home last night. Kellerman, a 50-year-old native of Autumn, resides with her husband on Baybridge Blvd. in the north end of town. Anyone with information on Sharon Kellerman's whereabouts should contact the Autumn Police Dept. as quickly as possible. And, in other news . . ."

He looked at the picture which flashed on the screen along with her description.

A creepy suspicion nagged him as he sat with his coffee. He took a sip as he watched local events which were not quite so distressing. The uncomfortable feeling grew worse as he stared at the screen.

Somehow, he suspected that there might be a connection between Sharon's disappearance and his house . . . and the mansion. He didn't know why he felt that way. It made no sense. What could the connection be? Perhaps it was just a coincidence.

Maybe not.

He continued to stare at the screen.

The weatherman came on. He promised more thunder storms that evening.

Still, he stared at the screen.

Suddenly, the doorbell rang. It snapped him out of his daze. He walked to the front door and opened it. "Mrs. Burgdorf?" he said. "I mean, Maria. How are you? Come on in."

He held the door for her as she carried in a fresh pie. "Good morning, Russell," she said. "I hope I'm not disturbing you."

"Not at all."

"I was up baking since early this morning," she said. "I had to make some pies for a church function. And, it occurred to me that you could use a nice cherry pie."

"That's very sweet of you, Maria," he said. "Thank you. That wasn't necessary."

"As I said," she reiterated. "I was baking anyway. Plus, Jerry told me you had this place almost in order last time he was here. I wanted to see for myself."

"I'll just put this in the kitchen," he said as he took the offering. He carried it into the other room, as his guest surveyed her surroundings.

"This place looks lovely, Russell," she said. "My husband was right. You've done a fine job turning it into a home."

"Thank you," he said. "I've done what I can with the resources at my disposal. By the way, here are your pans from the other night. You really have to stop bringing me food. It's very kind, but I don't know where to put it all."

"You're young," she observed. "You need to eat."

"Would you like to sit down?" he offered. "I have coffee made."

"I'll sit for a minute," she said. "But, I've already had enough coffee today. I'm fine. Thanks just the same, though."

As they sat in the main room, he asked, "So, what brings you here, Maria? I get the impression you have more on your mind than just pie."

"Well, I guess I just wanted to check on you," she admitted. "I wanted to see how you were getting along in your new place."

"You mean," he deduced. "Since this is the Beckenbauer house?"

She rolled her eyes. "Yes," she sighed. "I should have known it was a mistake to introduce you to Clayton Spencer at the barbeque. He loves those stories. And Jerry tells me you've been talking to that paperboy, Mitchell Lorenzo."

"That's right."

"Look, Russell," she explained. "Please don't listen to local gossip. This is a nice house in a pleasant little town. You seem like a fine young man, and I would be delighted to have you as a neighbor."

"Thanks."

"This property has been vacant for so long," she continued. "I want to see this house occupied and kept up. It would make the neighborhood more appealing over all. But, every time Sharon Kellerman sells this place, the residents start listening to people like Clayton and Mitchell. It's disheartening to see this place abandoned time and time again."

"Speaking of Sharon Kellerman," he said. "Did you hear she disappeared yesterday?"

"Yes," she said. "I saw it on the news this morning. I hope she's all right."

"Do you think there could be a connection between her and this place?" he asked.

"Now, see?" she said. "That's precisely what I was talking about. What possible connection could there be between Sharon and this house? Sure, she sold this place to you. But, so what? Who would care?"

"Have you ever met Elliott Van Pouck?" he asked.

"Not many people have," she said. "And what does he have to do with this conversation?"

"The man is absolutely insane," he imparted.

"You've met him?" she asked with sudden interest. "But, how could that be? You just moved here a few days ago."

"He still made a point of meeting me," he said. "He's crazy. And, I believe he's dangerous. He told me that Ingrid Beckenbauer wants me to leave her house."

"That's ridiculous," she scoffed. "Why would he say such a thing?"

"Maybe the legends are true."

"That's absurd," she commented. "There are no such things as ghosts or haunted houses. Elliott may be a fruitcake, but nobody is haunting anyone in this town."

"That's what I used to think," he began.

The phone interrupted him with a loud ring. His eyes grew wide. The phone rang a second time. "It can't be," he declared as a chill ran up his spine.

"What's the matter?" she asked as he jumped to his feet. She watched him rush over to the phone that hung from the wall.

"It's impossible!" he exclaimed as he stared at the phone. As it rang a third time, he said, "I unplugged this phone a few days ago. I swear!"

"You couldn't have," she said as she followed him. She pointed to the jack as she continued, "See? It's plugged in."

"But, that's exactly my point," he said. "I yanked that plug out days ago. Watch."

He pulled the jack out of the wall. The phone rang again.

Maria stared in amazement. "That's unbelievable," she stammered. "Maybe it's some sort of electrical glitch or something."

The phone rang again.

"That doesn't make any sense," he said.

"Well, I don't know what else to think," she replied.

The phone rang again.

"Aren't you going to answer it?" she asked.

He hesitated. The phone rang again.

Finally, he reached out and picked up the receiver. He put it to his ear and said, "Hello."

There was a heavy, eerie silence on the other end. He knew she was there. He knew what she wanted. The silence nearly seemed to crawl up his skin.

Then, he heard the meek, timid voice. She sounded alone and frightened. She said, "Help me. Please help me!"

He stood and listened to the ensuing click and dial tone. The tone was as steady and unwavering as the sensation of something slithering under his flesh.

Maria stared at him as he hung up the phone. "Who was it?" she asked.

"It was her," he muttered. "Ingrid Beckenbauer."

"That's preposterous," she replied.

"It's true," he insisted. "She wants me to help her. Or she wants her husband to help her. Either way, it's not the first time she called for that reason."

"How could she want you to help her?" she asked. "She's dead. Besides, what could she want you to help her with?"

"You know the stories," he reminded. "She wants me to help her find her husband. Or, that's what I'm guessing. I'm not sure what to believe anymore, because Elliott Van Pouck told me that she wants me to leave this house. Maybe that's how she wants me to help her."

"This is all getting too implausible," she remarked. "Next you're going to tell me you've seen ghosts."

"I have," he averred. "I know it's hard to believe, but it's the truth."

"Russell," she declared. "I'm losing patience with this conversation."

"You were right here when the phone rang," he reminded.

"See?" she pointed out. "As soon as you start talking about this place, people's imaginations start running wild. You almost have me believing this stuff."

"What about all those people who bought this house before me?" he pointed out. "They can't have all been crazy. Mitchell told me people have actually died in this house because of this."

"Mitchell is a teenager who believes kids' stories," she said. "No one died in this house with the possible exception of the Beckenbauers. That's just another reason not to believe everything you hear in this town."

"Aren't you at least concerned about Sharon Kellerman?" he pressed.

"Of course I'm concerned," she said. "I've known her for years. But, there's no reason to suspect Elliott Van Pouck had anything to do with it."

"Well, I don't have any evidence," he admitted. "It just seems like an odd coincidence. Still, it's nothing I could take to the police."

"That's for sure," she agreed. "What would you tell them? You live in the Beckenbauer house and you've seen ghosts? They'd laugh at you, just like they've done to everyone who's lived in this house before you."

"But, I've met Elliott," he persisted. "He's crazy. And, he thinks Ingrid doesn't want anyone in this house. However, that's no reason to go after Sharon."

"Just let it go, Russell," she said. "Throw that phone out. It's obviously defective. Forget whatever you think you saw, stop listening to Clayton and Mitchell, and have a nice life in your new house."

"I wish it was that easy."

"It is," she insisted. "If you let it be. Now, I really have to go. Thanks for returning my pans. Enjoy the pie. And stop thinking about ghosts."

He watched her carry the empty pans to the door. "Maybe you're right," he said. "Maybe it *is* just a coincidence. I don't know why I can't shake the feeling that lunatic is involved. Thanks for the pie."

"You're very welcome, dear," she said as she walked out the door.

He watched her walk down the steps.

"And, take my advice," she called back. "Throw that phone away."

"Will do," he said. "Would you like help with those pans?"

"No, thanks," she said. "Have a nice day."

He returned the sentiment as she disappeared in the shade of a row of trees by the side of the road. He still wasn't sure what to think when he went back inside.

Just to be safe, he took the phone off the wall. He threw it in the nearest garbage can.

* * * * * *

He sat in the study. He was in a big, comfortable chair by his desk. He was reading Charles Dickens. He was not wearing a pink bathrobe. In fact, he was dressed in casual menswear. He seemed calm. He seemed rather peaceful.

Then, a flash of light caught his attention. The iridescent shadow of a man stood at the far end of the table. It stood solitary and silent in the dim light of the study.

The old man in the chair looked up. He smiled with recognition. "Dad?" he called. "Is it really you? It's been such a long time."

The specter remained silent and motionless.

"Dad?" the old man called again. "Can you hear me? Can you speak? You have no idea how happy I am to see you. Do you remember Penelope? She's Joseph Hughes' daughter. She's such a beautiful girl, Dad. So charming and lovely. She agreed to marry me, Dad. We got married years ago. She bore me three wonderful children: Phillip, David and Kathleen. They're all wonderful. And so well behaved. You should meet them. Can you stay for dinner? I'm sure the maid can accommodate one more."

The shadow remained still and lifeless.

"You'd love my Penny, Dad," he continued. "She's a splendid wife and mother. I only wish you had stayed around long enough to see how perfect my life has become."

The apparition finally moved. It reached up above its head. It pulled a rope that appeared out of nowhere. The glowing rope seemed to drop out of the solid ceiling.

The noose was already tied. The knot was perfect.

"What are you doing, Dad?"

The shadow slipped the noose around his own neck.

"Dad? Stop that! What are you doing?"

The rope lifted, dragging the spirit up by its neck. The specter gasped and flailed as it hanged. It struggled for breath as it dangled from the noose.

"Dad!" screamed the old man. "No! Please don't!"

He jumped out of the chair. He ran around the table so he could help his father.

However, the image vanished before his eyes.

"Dad!" he wept hysterically. "Please don't leave me! Please don't go!"

He collapsed in a chair by the table. He put his head down in his arms on the table. He cried as he begged for his father's return.

Even through his tears, he recognized his father's voice. The voice spoke as if he were sitting in the next chair. However, no one was there. The voice warned, "My stepmother, Katalina. She is inside of you . . . as she was inside of me . . . and my father before me. She will always be inside you, Elliott. You will never know what she is capable of, my son. But, she will always be a part of you."

The voice fell silent. However, the old man cried into his folded arms.

In the dim light of the study, the coat rack behind him was partially obscured in dismal darkness. He had forgotten it was there. He just sat at the table and wept.

And hanging from the coat rack, an old bathrobe cast a long shadow against the wall.

* * * * * *

"I'm telling you," she insisted. "It scared the hell out of me."

"I'm starting to think you've been in this town too long."

"This isn't a joke, Jerry," she said. "The phone kept ringing even after he unplugged it. You should've seen the look on his face when he answered it. He said it was Ingrid."

"And you believe him?"

"You had to be there, Jerry," she said. "It was all so spooky."

"What's happened to you, Maria?" he argued. "You used to be the voice of reason. You used to have a firm grasp on reality. You saw them finally put that house on the market after it had been a vacant eyesore for too many years. You were glad we'd have neighbors instead of declining property values. You scoffed at the first few owners and their tales of ghosts and hauntings. Have you finally cracked? Have you buckled under the constant pressure of the local folklore?"

"The phone kept ringing, Jerry," she persisted. "I was there. I saw it with my own two eyes. And, I could tell someone was on the other end. I don't know how, I could just feel it."

"Oh my God," he declared. "You really have cracked."

"Who's to say the stories aren't real, Jerry?" she questioned. "How do we know for sure those things didn't happen the way so many people have claimed? It's difficult to believe that everyone who has owned this house was crazy."

"Common sense is all you need to disregard those people," he explained. "It's as pure and simple as that. I don't know what was wrong with all of them. But, I do know that there are no such things as ghosts and goblins. They just don't exist."

"I want to believe that," she admitted. "I used to believe that wholeheartedly. But, now I'm not so sure. Of course, I didn't say anything to Russell."

"That's good, at least."

"I'd like to see him stay there," she commented. "He seems like a fine young man. Whatever is happening over there, I hope he works it out. But, something's not right over there. Maybe I'm feeling the influence of Sharon's disappearance."

"That's very likely."

"She's such a dear woman," she said. "It's not like her to just take off. Someone must have kidnapped her. And it's so easy to blame the Van Poucks. They're the first conclusion anyone jumps to when something happens in this town. But, what motive could Elliott Van Pouck possibly have for going after Sharon Kellerman?"

"There is no logical explanation," he said. "You're just understandably upset. Put Sharon out of your mind. Try to think positive thoughts. And whatever you do, don't lose your grip. This is not a fantasy world. There are no such things as ghosts."

"I want so much to keep believing that," she muttered as she stared off into space. "But, if you had been there . . ."

She paused before finishing, "I still say there's something wrong with that house."

* * * * * *

159

Later that night, the darkness outside seemed assertive and formidable. The thunder and lightning had stopped, at least. However, the rain still hurled itself against windows and walls with an impressive force.

They listened to the rain as they sat together on her old, comfortable sofa. After a sip of coffee, he put his arm back around her shoulder.

"I'm glad you decided to come out with me tonight," he said. "Sorry about the short notice. If I had realized what day it was, I would have asked you out sooner. I wouldn't want to leave you sitting home on a Friday night."

"That's okay," she said. "With my work schedule, I tend to forget what day I'm up to, also. But, it's nice making a point to get out on a Friday evening for a change. I probably stayed out longer than I should have. I'm supposed to be at work tomorrow morning."

"You can always take the day off," he suggested. "It's not as if I'm going to fire you."

"I really don't want to get into a situation where either one of us exploits our working relationship," she explained. "That's one of the reasons I hesitated to start anything with you. If we're going to do this, we have to keep the store separate from our personal lives."

"You're right," he said. "I'm sorry."

"That's okay," she said. "I wish we could spend more time together, too."

"I had a wonderful time tonight," he said. "I don't believe we stayed out this late, went as many places as we did, and still haven't been to the same place twice. I never would have suspected a town like Autumn would have such a night life. I was expecting us to end up back in Sky Shards again."

"I thought you liked Sky Shards."

"I do," he said. "But, there were so many other places to go, we didn't need any repeat performances. You're doing a great job of showing me around."

"We really didn't go to that many places," she informed him. "It just seemed like a lot because you were with me."

"Is that right?" he asked. "Does that even make sense? Well, it doesn't matter. I'm in my favorite place right now."

She allowed a quick laugh before they kissed. One kiss turned into two, and then three. An omnipresent mood was becoming more difficult to ignore.

When she pulled away, she commented, "I knew it was a mistake to invite you in for coffee tonight."

"Why do you say that?"

"Because I have to go to work tomorrow," she reminded.

"Do you want me to leave?"

"No," she said. "Not right away. I just have to keep my priorities straight. I'm glad you're here. It feels nice having you around. I just don't want it to get too easy to . . ."

Her voice trailed off in discomfort.

He broke the awkward pause by saying, "I hope you're not feeling any pressure from me. It's not my intention to rush you."

"No," she said. "You're all right. I guess I just don't know what I want or expect yet. But, that's my problem, not yours."

"Well," he said. "As long as I'm included somewhere in the picture, I'll be happy with whatever you decide."

The smile she gave him was delicate and enticing. This kiss was invited and almost vital. Subtle decisions were won, lost and forgotten.

"By the way," she observed afterward. "We always come back to my place after a date. When do I get to see your place? Your house has got to be much bigger and nicer than my tiny apartment."

"I told you," he reminded. "I just spent all afternoon regrouting the bathroom. There's a few other projects I'd also like to finish. The place is still a work in progress."

"I don't care about a few imperfections," she said. "I know you just bought the house. I'll understand if it's not the ideal example of a palace in the country."

"Okay," he acquiesced. "I promise I'll let you see it soon."

"You'd better," she smiled. "I'd hate to think you were hiding something from me."

"What could I possibly be hiding?"

"I don't know," she poked. "Maybe you're farming sheep. Maybe you're harvesting cow dung for fun and profit."

"Cow dung?" he replied. "I gave that up years ago. Sure, the money was good. But, I couldn't keep the flies out of the house."

She laughed as they began to kiss. She even told him that he was sick before they kissed again. Uncertainties were washing away like the dirt from a fine chassis in a carwash.

Her head was resting comfortably on a cushion near the armrest. She was lying beneath him on the sofa. She looked up at him with sweet green eyes as she reiterated, "I said it before, and I'll say it again. I knew it was a mistake to invite you in here tonight."

"That's too bad," he teased. "Because now you're stuck with me."

"What if I don't want to be stuck with you?" she asked playfully.

"Well, it's easy enough to find out whether you do or not," he suggested. "I can always use my own patented lie detector."

"You have a lie detector?" she asked. "Where is it?"

"Right here," he said.

They kissed again. And, he was right. Her kiss told him exactly what he wanted to know. She knew it, too. She allowed the slow, natural process of communication to unfold amid their mutual affection.

"You have a patent on that?" she managed to ask with a giggle.

"You bet," he whispered. "I'll show you the paperwork tomorrow."

The open truth was so soft and warm underneath. The gentle current which brought them together flowed evenly and uninterrupted. And like the falling leaves of autumn, they traveled with an elegant flourish to where they had always been destined to go.

CHAPTER 9.....
A_LEGACY_OF_
MADNESS_____

He glanced around the ostentatious front room. It seemed even gaudier than before. Under the layers of dirt and corrosion, everything maintained an air of the splendor it once held. The sparkling chandelier hung broken and dusty from the ceiling. The grand fireplace stood not as proudly as before. It was grimy. Stones were chipped, cracked and needed to be replaced. Picture frames were without photographs. One of the tarnished gold candlesticks was missing.

The stairwell at the far end had once been such a regal and elegant fixture. At this moment, it was a crumbling tribute to neglect and decay.

He wished he could have seen this room in its heyday. He wished he could have witnessed the glory that had been a hallmark of this prestigious family. But of course, it was too late.

Somehow, he felt at home here. It almost felt as if he belonged in these dilapidated halls. He watched a shadow slink by. It didn't startle him. It didn't make him feel uneasy.

He glided up the stairs as if by choice. He would have sworn that he knew where he was headed. Everything seemed so incredibly natural.

Then, he heard a raised voice in the other room. The speaker sounded a bit testy. Without a sound, he followed the noise. He positioned himself outside a door so he could see without being seen.

He recognized the mysterious vision of the woman. She wore the same hat. She almost looked as though she were actually in the room. She sneered at the balding old man in the chair before her.

"You're a sniveling little coward, aren't you?" she averred. "You're just like your father. No wonder Penelope wants to leave and take your children away. She can't bear the sight of you."

"That's not true, Grandma Katalina," he tried to argue. "My Penelope loves me. That's why she married me. We have three wonderful children together."

"Those insufferable little brats?" she scoffed. "You consider them to be an accomplishment to be proud of? I've seen inside their souls, Elliott. They're as wretched as you. They will amount to nothing, just like their worthless father."

"I'm not worthless," he demanded. "And neither are my wife and children!"

"I never said Penelope was worthless," she grinned. "She made a mistake marrying you. She knows that now. That's why she wants to take the kids and leave. There may be hope for her and those brats if she does."

"Penny doesn't want to leave me!" he insisted.

"Then, why do you need to keep her in the cellar?" she questioned. "You have to keep her down there . . . with the children. You have to keep them, or they will leave."

"Penny would never leave me!" he shouted.

"She'll never stay with you, Elliott," she said. "Not if she's given a choice."

"She won't leave me!" he bellowed through tears. "She loves me! I know she does!"

The woman vanished right before his eyes. The old man jumped to his feet in shock. He glanced frantically about the room. The woman in the hat was nowhere in sight. However, her voice continued its haunting strain without any apparent visible source. "She will never stay, you fool. Not unless you force her. She will never stay if you let her out of the cellar."

"No!" he cried. "Please, Grandma Katalina! I'm not a fool!"

" . . . Never . . ."

The old man was nearly hysterical. It was difficult to watch him.

He left the old man weeping in his solitude. He drifted backward through a hall. He felt weightless. He felt alive. He felt at peace with his surroundings. Then, he saw another image approach him. It almost glowed in a dim, murky fashion. It caught him off guard. Before it even drew near, he knew it seemed out of place.

Something wasn't right.

Somehow, he knew who she was before he caught a clear glimpse of her face. He saw the torn gashes in her blouse. Her eyes were still wide with terror. It almost seemed as if she had just died moments before. He wondered if she had even realized what had happened. Her movements were awkward and unsure.

He felt a chill as she stepped out of the shadows. He could no longer deny her identity. He could no longer hope he'd been wrong.

"Sharon Kellerman!" he gasped.

The shock of his discovery awakened him with a start. He sat up in bed. It took a few moments to catch his breath. He glanced around the darkened room. It was small and unfamiliar. This added to his immediate sense of distress.

Then, he recognized something. He remembered where he was. He gazed down at the girl sleeping beside him. He breathed a sigh of relief. She looked so sweet and peaceful . . . almost child-like.

He brushed a strand of hair from her face with his hand. She made a gentle sleeping noise. She moved a bit. Then, she was still.

He settled down beside her in bed. He felt better. Certain thoughts continued to trouble him, however.

For instance, he wondered why he would have had such a dream if he weren't at home. The image of the spirit taunting the old man replayed in his mind. And, the last thing he saw kept gnawing at him. He knew it was a sign. It confirmed his fears.

These thoughts rolled over in his head as he struggled to go back to sleep. After a while, he was able to drift off again.

The next time he awoke, he was alone. The covers were crumbled and wrinkled in the empty space beside him. Sunlight spilled through the curtains and splashed up along the bed. Its faint glow illuminated the tiny room with a murky atmosphere. An alarm clock on the nightstand read 9:21.

He got up and walked to the other room. The apartment was still and quiet. It almost appeared to be abandoned.

There was a note on the kitchen table. He turned on the light and picked up the note. It read:

> Russ,
>
> I had to go to work this morning. Had a great time last night. Thanks for everything. I left the coffee pot on for you. We'll talk soon. Call me.
>
> —Heidi

* * * * * *

"I'm glad you decided to join us today, honey," she said. "I was beginning to worry."

"Why would you worry?"

"It's almost time to open," she said. "It's not like you to be this late."

"I'm always a little late."

"Yes," she admitted. "But, not quite this late. If I didn't know better, I'd swear you went out with someone special last night."

"Give it a rest, Daisy," said the girl with the tired, green eyes. "I just got a late start this morning. I overslept a little. That's all."

"Okay. If you say so."

"I do say so, Daisy," she averred. "And, don't you even start, Tamara."

"What are you giving me a hard time for?" Tamara defended. "I haven't said a word. I had no intention of implying that you went out last night with any certain store owner. What do you take me for, Heidi?"

"Just let me count my money before we open," she snipped. "All right?"

"Fine," Daisy said.

"You can tell us when you're ready," Tamara allowed.

"Tell you what?"

"Whether or not you went out last night with a certain store owner," Tamara said. "But, remember. I didn't bring it up."

"Yes you did."

"Fine," Tamara surrendered. "So, did you?"

"Yes," she begrudgingly confessed. "I went out with Russ last night. That's why I'm late. Are you happy? Can I count my money now, please?"

Tamara opened her mouth to speak. However, she saw Daisy shaking her head as a signal. She acquiesced with a sigh. She watched her friend count a stack of bills.

Daisy and Tamara shared a glance.

As their friend opened her register, she made an awkward attempt at a recovery. "So, Tamara," she asked. "How are things between you and Josh?"

"Great," Tamara said, as if she didn't notice. "Just wonderful."

And after an uncomfortable pause, she repeated, "Everything is just wonderful."

* * * * * *

"I remember you," she said. "You're the guy who bought the Beckenbauer house."

"That's right," he said. "It's nice of you to remember."

"I always like to keep track of my customers," she relayed. "Of course, I try to make more of an effort with those that I think will become regulars. Don't take it personally, but it's hard to list you in that category."

"I don't plan on going anywhere."

"No one ever does."

169

"Can I please just get a cup of coffee, Amy?" he asked.

"Sure," she said. As she went to grab the pot, she added, "Will you be having lunch here today?"

"I haven't decided yet."

As she poured him a cup on the bar, she observed, "You look troubled this morning. Is something on your mind?"

"Well," he began. He paused before explaining, "I've had some problems at the house. I wasn't sure if I should tell anyone about this. But since you know where I live, I guess I can talk to you. Things are getting a little scary over there."

"I see," she said. "And you figure I'm the person to talk to? Is it because I'm a bartender?"

"If you don't want me to tell you, I won't," he said.

"No, no," she said. "Don't let me stop you. If you need to talk, I'm all ears. I'm sorry if I seemed a little cold. It's not you. It's just that you hear a lot of people tell a lot of strange stories in a place like this. And, the people involved in the Beckenbauer house are reputed to tell some whoppers. I've never heard any, personally. But, I know that it's not a good idea to put any emotional investment into anyone connected with that place. Most folks don't stay there too long."

"I'm not looking for emotional investment," he informed her. "I just need an uninvolved third party to listen."

"Then, I'm your girl."

"Weird things are still happening over there," he said. "I won't go into detail. That's not necessary. But, I think I told you that my new girlfriend wants to see my house. I'm afraid to take her there. I don't want her to freak out on me. She's already a bit skittish over rejoining the world of dating."

"Why?"

"She's had some bad luck in the past," he replied. "And, I don't want her to think of me as another link in her chain of bad luck. We could both use some good luck right about now. Plus, I have to wonder if the situation is dangerous over there. I don't want her to get hurt."

"I think we've already had this conversation before," she said. "I remember telling you that you can't keep her away from your house forever. She's going to get suspicious. And if she's already nervous about dating, she'll get suspicious more quickly than normal."

"So, what do I tell her?"

"Tell her the truth," she said. "I'm sorry, pal. But, there's no graceful way around it. You're going to have to tell her what's going on, and hope that she likes you well enough to stick it out."

"That's not very comforting."

"Love's a bitch, Russell," she imparted. "The sooner you face up to that fact, the sooner you'll move past your whining stage."

"That's kind of harsh, Amy."

"I'm sorry," she said. "But if you really care about this girl, you're going to have to come clean. That's all there is to it."

"I guess you're right," he admitted. "Especially now that things are getting complicated at the house. Elliott Van Pouck is a dangerously insane old man. And, I'm not sure how to say this. Have you heard about the disappearance of Sharon Kellerman?"

"That name sounds familiar," she said. "I think I recall hearing about her on the news. Her husband just offered a reward for information about her whereabouts."

"Really?" he asked. "I hadn't heard that yet. But, the weird thing is . . . I have reason to believe that Elliott killed her. I'd almost stake my life on the thought that her body can be found somewhere on the Van Pouck property. Probably in the mansion."

Her eyes grew wide as she listened. "Why do you think that?" she asked.

"I had a dream last night," he explained. "I saw her ghost in the mansion. I think she's trapped there because Elliott killed her."

"The guy who owns the Beckenbauer house had a dream?" she scoffed. "I'm sure that will impress the world at large. I'm sorry. I don't mean any disrespect. But, nobody's going to listen to you, if that's all you have to offer."

"I know," he said. "You're right . . . about everything. I have to do something to stop what's happening. I can't even think of a motive for why Elliott would want to kill Sharon. But, I can't just stand by and watch this anymore. I'm going to have to take action, and come up with some proof about what I know."

"And, how do you plan to do that?"

"I'm not sure," he said. "I guess I'll have to get into the mansion. Maybe I can search the grounds. I need some sort of tangible evidence. I need to show that I'm not crazy. I know I have to show the cops something. I can't just run to the police and tell them I see ghosts. They'd just laugh at me."

"That's right."

"I'm beginning to see the pieces of this puzzle come together," he said. "Somehow, someone has been showing me what happened between the Van Poucks and the Beckenbauers back when this all started. But, everything is happening so slowly."

"You're losing me again."

"That's okay," he said. "I know what I have to do to start things rolling. Someone wants me to solve this. And, I think I know who it is. I just have to speed things up a bit. Even if Elliott Van Pouck is a frightening little guy, I'm going to have to search for answers right in his back yard."

"Isn't that trespassing? And dangerous?"

"Probably," he admitted. "But, it has to be done. Besides, I even know why Elliott is so crazy. In my dream, I saw the spirit of Katalina haunting the old man."

"What?" she asked.

"Katalina's behind everything," he said.

"A lot of people have suspected that all along," she said. "Or at least, those people who believe in ghosts. Those rumors have been floating around for years."

"But, I saw her," he said. "In my dream, she was taunting Elliott. She is the reason he killed his wife and children."

"You still believe he did that?" she asked.

"Of course," he said. "And, Katalina made him do it. I am convinced she has intentionally driven him insane, along with every other member of that family. She's a bitter old hag who couldn't cope with her husband's infidelity. So, she's been torturing the entire family since her death. Her inability to let go of her past has trapped her spirit in that house along with the spirit of every other person who died there."

"That's an interesting theory."

"And, it's up to me to prove it," he averred. "I may have even discovered how she linked her family with my house. But, I need to know more. I need to prove it. And, I need to stop Katalina. She has tormented these two households long enough. She has poor Elliott so twisted up, he doesn't know if he's coming or going. No wonder he doesn't know who he is from one minute to the next."

"Well, listen," she said. "This is all quite fascinating. But, I have other customers coming in. Are you going to order lunch?"

"No," he said. "I'm not hungry. But, I'll take one last coffee for the road."

"Okay," she said. And as she poured him a cup, she added, "Good luck with whatever you decide to do. It would be nice to see the Van Pouck mystery come to an end. And, it would be nice to see you stay in town for a while."

"Thanks," he said. "I plan on living a long time in that house."

She smiled at him before going off to attend her new customers. He stared down into the steaming cup. He regarded the dark beverage as he considered strategies.

* * * * * *

They watched her run off to the rest room.

"I'm glad she's gone," she said. "I'm dying to talk to somebody about this. Of course, I'd rather discuss this with Heidi. But, she's not talking."

"Give her a break, Tamara," her friend said. "She's just getting back into the swing of things. Remember, it's been over a year since she's seen anybody. And, those three years with Charlie was quite an ordeal."

"I know," Tamara said. "But, we're her friends. She should want to share this with us. This should be a happy time for her. Why won't she tell us what's going on?"

"She's afraid to admit to herself that she feels something for Russell," she imparted. "So, what makes you think she'll admit anything to us?"

"I'm almost certain she's slept with him," Tamara said. "All the signs are there."

"Of course she has," she said. "But, don't push her. She'll tell us when she's ready."

"Do you think she falling in love with him, Daisy?"

"Why do you think she's so scared to talk about this?" she said. "If this was just a casual fling, she'd be much more open about it."

"I hear you," Tamara agreed. "But, I love Heidi. I want to be happy for her."

"We both do, honey," Daisy said. "But, you just have to give her time. She's being overly cautious because of her recent past. She'll come around and loosen up when she's ready. Don't drive her away. Just be patient. Sometimes, that's what friends have to do."

"All right," she said. "You probably have a point. But, this is going to drive me nuts."

"Me too," Daisy said. "But, you'll just have to suck it up. Ssshhh. Here she comes. Hi, Heidi. You didn't miss anything. The store's been quiet."

"What are you guys talking about?" Heidi asked.

"Nothing," Daisy said. "Tamara was just telling me that Josh is thinking of getting a new car. I told her to steer him towards a Camaro."

"A Camaro?" Heidi asked. "Can he afford something like that?"

"I hope so," Tamara answered smoothly. "I'm getting sick of that old Dodge."

* * * * * *

The iron gate was locked. He was disappointed, but not surprised. It had been a good idea to walk here from home. The sky was clear and sunny. It was warm, but not too hot or humid. It was a great day for such a project.

Scaling the fence didn't seem like his best option. It was too high. The rusted metal posts were pointed at the top.

He followed the gate along the side of the mansion. The other houses were set far away from this building. He figured the mansion had been alone on this block for centuries. These newer dwellings must have been added within the last hundred years. Still, he hoped no one could see him as he circled around the rim of the property.

Behind the mansion was a spacious parking area. The pavement was crumbling and cracked. Behind the parking area stood an old, abandoned carriage house. It had probably been an impressive structure in its day. Although, it had fallen into a state of disrepair. Rotting wood and chipped paint added to the unstable appearance of the building. It could barely be seen from the road. In fact, he hardly noticed it before. It seemed like a good place to hide things. He watched the structure as he moved farther down the fence.

Beyond that, there was an overgrown wooded section that eventually dropped off into a steep decline. He lost his view of the mansion and carriage house. This plot of land was more secluded. It seemed to be out of everyone's visual range.

He took his time searching the iron fence at this point. The woods began to surround him as well. He welcomed the sense of privacy afforded by these conditions.

Just before the steep drop off, he noticed a weak spot in the fence. It was raised, rusted and broken. Years of erosion and small animal intervention left a hole in the iron barrier. It wasn't big enough to crawl through. However, the rusty, warped bars looked weak and penetrable.

He grabbed two of the bars near the opening at ground level. He began to lift. It was difficult to gain proper footing in the mud. The bars creaked and complained. They began to give way. He braced himself and pulled harder.

Luckily, rust had consumed enough of the two bars. They bent a little, then broke off in his hands. He tossed them aside. The gap was almost big enough for him. Still, he bent a third bar far enough away to give him the necessary room.

He nearly had to crawl through the opening in the mud. However, he was able to gain access to the Van Pouck property. He stood and brushed the dirt from his pants as best he could. Then, he looked around.

A quick survey of the vicinity suggested that he should head back in the direction of the carriage house. The undergrowth was dense. However, it was passable. This place did not quite resemble a forest. The trees were not packed too closely together. Still, it appeared to be a wild, untamed terrain. It was a place that could easily conceal secrets. Anything could get lost here. Anything could be found.

He wandered farther away from the fence. He kept walking toward the mansion. This small patch of the world seemed so tranquil and serene. It was difficult to imagine the atrocities that must have transpired on this property.

The restful shade of the oaks and elms that stood proudly on this site made it feel like the most relaxing place on earth. Birds chirped casually. Sunlight floated down in calm, bright wedges between the green, leafy branches overhead. It was the perfect setting for a daydream.

He finally stepped out of the shade. He was in a clear spot of land behind the carriage house. He glanced around the area. Nothing caught his attention. He circled around to the front of the building. It was easy to see how this could have been a barn or a stable once. Like the mansion, it was a sagging, decaying symbol of the affluent past which had been enjoyed on this site so many years ago.

As he stood at the entrance, he looked up at the back end of the mansion. It stood nearly fifty yards from his position, across the crumbling parking area. There must have been some great parties here back in the old days, he thought.

Still, he didn't want to be seen from the house. He grabbed the latch to the giant front door. Luckily, it was unlocked. It easily swung open with a creak and a groan. He quickly slipped inside. He closed the door to a slit to avoid drawing attention.

Flipping a light switch on the nearby wall brought a few bulbs to life. However, the view was still dim and dusky. He glanced about the large, cluttered room. Dirt and grime covered everything. There were tools, machines and even a tractor.

Wooden compartments on the far end looked like the remains of a stable for horses. There were tables covered with cloth sheets draped callously over anonymous piles like filthy tarps. However, he didn't see any clues that could prove anything about what happened to Mrs. Kellerman.

There were so many things he wanted to prove about this family. However, Sharon was the most immediate concern. He also wanted to bring an end to the alarming incidents that seemed to plague his own home. He moved through the big room quickly, looking around as he went. He even lifted a few sheets from tables to see what was piled underneath. After a few rancid though worthless discoveries, he decided to stop doing that.

Eventually, he stepped on a loose section of boards. He looked down and saw that he had detected a sort of platform. Glancing around, he noticed a few ropes leading up toward the ceiling. The square hole in the ceiling seemed to roughly match up with the size of the platform on which he was standing.

Purely on a whim, he grabbed one of the ropes with both hands. He pulled the rope firmly downward. It didn't surprise him that his platform raised a foot or two off the ground. After a grin of self-satisfaction, he continued to pull the rope until he had lifted the platform up to the second floor.

He tied the rope to a metal handle that was attached to a nearby wooden pillar. As he stepped off the platform, he observed, "Well, that certainly came in handy. And to think I was going to go looking for a flight of stairs."

He glanced up over his head. As he suspected, a few of the ropes were attached to pulleys up by the rafters.

The second floor was still disturbingly dark. As his eyes panned the dismal surroundings, a flash of light startled him. A sudden movement made his muscles tense.

Upon closer inspection, he realized that he was seeing his own reflection. Apparently, a large, dusty mirror was leaning up against something not far from where he stood. He took a moment to laugh at his undue apprehension.

Cautiously, he began to move away from the platform. He searched for anything that might prove useful. He also searched for some light to aid in his investigation. He made his way carefully over to the nearest wall. However, he tripped over something on the floor. It felt like it was the approximate size and shape of a human body.

He fell to the hardwood floor with a clunk. He winced at the feeling of having skinned his knees. He turned to look at what he had tripped over. It was difficult to see in the incapacitating darkness. However, he thought he saw something that made him feel suddenly cold.

"Is that a hand?" he gasped.

He reached out to touch the object.

Then, he was interrupted by another flash of light. He looked up and recoiled at the terrifying sight before him.

The illuminated figure seemed to glow. The tall, gaunt man appeared to be overdressed. His eyes were vacant and hollow. His mouth curled down in a malevolent frown. And, he held a long, sharp knife in his right hand.

The intruder stared at this ghastly vision in disbelief. He jumped back up to his feet as the apparition slowly approached. He instinctively took a step backward. The glowing figure raised the knife as he moved toward the unwelcome visitor.

The intruder kept an eye on his grizzly attacker. He felt his way backward with his hands in an awkward attempt to escape. The ghost brandished the knife in a menacing fashion as he continued his advance.

The intruder stumbled against unseen obstacles as fear overshadowed caution. However, he managed to stay on his feet as he retreated from the oncoming threat.

He stumbled backwards. His retreat grew quicker. His footing grew more confident. There seemed to be a light behind him. It wasn't as dark in this corner of the building. The eerie attacker displayed the blade for his intended victim. There was no doubt that he wanted to stab his uninvited guest.

The intruder looked over his shoulder. The light was coming from below. He could see a stairwell in the corner. He turned and ran toward the light. He stepped over a few carelessly discarded items as he fled. At the top of the stairs, he glanced over at the creepy aggressor on his heels. The mysterious assailant was following him with a quicker pace. It still wielded his weapon in a hostile manner. Its face was twisted in a ferocious scowl.

The young man ran down the stairs to the first floor. There was enough light down there to afford adequate vision. He ran toward the huge front door of the building. He dodged the many impediments as he raced for the exit. The door was still open a crack as he approached.

As he flung the door open, it creaked and groaned. He glanced over at the stairwell. He could see his fearsome enemy making its silent, swift descent to the ground floor. The knife blade gleamed proudly in plain view.

As soon as he was outside, he pushed the door shut with all his might. It closed with a heavy thud. He wasted no time charging around to the back of the building and across the parking area. Then, he began to wade through the thick underbrush as he entered the wooded area at the back end of the property. Trees began to surround him as he fell under the shade of this untamed expanse.

Then, something peculiar caught his eye.

Near the edge of the woods, he noticed a few disruptions in the undergrowth. There were two parallel lines carved through the brush heading away from the mansion. They looked as though they could be tire tracks. It was as if someone had recently driven a car from the parking area through the woods.

He wanted to investigate. He looked back toward the carriage house. Even in the sunlight, he could make out the dim figure moving across the parking area. Apparently, the specter was still pursuing him.

Despite the inherent obstacles of the terrain, he followed the tracks through the woods until he approached the spot where he could see the drop-off up ahead. He glanced back over his shoulder. The shade from the trees made the frightening assailant easier to see. It showed no intention of giving up the chase.

181

He knew he was getting close to the hole in the iron fence. It seemed prudent to abandon the investigation for the time being. So, he swung off his course. He headed quickly for the spot near the steep decline that had helped to create his only possible escape.

The undergrowth got progressively thicker as he ran farther from the mansion. Roots and dead branches from the trees also hindered his race for freedom. He tripped over a short, dense growth of some kind and landed on his face. He quickly jumped up and checked over his shoulder again. The specter glowed with a murky haze in the shade of the trees. It glided effortlessly over the inhospitable terrain. It still held the long, sharp knife tightly in its bony hand. It was closing in on him with silent malice.

He resumed his race for the fence. He could see the rusty obstacle through the trees. It wasn't too far up ahead. His heart beat heavily as he reached the iron barrier. He quickly followed it toward the steep drop. He knew he was getting close, but he didn't have much time to search.

The malevolent spirit continued its steady pursuit. It didn't seem likely that a ghost would be willing or able to do him any harm. However, he had no time to quibble over such issues. He had to get out of there. That thing with the knife was narrowing the gap between them.

Finally, he saw the hole he had helped to create. He used the posts of the fence as a banister as he rushed toward his makeshift exit. His attacker was only a few feet behind him when he reached the aperture. It grimaced with anger as it raised the weapon to strike its intended prey.

He squatted down and leapt through the opening. He didn't have time to aim. And, a bent, broken post from the enclosure caught his upper arm. He cried out in pain as the jagged metal object tore a gash in his flesh.

He tumbled through the grass outside the Van Pouck property. Then, he looked over to see where the ghost was as he rose to his knees. He didn't see anything. He glanced all around him, both inside and outside of the fence. There was no sign of his pursuer.

Evidently, the apparition had vanished.

"Katalina," he whispered to himself as he stood. "She's behind this. She sent that thing after me. Obviously, she's determined not to let this mess come to an end."

He held his arm to control the bleeding. The cut wasn't massive, but it needed attention. He still felt a knot in the pit of his stomach. He didn't trust anyone or anything in this situation. He kept an eye over his shoulder as he hurried home to tend his wound.

CHAPTER 10.....
CHASMS_OF_FEAR_____

The days were getting noticeably shorter. Even on sunny days, it was nearly dark by 7:15 in the evening. The clouds were beginning to gather again, so it grew dark and dreary even earlier than expected.

She threw her purse on the kitchen counter as soon as she walked through the front door. She plopped herself down on the sofa. She turned on the television. She didn't care what show was on. She just didn't feel like making dinner for one.

The local news was finishing a story about a tragic tornado in the mid-west. Then, they started talking about something closer to home. A man named Kellerman was offering a reward for information about his missing wife. Apparently, he loved her very much and would do anything to ensure her safe return.

She shook her head and rubbed her weary eyes.

When a commercial started hocking laundry detergent, she got up. Luckily, the coffee pot had been turned off and the note on the table was gone. She was about to check the bedroom when the phone rang.

She answered, "Hello?"

"Hi, Heidi," said the caller. "This is Russ."

"Hi, sweetie," she beamed. "I was just thinking about you. How are you?"

"Not too bad," he said. "And, how about you?"

"I'm kind of tired," she said. "The first day back to work is always hard after a few days off. I'm glad that after tomorrow, I'm scheduled for a few more off days."

"That's strange," he commented. "Why is that?"

"I don't question the schedule rotation," she said. "It's a bit unusual, I grant you. But, Bill Green is a nervous, odd little guy. Who knows what he's thinking? I've learned to just roll with the punches. Frankly, I could use a break from Daisy and Tamara anyway."

"Why?" he asked. "I thought they were your friends."

"They are," she said. "But they won't stop prying into our business. And, I'm not ready to tell them everything they want to know."

"So, you haven't told them . . . everything?" he asked cautiously.

"No," she said. "I'm sorry, but I don't want to get too vested until I'm sure things are going to . . . work out."

He could hear the reluctance in her voice. "You mean, with me?" he gently prodded. "You're still not sure about me yet, are you?"

"I'm sorry," she said. "It's not you. It's me. I promised myself I would never make certain mistakes again. Maybe I'm being paranoid, but I have to be sure."

"It's okay, honey," he said. "Don't sweat it. You can be as paranoid as you want. I don't care. And, you can tell your friends whatever you want whenever you'd like. It doesn't matter to me. They're your friends, not mine."

"Thanks."

"No problem," he said. "Actually, I just called to see if it was too late to invite you to dinner tonight."

"I don't know," she said. "I'm exhausted."

"We can just get a quick bite somewhere and call it an early night," he suggested.

She considered the proposal for a moment. "I'll tell you what," she finally said. "You can take me to dinner if you let me see your house."

"You want to see my house?" he asked. "Tonight?"

"Is that a problem?"

"Not really, I guess," he sputtered. "I told you it still needs a lot of work."

"And, I told you I understand all that," she said. After a suspicious pause, she added, "I'm beginning to get the impression that you don't want me to see your house. Is there any particular reason for that, Russell?"

"No," he defended. "Of course not. I just thought you were too tired to . . ."

"We're not going to do anything, Russell," she interrupted. "After dinner, we can have a quick cup of coffee, I'll check out your new house, and then you can take me home. If you're not keeping any secrets from me, it shouldn't be a big deal."

"All right," he said. "Calm down. If it's that important to you, I'll bring you back to my place after dinner. Okay?"

"Fine," she said. "You can pick me up in about an hour."

"Sounds good," he said. "I'll see you then."

She sat for a moment after hanging up the phone. A fleeting picture of Russell drifted across her mind. She wondered what was wrong.

At least, she hadn't let her guard down yet.

* * * * * *

"So, what do you want to do tonight?" he asked. "Do you want to go back to The Scathing Cauldron?"

"Sure," his friend said. "But, I might want to turn in early tonight."

"What's the matter?" he asked. "It's Saturday night."

"Yeah," his friend said. "But, I don't feel much like drinking. Hell . . . it's only 7:30, and you're trashed already, Charlie. Why don't you give it a rest. Remember, drinking is what killed Paul in the first place."

"The Sheep Man?" he said. "You don't have to tell me what killed The Sheep Man. He was my best friend. I know what killed my best friend."

"His name was Paul Sheppard, Charlie," his friend reminded. "And he was almost as drunk as you are when he wrapped his car around that telephone pole last week."

"I know what his name was, Jack," he snapped. "I just finished telling you he was my best friend. And where do you get off telling me how he died? What's with you lately, Jack? You used to be my friend. You used to be a cool guy to hang out with. But lately, you've been a whiny little wimp. You're turning into a real asshole."

"I'm an asshole?" asked Jack. "Why? Because I don't want you to wind up like Paul?"

"I'm not going to wind up like Paul," he protested. "Don't get me wrong. The Sheep Man was a great dude, God rest his soul. But, he drove like a woman. Even when he was sober. God, I miss him. We have to bury him on Monday, and you won't even drink to his memory."

"We've been drinking to his memory all week," Jack said.

"I know," he said. "But, The Sheep Man deserves a whole month. Maybe two."

"Let it go, Charlie," Jack persisted. "Your drinking is getting out of control. You saw it kill Paul. You lost the best girl you ever had . . ."

"Heidi?" he said. "Don't remind me about Heidi. The little bitch! Wouldn't you know I'd run into her right after The Sheep Man died. I didn't even get to tell her about it."

"I'm sorry," Jack said. "Forget I mentioned her."

"I almost did forget about her until I saw her the other night," he said. "Man, that brought back some memories. What a girl! Say, what were we even doing, going to a shit trap place like that, anyway?"

"We've been there before," Jack reminded. "You usually like that place."

"Well, not anymore."

"Just forget I brought it up."

"Heidi," he said in a nearly reflective tone.

"Don't even think about her, Charlie."

"Do you believe she ran out on me like that?" he said. "No warning. Not even a good-bye. She moved and won't give me her address. She slaps me with a restraining order, so I can't even see her at that damned store she works at. What the hell?"

"It's your drinking, Charlie," Jack said. "It was way out of control even back then. And, it's only gotten worse ever since. You used to beat her up, Charlie. You'd be surprised, but a lot of girls don't like that."

"I only did it when she didn't do what I fucking told her to do," he argued. "If she listened to me every once in a while, I wouldn't have to hit her. I never enjoyed doing it, you know. I'd never want to hurt my girl. She just wouldn't listen."

"Do you even hear yourself, Charlie?" Jack asked. "You sound like a lunatic."

"And, did you see that fucker she was with the other night?" he rambled. "What is she thinking? How the hell is that bastard better for her than I am?"

"Let her go already," Jack advised. "It's been over a year. She's not coming back. There are millions of other girls out there."

"I've had other girls," he replied. "None of them compare to my Heidi. She's the only woman I'll ever love."

"For God's sake, Charlie," Jack argued. "She's gone. You're not the only man who's lost a woman and had to move on. Get used to the fact that she's not coming back."

"Oh, she'll be back," he said with confidence. "She'll get sick of that twirp. Or, I'll take her away from him. Or, whatever. I don't know how, but I'll get my Heidi back. You can count on that, pal. Now, I need a drink. Are you coming or not?"

Jack rolled his eyes with a sigh. "Yeah, I guess," he said. "I'll drive."

* * * * * *

They sat in a booth by a window. The austere darkness outside made it impossible to enjoy the beautiful, secluded setting. They had already ordered dinner. He watched her in the wistful glow of candlelight.

"This is nice," she said. "Thanks, Russ. I'm starting to like this Nicole's place. It's kind of funny that you introduced me to it. I wonder why I'd never heard of it before."

"As the name implies," he reminded. "It's a 'Secret Retreat'."

"But, how did you find it?" she asked.

"Research, my dear," he stated. "I put some time into looking, because I knew you would be worth the effort."

"Thank you," she said with a coy smile. "But, if we're just going to have a quick dinner and call it a night, why did you take me to a place like this?"

"What were you expecting?" he responded. "Fast food at a drive-through window?"

"No," she said. "Just something . . . not as fancy."

"If you want to leave," he suggested. "We passed a burger joint about a mile down the road. We can always . . ."

"Don't you dare," she interrupted playfully. "This is much better."

"But, you can't get a jumbo order of fries here," he continued.

"Stop," she said with a delightful little laugh. "I don't want any food that requires opening those annoying little catsup packets."

"Too bad," he said. "I brought a few in my back pocket just in case."

"Maybe we can use them with our dessert," she teased.

Her green eyes sparked and toyed with him in the deliciously subtle candlelight.

"So," she said, to break a momentary silence. "I finally get to see your house, huh? I was wondering when you were going to give me security clearance."

"I'm sorry, Heidi," he said. "I wasn't trying to keep anything from you. I've only been living here for about a week. I just don't want your first impression to be that I live in some half-constructed barn or an asylum."

"And, I'm sorry, too," she said. "I keep letting my paranoia get the best of me. You've been so great about everything. I guess I'm looking for the catch. I'm looking for the down side. I really shouldn't be so anxious to find whatever it is that will make you appear less than perfect. I'm sure I'll see something eventually. I should try to be happy as long as it lasts."

"Well, I do have a mole in my armpit," he admitted.

"I know," she said. "It's hideous."

"And, it hasn't driven you away?"

"It's not as scary as that thing on your back," she informed him.

"What thing on my back?"

"Oh, relax," she said. "Any good doctor can remove it with a hot needle and a sharp scalpel. By the way, you still haven't told me what happened to your arm."

"I mentioned I was fixing up the house, didn't I?" he said. "I must have cut it on a broken piece of piping."

"Sounds nasty," she said. "Did you have a doctor look at it?"

"That's not immediately necessary," he said. "Perhaps I'll show it to someone when I go in for that thing on my back."

She giggled before taking a sip from her drink.

Rain began to splatter lightly against the window. The drops became larger and more numerous as their meal progressed. By the time they got back to his place, they were in the midst of a downpour. He parked in the garage, so they could enter the house without getting wet.

As she walked through the house, she gave it a quick visual inspection. When she got to the main room, she commented, "This is a great place. Why were you afraid to let me see it? It's fabulous."

"Thanks," he said. "I guess I'm a bit of a perfectionist. It still needs work in a number of spots. Just don't cross any police crime scene tape that you find strung up anywhere."

"Okay," she snickered. "It's a deal."

"Sit down," he offered. "Make yourself at home. I'll go start the coffee. If you want to turn on the TV, feel free. I think Channel 36 is showing some 'Mr. Ed' reruns right about this time of night."

"Actually, coffee seems a bit ridiculous at the moment," she said. "I'm tired, and I need to go home and get some sleep. Do you have any wine?"

"As a matter of fact," he said. "I just put a wine cellar in here yesterday. I haven't done much to fill it, though. I can probably fine some red or white . . ."

"Red would be fine. Thanks."

He ran off to find a bottle and a corkscrew.

She called after him, "You built a wine cellar in your kitchen?"

"It's a big kitchen," he called back. "And a very small wine cellar. Some might call it more of a cabinet."

He pulled a bottle from a shelf. He nodded at his choice. He fished around in a drawer for something to remove the cork.

Then, he stopped. He thought he heard a noise in the other room.

He listened for a moment, but it was gone.

"Heidi?" he called.

There was no reply.

He put the bottle on the counter. "Heidi?" he repeated.

Then, he heard a scream. He raced into the other room as another scream tore through the air.

Heidi was sitting on the sofa. She was visibly shaken. She was trembling so much you could almost hear her clothes rattle. Her stark face had gone completely white. Her eyes were wide and fearful.

He glanced around the room. Nothing seemed out of the ordinary.

"What's the matter, honey?" he asked.

She managed to look at him with a terrified stare after a few moments. She finally stuttered, "Y-you're not going to believe this. B-but, I saw a man standing right over there in the m-middle of the room."

As she pointed at the spot, she continued, "I almost thought it was Charlie for a second. But, it didn't look like him. And, the clothes were all wrong. L-like some old movie. Then, he just vanished. I know it sounds crazy, but it's almost as if it were a g-ghost!"

He stood very still and silent.

"Maybe Charlie's having a greater effect on me than I thought," she deduced through her panic. "Maybe he's got me so scared of seeing anyone, it's got me seeing things."

"Don't say that," he said with a nervous sigh. "It's probably not you."

"Why?" she asked. "What are you saying?"

He sat on the sofa and put his arm around her quivering frame. Then, he asked, "First of all, are you all right?"

"I suppose," she replied. "What's going on?"

"Well . . .," he began, while searching for an explanation "I'm not sure what . . ."

Before he could finish, Heidi cut him off with another blood-curdling scream.

He followed her gaze back to the center of the room. The faint shadow of a specter stood near the armchair. It was thin, and wore old period clothing. It looked vaguely familiar. It was too short to be the creature that had attacked him in the Van Pouck's carriage house. Still, he knew he'd seen this spirit before.

Then, it occurred to him. This was the man he'd seen curled up by the entrance of this very room. This was the corpse that had disappeared before his very eyes. Even though he had no way of knowing, he was sure of this man's identity.

"Edgar!" he whispered in shock.

The vision scowled with empty eyes. It raised a knife in it's clenched fist. It began to march toward the sofa. Heidi shrieked as Russell leapt to his feet to protect her.

Then, the image vanished.

The couple gawked at the vacant space near the armchair. There was no sign that anything strange had transpired.

After a long pause, she was the first to speak. "What was that, Russell?" she asked.

He sat back down beside her. He chose his words carefully. He spoke slowly, as he imparted, "What would you say if I were to tell you that this is the Beckenbauer house?"

All color drained from her face again as she stared at him. She finally asked, "This house? This is the Beckenbauer house? *The* Beckenbauer house?"

He nodded silently.

It had to sink in. It took her a full minute to respond.

"Oh my God," she muttered. "I don't believe it. I thought I heard you say, 'Edgar.' Is that what you meant? I was just accosted by the ghost of Edgar Beckenbauer?"

"I think that's who it was."

"That's just perfect," she complained, almost to herself. "That's the story of my life. After all this time, I finally . . . *finally* meet a guy I like. I nearly even let my guard down for a second. And now, he turns out to be the guy who owns the Beckenbauer house."

"Don't flip out on me, Heidi," he began. "Let me . . ."

She either didn't hear him, or else she ignored him. She was still speaking to herself as he tried to explain. In her shock, she was attempting to process information.

"So, it's true," she said. "All those rumors and legends are true. This place is really haunted. I was just attacked by a ghost. That's why nobody who buys this place stays here for more than two weeks before they go screaming off into the sunset, never to be heard from again."

"Are you okay, Heidi?" he asked. "Are you even aware that I'm here?"

She was still talking to herself while staring at the carpet. "I'm finally interested in a guy," she explained to herself. "But, he bought the Beckenbauer house. It's really haunted by ghosts who attack people with knives. Now, the man I started to like is going to go screaming off into the sunset. In a week or two, he's going to leave this town and never return. I'm never going to see him again. And, oh my God! I nearly let myself feel something for him. I almost allowed myself to feel something!"

"Come back to me, Heidi," he said. He grabbed her shoulders and shook her gently. He didn't want to be violent. He only wanted her to snap out of her shock.

She stopped speaking. Her green eyes drifted away from the floor. She suddenly looked back at him as tears dripped down her cheeks.

"Russell?" she said. "It's true. I almost let myself have feelings for you."

"You still can," he told her. His hands were still on her shoulders as he continued, "I'm not going anywhere. I'm not leaving this house. I'm not leaving this town. And, I'm not going to leave you."

"Of course you are," she said. "Everyone leaves this house. And, now I know why. I certainly can't blame you. But, once you're gone . . . you're gone."

She was weeping by the time she rose to her feet. "I can't do this, Russ," she said. "I can't stay with you if you're going to leave in a week."

"I'm not going anywhere," he insisted as he stood. "I don't care what other people have done. I'm not going to be driven out of my own house."

"Good," she said. "Then, maybe Edgar can kill you in your sleep, instead."

"Nobody's killing anybody," he said. "Not here, anyway. Don't you see? That's why I didn't want you to come here. I knew you'd react like this. I didn't want to scare you off. Everyone in this town goes nuts whenever you mention this subject."

"Now we both know why," she said. "I . . . I have to get out of here."

As she turned toward the front door, he asked, "What do you mean? Where are you going? Don't leave like this."

She didn't even face him. She just walked slowly toward the door as she replied, "How should I leave, Russell? Is there a better way? Tell me. I'd love to know what it is."

"You're upset, Heidi," he said. "I understand completely. But, this isn't the solution. Believe me. This little situation is only temporary. I'm looking into what's going on. I've already found out some of the real story. It's only a matter of time until I figure out how to fix this whole mess."

"Oh, really?" she said as she finally turned to face him. She stood at the front door as she continued, "And, where are you getting the story from? Are you talking to ghosts, Russell? Am I dating a guy who talks to ghosts?"

"Well, no," he tried to explain. "I just . . . well, I talked to Elliot Van Pouck. He lives in the mansion up the road. He's the last surviving member of that family. He's very old, and incredibly insane. Potentially dangerous . . ."

"So, talking to old, dangerous, crazy people is going to help you?" she argued. "You don't have to rehash the legend for me. I've lived in this town a lot longer than you have. I've heard all there is to hear. Maybe the old guy will die next week. Maybe not. But even if he does, you're not in the clear. The Beckenbauers will continue to haunt this house and attack people with knives until someone finds out what happened to the wife's body. She could be anywhere on that property. She doesn't even have to be on that property. She could be anywhere in the township of Autumn, and no one would know. The Van Poucks used to own this town back in those days. They could've done anything with that body, and nobody would have asked any questions."

"Will you let me explain?"

"How did you even meet Old Man Van Pouck, anyway?" she inquired.

After a reluctant pause, he answered, "He sort of invited me to the mansion."

"He invited you?"

"I can't tell you every detail right now," he said. "But, trust me. I'm getting the answers I need to solve this mystery. I've even been to Nobody's Grave."

"Nobody's Grave?" she asked. "You mean that children's story about where the wife wants to be buried? Now I know you're crazy. Oh my God! First, Charlie Putnam and now you. I always wind up with the crazy men. How does this happen?"

"I'm not crazy," he insisted. "You just saw Edgar's ghost. You know the legends are true. I'm asking you to believe in me."

"All the rumors say that whoever owns the Beckenbauer house always sees Nobody's Grave just before they go running out of town," she imparted. "So, not only are you insane, but you'll be leaving Autumn any minute now."

"I'm not leaving this house," he repeated.

"I have to go," she said as she reached for the doorknob.

"I understand if you need time to think," he said. "But, please don't just run out of here like this. Promise me that you'll talk to me about this. Promise me that you'll give me some time to iron this out."

"No, Russell," she said. "I'm not promising anything. I'm not going to get involved with a guy who's going to leave town in a day or two."

He watched her open the door as he said, "I bought this house, and I'm not going anywhere. Don't leave. Be reasonable. At least let me drive you home. It's raining outside."

"I can call a cab from my cell phone," she told him.

"You can't wait out there," he said. "You'll catch your death."

"Do you think my chances are better in here where ghosts run around with knives?" she asked. "And crazy guys tell stories about visiting graves that don't exist? Good-bye, Russell. Thanks for the lovely evening. Thanks for everything. It's been a blast."

"Please don't do this, Heidi," he begged. "Please?"

She didn't say a word as she stepped out onto the porch. He could hear the rain pouring outside before she closed the door behind her. There was a heavy, dull pain in his stomach as she quickly disappeared into the dreary darkness and the cumbersome burden of rainfall.

He wanted to go after her. He desperately needed to talk to her. It seemed nearly imperative to save her from both the rain and her clouded judgment. However, he knew that pursuing her would be pointless.

She was in no condition to be receptive to anything he could say.

He turned away from the door. The rain outside sounded intimidating in its aggressive assault on the neighborhood. It was difficult to assume she could stay dry even hiding under the cover of the many trees that lined Agnes St.

It hurt him deeply to return to his living room. However, he knew she needed time. He could only hope that time would make a difference.

The pain grew deeper and more agonizing as the night progressed. It surprised him to note the effect this girl had on him. He had met her nearly a week ago. And, the dreadful fear of losing her almost paralyzed him.

He tossed and turned in bed. He couldn't get to sleep. He could no longer hear the rain. The totalitarian darkness closed in around him.

Suddenly, he saw something. A bright, glowing figure stood beside his bed. He recognized her face from before. She stared at him with beautiful, sad eyes. Her long, white dress flowed gracefully to the floor. And for the first time, he noticed the delicate chain she wore around her dainty neck.

Before he could stop himself, he whispered, "Ingrid!"

She watched him silently for a minute. He was afraid to move. The spirit did not seem angry or vengeful. She appeared almost as if she had something to say. She continued to watch him as she glided toward the bedroom door. He couldn't help feeling as though she wanted him to follow her.

Slowly, he rose up out of bed. He didn't take his eyes off her. He watched her walk through the closed bedroom door. It startled him. However, it did not frighten him. He just opened the door and stepped out into the hall.

She was already standing at the top of the stairs. She began her graceful descent as he followed behind her. The crisp darkness beat down on him like the opposite of sunshine. The stillness seemed to wrap around him with all the intent of a hungry boa constrictor. Still, he felt compelled to follow this bewitching apparition.

He didn't even hesitate when she passed effortlessly through the front door of the house. He just opened the door and followed her to the sidewalk. He knew where she was leading him. He had felt this compulsion before. He just never realized its source.

The rain appeared to have stopped. The air was moist. Large puddles reflected the lights which lined the road from the street lamps. He walked behind this glowing mistress without insolence. The air had cooled considerably. The night was calm and passive.

He wondered if she had been responsible for the similar compulsions he had felt earlier. Still, he followed her up the hill.

He wondered if she had been the hand who had pushed him into Nobody's Grave. Still, he followed her up the hill.

He wondered . . .

They walked past houses. No one stirred. No cars drove by. Nobody else strode along the drenched sidewalks. No one with beautiful green eyes waited under trees for cabs. There were no witnesses to this vital journey.

They walked past the Van Pouck mansion without slowing down. He followed her right to the gate of the cemetery. She glowed even brighter as she glided over the soil of the dead. He pursued without question as she led him where he knew he had to go.

Her illumination reflected off the smooth surfaces of gravestones.

Then, she disappeared rather suddenly.

He stared in disbelief.

After a moment, he continued his stroll to Nobody's Grave. He knew that he was destined to go there. And as suspected, the neatly dug hole in the earth awaited his arrival.

He didn't hesitate to gaze down into the grave. His new troubles with Heidi gave him added incentive to see what the spirits had to show him.

The daunting spectacle of the skeleton lying on its back didn't even phase him. He stared down at the human remains with a brave determination.

He recognized the chain and locket the skeleton wore around its neck. It was identical to the jewelry worn by the specter that had led him here. Things grew clearer in his mind. He was beginning to see Ingrid as an ally rather than an enemy.

He jumped down into the grave without worry. He didn't flinch when the figure lifted its bony arm and pointed a slender finger at him. He watched anxiously as the skeleton traced four letters into the muddy wall of the grave. It wrote, "K-A-T-A".

Then, the floor dropped out beneath him, as expected.

The feeling of falling into an endless pit of despair engulfed him again. He tumbled helplessly down through the chasm of fear and desolation that had claimed him before. He kept falling through the anguish of loss.

He kept falling . . .

Then, he found himself back in the grand front room again. Everything was beautiful, elegant and polished. A fire was slowly burning itself out in the fireplace. It was late at night. It was nearly time for bed. She was calm and relaxed as she watched the flames dance and dwindle before her eyes.

She sat leisurely in a soft, comfortable chair. She wore her favorite pink bathrobe with white trim. She was accepting a drink from a maid as he marched angrily down the ostentatious staircase. He appeared to be gripping a string of cheap beads in his white-knuckled fist.

She glanced at his approach with a dismissive sense of amusement. She quietly said, "Thank you, Lillian. You may go."

"Yes, ma'am," Lillian replied with a quick bow. She quickly carried a tray out of the room in silence.

"Katalina!" he bellowed as he reached the bottom of the stairs. "Katalina! What is the meaning of this? What are these accursed baubles, and why did I find them on my pillow upstairs?"

"Why, Gordon, darling," she said with a touch of arrogance. "They're simply Gypsy Reprisal Beads. I bought them from a charming little lady downtown. She owns an absolutely delightful little shop where one can purchase all manner of such enticing trinkets. I should take you there sometime."

"Never mind that!" he grumbled. "What are these hideous beads doing in our bed? And, on my pillow?"

"It's the most curious thing, really," she explained. "The darling little woman told me that she cast a spell on those beads. If I chant a certain phrase when I place them on your pillow, it will cause a rather intriguing consequence."

"And, what might that be?"

"Well, absolutely nothing," she said. "If you've been faithful to me. However, if you have shared our bed with anyone other than your wife . . ."

She paused to grin confidently. There was a look in her eye that he found disturbing.

"Let's just say, dear husband," she finally continued. "I sincerely hope you don't find out."

"Are you telling me," he pressed while stewing quietly. "That you put some sort of a Gypsy curse on me? Using these pathetic little beads?"

"It's only a curse if you've been unfaithful, darling," she expounded. "If you have been loyal, you've nothing to fear. It's the perfect stroke of justice, really."

"I will not be made sport of in this manner!" he shouted. "I will not have our marriage rely on games with cheap trinkets purchased from hooligans and ne'er-do-wells!"

He stormed over to the fireplace and tossed the beads into the dying flame.

They both watched the fire rise up around the beads. They sparked and burned for a moment. Then, the flame instantly extinguished itself. Everything in the fireplace became instantly cold.

His jaw dropped in amazement.

"It doesn't matter anymore, Gordon," she said. "You can throw them out, or burn them. Do whatever you like. They have served their purpose. It all depends on you now."

"You think you're so clever, don't you?" he scoffed. "Do you really think some silly Gypsy curse is going to scare me? Only a fool would believe in such nonsense."

"Then, why are you so angry, dear?"

"I'm not angry anymore," he said. "In fact, I'm beginning to find this entire episode rather humorous. My wife wastes money on frivolous beads sold in worthless trinket shops downtown."

Then, the string of beads moved. It appeared to hop by itself out of the fireplace and onto the hearth. That's where it stayed silent and still.

He recoiled from the sudden interruption. His eyes grew wide as a wisp of smoke still rose from the inanimate object.

"What was that?" he asked. "How did you do that?"

"It wasn't me, dear," she said. "It was the beads. They don't like to be mocked."

"If you're trying to scare me," he warned. "It won't work. I don't fall for parlor tricks, Katalina. I'm the richest, most powerful man in this town. I didn't get that way by believing every magician and con man who comes down the pike."

"That's true," she admitted. "You were born into the family fortune."

"You're not funny, Katalina!"

"Oh, aren't I?" she said as she stood. "Don't I amuse you, Gordon? Perhaps it would be amusing if I welcomed inappropriate intruders into our marital bed, like my darling husband. Would that be funny?"

"Katalina!" he gasped. "Such language from a woman of your stature! It's unthinkable! It's unforgivable to even joke about such things!"

As she stepped away from him, she added, "Why? Is infidelity an indulgence only to be enjoyed by men? I should hardly think so. Who would they be disloyal with? How would your common Mrs. Ingrid Beckenbauer answer such questions, my love?"

"You leave her out of this!" he warned. "I told you nothing happened between us."

Although she wasn't facing him, she asked, "Then, why are you so mad? Why are you defending her? Why is your face so red?"

"Because I'm sick of your unwarranted accusations!"

"As I mentioned," she reminded. "If you're telling the truth, you have nothing to fear. However, if you are lying, the consequences will stretch far beyond the two of you."

"Your threats are meaningless to me, woman!"

"Are they?"

"I'm sick of your smug attitude and righteous indignation!" he snapped. "Stop this foolishness this instant! And, don't you dare threaten Ingrid!"

"Why, Gordon?" she prodded. "What will you do? Whatever will you do if I choose to threaten that little tart of a smuggler's wife?"

"Shut up!" he shouted. He grabbed a solid gold candlestick from the mantle with such force, the candle it held was propelled across the room. He brought the candlestick down upon the back of her head with a fierce blow that sent her crashing to the floor.

She managed a scream or two. However, he was on top of her immediately. He continued to beat her mercilessly with the solid gold instrument again and again, while furiously barking, "Shut up! Shut your filthy mouth . . .!"

He kept shouting and beating her long after she fell silent and still. Then, he stopped when he realized what he had done. Slowly, he rose to his feet. He looked down at his wife's bloody, lifeless face. He looked at the blood-stained candlestick in his hand.

He could only stand there as the shock of his actions rolled through his brain like a tidal wave of guilt and despair.

Then, he heard another scream.

He looked up to see the maid standing just inside the doorway. She was staring in horror at the terrifying sight before her.

"Lillian!" he cried as he dropped his weapon.

She could only stand petrified as he ran up to her. He grabbed her by the shoulders. He shook her violently while sternly advising, "Lillian! Don't you dare breathe a word of this to anyone! Not a soul! I swear if you tell anyone, I will kill you with my bare hands! Do you understand? Do you understand?"

She cowered beneath his threatening gaze. She trembled as she peered frightfully up at her menacing employer. "Yes, Mr. Van Pouck," she answered meekly. "As always, I remain your humble servant, sir."

She was still quaking in his grip. As he glared down into her horrified eyes, his gaze eventually softened. Finally, he let go of her shoulders. He grew calm and in control.

"Of course you are," he admitted. "You have always been a faithful, valuable treasure to the family, Lillian. Your loyalty is a commendable asset, my dear."

"Thank you, sir."

"You may go."

"Yes, sir."

As she scurried off, he turned his attention to his motionless wife . . . the blood-stained candlestick on the floor . . . and the string of beads which sat harmlessly on the hearth.

When Russell awoke, he suddenly sat up in his bed. His breathing was labored. He was drenched with sweat. And, an eerie darkness still cloaked his room under the mysterious cover of night.

CHAPTER 11…..
A_PLEA_IN_BLOOD_____

She was being brave. She wasn't going to cry. It wasn't even that big a deal. She followed her morning routine. She skipped breakfast, because she wasn't hungry. There was time for a leisurely drive to work.

It was a superficial pain. It was unnecessary. It was temporary. It would pass. She wouldn't let it ruin her day.

The air was cool and pleasant. It smelled of wet grass in morning sunshine. The faint rainbow reminded commuters of the previous night's storm. The sun was bright, but unobtrusive. A gorgeous blue sky allowed a few fluffy clouds to drift aimlessly by.

. . . She wouldn't let it ruin her day.

She wasn't in the mood to face the girls. She knew she could sidestep the questions. She just wasn't in the mood.

The usual eight or nine cars were in the parking lot. Aside from that, the place looked deserted. She parked in her favorite spot, and took a moment to brace herself. She reminded herself how easy it was going to be to keep from crying. She took a deep breath. Then, she entered the building.

Music played softly in the background. Bright lights illuminated well-stocked aisles in an amiable fashion. The store was nearly ready to open.

She put on a smile for greeting coworkers as she picked up her money. She made a point of being nice to Danny when she signed out her cash drawer. However, her stomach tensed as she approached her station. She wished there was a way that she could avoid this. The knot in her stomach grew tighter when she saw the girls and the cash registers. This was going to be harder than she thought.

. . .She wouldn't let it ruin her day.

"Good morning, ladies," she said through a forced a smile.

"Hi, Heidi," Daisy said. "How are you today?"

"Fine."

"Hi," Tamara said. "You'll be proud of me. I'm not even going to ask what you did last night, because I wouldn't want to pry. I'm sure you'll tell us when you want to."

"There's nothing to tell, really."

Daisy watched her count her money. She didn't want to interrupt her. Still, she couldn't wait. She tried to be delicate when she asked, "Heidi? Are you all right, honey?"

"Yes," she said. "I told you I'm fine. Everything's wonderful."

Tamara looked over with sudden concern.

"Are you sure?" Daisy asked as she inspected her friend's face with growing apprehension. "You don't look too happy."

"Now that you mention it," Tamara agreed. "Daisy's right. You look terrible."

"Thanks, girls," she said sarcastically. "That's just the kind of ego boost I need."

"What's wrong?" Daisy asked. "Did you have a fight with Russell last night?"

"Why do you automatically assume I had a fight with Russell?" she defended. "Does everything in my life have to revolve around Russell? Can't I just have a bad morning without it being about a guy? I have a life, you know. The key to my happiness does not depend on any one man."

"Sounds like boy trouble to me," Tamara surmised.

"Cut it out, Tamara."

"So, what happened?" Daisy asked. "You guys were getting along so well yesterday."

"What did he do?" Tamara said. "Is he married? Is he gay?"

"No," Heidi said. She took a deep breath. Then, she continued, "You're never going to believe this. He lives in the Beckenbauer house."

The girls gasped in shock.

"*The* Beckenbauer house?" Daisy inquired.

"Wow!" Tamara declared. "I didn't see that coming."

As Heidi nodded, Daisy asked, "How do you know? Did he just come out and tell you?"

"No," Heidi replied as her mood steadily declined. "He took me to his house for the first time last night. I saw a ghost."

As the girls gasped again, she added, "It attacked us. Then, it vanished. Russell said it was probably Edgar."

"You saw Edgar Beckenbauer's ghost?" Tamara inquired. "You mean, the rumors are true? That house is really haunted?"

"Yes," she said through sniffles.

"So, what did you do?" Daisy asked.

"I left him," she said. "I told him good-bye forever."

"What?" Tamara pressed as delicately as she could. "You left him because of a ghost in the house?"

"What else was I supposed to do?" Heidi asked as tears welled up in her eyes. "You know what happens anytime anyone buys that house. They never last a whole month. That house has been sold at least ten times, and nobody ever stays there past a couple of weeks. Sure, I know why now. They weren't all crazy. But, it doesn't matter what his reasons are. When Russell runs off like the rest of those people, he'll still be gone. Why should I stay with him and drag this thing out?"

"How do you know he'll leave?" Daisy asked.

"Everybody does!" she said through a trickle of tears.

"But, if you stay with him," Daisy explained. "He'll have one reason to stick around that no one else had."

"I didn't want to even get into this in the beginning," Heidi said as a few more tears leaked out. "Remember? You talked me into it. And, what's the use, now? Even if he stays there, who wants to date a guy who lives in a haunted house? Would you like to go to a guy's house if you knew Edgar Beckenbauer's ghost is going to chase you around with a knife any time he feels like it?"

"Wait," Tamara said. "I know that legend. The house will only be haunted until the wife gets buried beside her husband, right?"

"Yes," Heidi said. "But, no one knows where the body is. It could be anywhere in Autumn. They've been searching for it for over seventy years. What makes you think Russell can find what nobody else can?"

"You could help him," Daisy suggested.

"What?" Heidi asked. "Are you nuts?"

"Well, what do you know so far?" Daisy asked.

"I know that you're as crazy as Russell is," she said. "If you think I'm getting mixed up in this. Why should I? What's in it for me?"

"Russell," Daisy replied simply.

Heidi didn't speak.

"How do you really feel about him?" Tamara asked. "I mean, how much . . .? Or I mean, did you . . .?"

She couldn't bring herself to finish the question.

After a pause, Heidi snipped, "What, Tamara? Did I do what? You mean, did I sleep with him? Is that what you were going to ask, Tamara? I'm sure you've been dying to ask me all week. Let me save you the trouble. Yes, Tamara! Yes, I slept with him. Are you happy now? You can run out and tell the whole world that I had wild, passionate sex with Russell Wilburn!"

"Please don't take it like that, honey," she said. Her guilt grew deeper as she saw a new stream of tears on Heidi's cheeks. "I didn't mean it that way."

"Didn't you?"

"Of course she didn't," Daisy said.

"I haven't said anything to anyone. I promise."

"She cares about you," Daisy added. "You know we both love you very much, Heidi. We just need to know how you feel about Russell. Do you . . .?"

After a pause, Heidi asked, "Do I what? Do I love him? Of course not! How could I? I've only met him a week ago. How could I possibly . . .?"

She stopped. She was silent for a full minute. Her friends waiting patiently for her to finish. Then, she said, "I don't know. Oh my God! How stupid is that? What's wrong with me? How could I not know? I shouldn't even be thinking about that crap yet. You ask me if I love him, and I have to answer, 'I don't know.' I must be an idiot."

"It's okay, honey," Tamara said. She held her sobbing friend. "Everything will be fine. You'll see."

She let her friend cry on her shoulder for a minute.

As Heidi's tears subsided, she said, "This is so pointless. I promised myself I wouldn't cry over some guy that I've only known for a week."

"That's okay," Tamara said. "There's nothing wrong with feeling something for someone. There's no such thing as a wrong emotion."

"Yes there is," Heidi argued as she pulled away and wiped her eyes. "Believe me. I know. Where are you getting your fortune cookie philosophy from?"

"The Amazing Dragon on Western," Tamara said. "I like their Moo Shu Chicken."

Heidi began to laugh.

Then, Tamara added. "I think you owe it to yourself to talk to him, though."

"But, he's crazy," Heidi said. "He told me he's been to Nobody's Grave."

"You mean, that kids' story?" Tamara asked in surprise.

"Yes," she said. "That's how I know he's going crazy, just like anyone who's owned that house. That's one of the main reasons I left him. I don't need any more raving maniacs in my life. I've already had enough of those."

"Maybe Nobody's Grave is real," Daisy suggested. "You saw the ghost in his house, right? Maybe all the stories are true."

"You must be kidding me!"

"It's like Tamara said," Daisy reminded. "I think you owe it to yourself to find out. At least, talk to him. After all, he's going to be your boss soon, too."

"Not if he goes screaming out of town before October," Heidi argued.

"Just talk to him," Tamara quietly insisted.

"I don't know," she said. "Maybe."

"Would you like to get out of here today?" Daisy offered. "Take the day off and think? Perhaps make a phone call or two?"

"That's a good idea," Tamara agreed. "You have the next few days off anyway. You need some time to sort things out. I think Stacy is back from Florida already. She's scheduled to come in tomorrow. Maybe we can get her to come in a day early."

"Or, the two of us can handle it," Daisy said.

"Thanks, guys," she said. "But, I'd rather work today. This whole thing is not such a big deal. I could use the money. Work will keep my mind off my troubles. Plus, if I want to call Russ, I can do it later."

"Are you sure?" Daisy asked.

"Positive," she said. "But, thanks. You guys are the best."

"Don't forget to count your money," Tamara reminded. "The store will be open in about fifteen seconds."

* * * * * *

He took his time in the shower. Standing under the steady stream of hot water felt soothing and relaxing. It promised to be a long, unpleasant day. He wasn't looking forward to facing it.

Eventually, he had to turn the water off. He dried himself off, and stepped out onto the tile floor. He stood at the bathroom sink with a towel tied around his waist. He wiped the steam from the mirror and prepared to shave. He shook a can of shaving cream. He was about to dispense the foam into his hand when he looked back in the mirror.

He saw a reflection of a familiar face watching him from behind. It startled him to see the image of a spirit in his mirror.

He spun around to face the intruder. However, she was gone. He glanced around the room. There was no sign that anyone else was present.

He even politely called out, "Ingrid?"

However, there was no reply.

He dismissed the incident with a shrug. Then, he turned back around to resume his morning routine. But this time when he looked in the mirror, he was confronted with a more gruesome sight.

A dark red liquid appeared to be smeared along the wall behind him. It looked as though someone had tried to write a message on the wall in blood.

He gasped while staring in wide-eyed terror. He spun around to see if it was really there.

The wall was still stained with thick, crimson smears that resembled crude lettering. The edges of some of the letters dripped blood down the vertical writing surface, which added to the horrifying effect of the message. It read:

"PLEASE FIND ME . . ."

He dropped the can of shaving cream. It bounced off the tile with a loud clank. He was trembling as he leaned back against the sink.

A number of thoughts ran through his mind. A lingering sense of fear was the most prominent. Until recently, he was under the impression that these spirits were harmless. But, after being attacked by ghosts with weapons (both in his home and in the Van Pouck carriage house), it seemed logical to reconsider that opinion.

At this moment, he was facing messages written in blood on his wall. It was getting more difficult to ignore the fact that his life was in serious danger.

He was still a bit shaky when he bent down to pick up the shaving cream he'd dropped. When he stood back up, the message was gone. The wall was clean.

He stared at the blank wall in disbelief.

Under the circumstances, he decided to hurry as he shaved. His stomach was tied in knots. He felt vulnerable in that small, unprotected room.

When he was finished, he dressed and went downstairs for breakfast. He decided to watch television in the main room while waiting for the coffee to brew. After ten minutes or so, he went back to the kitchen. He chose his favorite route through the hall where he had once hung his phone.

As he entered the hall, he saw something that sent a chill up his spine. He shivered as he stared at another message scrawled in blood. This time, the thick, sloppy letters dripped blood down the wall in the hallway just outside the kitchen. This time, the creepy correspondence read:

"BEFORE I SPELL HER NAME . . ."

He couldn't take his eyes off the frightful spectacle as he cautiously continued down the hall. He tried to stay as far away from the wall as he could. Once he made it to the kitchen, he was able to pour himself a cup of coffee with unsteady hands. However, he decided to forget about breakfast. He wasn't particularly hungry before. At this moment, eating was unthinkable.

He glanced down the hall as he came out of the kitchen. He wasn't too surprised that the writing had vanished.

However, he still chose to gain access to the main room by way of the dining room, instead of the hall.

His mind wasn't on the show he watched as he drank his coffee. He jumped up a few times to check the hall. The wall was completely free from any kind of stains.

He was glad when he finally left the house. It felt good to get away from the building. He wasn't sure what to make of the dreadful messages he had received. However, there were other concerns he needed to address. Not only was his house becoming a supernatural hazard, but his personal life was falling apart.

These visitations had distracted him in an unpleasant way.

Still, he had to wrestle with his feelings regarding a certain grocery store cashier. She had always been a bit squeamish. But at this point, she was downright frightened. And, who could blame her?

He'd only known her for about a week. Still, her abrupt departure had a tremendous impact. Even with the turmoil of living in a haunted house, all he could think about was getting Heidi to talk to him.

The weather was incredible. It was delightfully mild and sunny. Traffic was brisk for a Sunday. Families were out enjoying a marvelous September weekend in Rhode Island. Soon, the nights would be getting colder, and the leaves would change their colors. And, everyone knew that a brutal winter was not far behind.

For the time being, however, the streets of Autumn were filled with people who gladly accepted the beautiful day at hand.

He needed to collect his thoughts. He didn't want to just run to the store. It was not a good idea to push her too quickly. There was also the matter of the house . . . not to mention Sharon Kellerman or Elliott Van Pouck.

Fehr's Steak and Ale would not be open this early on a Sunday. He drove through town while running errands that seemed meaningless. He picked up a few things at the hardware store. He picked at a greasy omelette with home fries in a diner. He made a few other stops that seemed important at one time.

Around mid-afternoon, he decided he needed to pick up some groceries. It only made sense to go to the store that would soon be his responsibility. It was a short drive to Thornton Ave., anyway. So, he had all the more reason to go there for the miscellaneous sundries he required.

There were only a few cars in the parking lot. It looked as though The Golden Eagle could use a few customers. He parked near the front of the building. He took a deep breath before entering. Going into the Van Pouck mansion wouldn't even make him feel this jittery.

He walked through the sliding glass doors. The first thing he looked for was the cash registers. Each register was attended by a cashier. They sat idle at their stations. They were not burdened by patrons. They weren't talking much at all. He maintained a casual stride as he approached.

He greeted Daisy and Tamara as if nothing were wrong. They politely returned his greeting. However, their faces told him that they knew.

Next, he greeted Heidi. Her response was not very warm. She hardly even glanced in his direction.

He took it as a sign. Without a word, he walked back to the food aisles.

He found a few necessary items. He had no list. He couldn't remember why he'd come here. Paper towels ...

aluminum foil . . . he got them both. He put a few more items in a cart and brought it up to the front.

The cashier looked up without interest when he placed the merchandise on her counter. Her big, green eyes immediately focused on ringing up the purchases.

"How are you, Heidi?" he asked.

"Couldn't be better," she muttered as she scanned the cold cuts.

"Can we please talk?" he asked.

"I guess I can't stop you from talking," she said. "You chose my cash register."

"I mean, can we go somewhere?" he asked. "Just for a little while? We have to discuss this."

"Why don't you wait 'til you move back to Yonkers?" she suggested. "Or wherever the hell you're from? You can send me a postcard."

"Why are you so sure I'm going to leave Autumn?" he pressed.

"Nobody else can stay in that house," she stated. "Why should you be any different?"

"Can we just get a cup of coffee somewhere?" he said. "Please?"

"I don't get off 'til 7:00," she said. "There doesn't seem to be much point in talking, though. Why don't you take your things and go? As soon as I get these paper towels through the scanner."

She passed the item over the scanner again. And, again. And, again.

Finally, she slammed the roll down on the counter two or three times while crying, "God, Russell! Did you have to get the cheapest Goddamned paper towels you could find in the whole damned store?"

Daisy and Tamara watched their friend with growing concern as tears streamed down her cheeks.

He reached out to her over the counter.

"Don't, Russell!" she snapped as she pulled back. She wiped her eyes, and said, "I'm working."

She punched the code for the merchandise into the register. Then, she hit the Total button. You almost couldn't hear that she'd been crying when she said, "That'll be $22.76, please."

He reached for his wallet. "I think we both need to talk, Heidi," he said. "Can I please pick you up at 7:00? Can I call you, at least? I'll take anything."

She looked over at her friends. She had forgotten that they were witnessing this entire episode.

"Get out of here, honey," Daisy told her. "Just go. We can handle the rest of the day without you."

"Yeah," Tamara agreed. "Go on. It's been like a morgue in here all day, anyway."

Then when she noticed the callousness of her remark, she shrugged and added, "Oops! Sorry."

He watched those green eyes expectantly as she silently considered her options.

"All right," she finally consented. "Let me cash out, and we can get a coffee somewhere. But, I'm not going back to your house."

Russell, Daisy and Tamara all breathed a huge sigh of relief.

"No problem," he said. "Thanks, Heidi."

"Don't thank me yet," she said. "I'm not agreeing to anything. We're just talking."

"Fair enough," he said with a smile.

He waited patiently for her. There was a tense silence when she went to the back room with her money. He and the girls could hardly look at each other.

Tamara couldn't stand it. She had to speak. "So," she said. "I hear you live in the Beckenbauer house."

He noticed the nasty glance Daisy gave her friend. The knot in his stomach pulled tighter. "Yes," he said. "Evidently, I do."

"Then, it's true what they say?" Tamara inquired. "It's really haunted?"

"I'd rather not talk about it," he said. "If you don't mind."

"Sorry."

"You'll have to excuse her, Russell," Daisy said. "Sometimes, she can be as subtle as a bulldozer in a pottery shop."

"That's okay," he said.

"I didn't mean anything by it," Tamara said. "I was just worried about my own interests. We all thought you were going to be around long enough to save this store."

"If you're worried about whether or not I'll be leaving town in a big hurry," he said. "Allow me to put your mind at ease. I'm not going anywhere. I bought that house, and I have every intention of staying there. I promise that any problem with that place will be resolved. And, believe me. This store and your jobs are safe."

"You sound awfully sure of yourself," Daisy observed.

"I am."

"That's good to hear," Tamara said.

"However," he added. "I would appreciate it if you girls keep quiet about the whole Beckenbauer house issue. That's not the sort of thing that should be spread around. My house is my business. I don't need rumors, or people prying into my life. Plus, I don't need all my employees being concerned over job security. Do you understand?"

"Yes, sir," they chorused.

"Good."

Luckily, a few customers came up to the registers. The girls were occupied until Heidi came back carrying her purse.

They said good-bye to the cashiers as they left the building.

As they walked out through the sliding glass doors, she said, "There's a little diner just a few blocks down the road. It's called Crystal's. It's nothing to brag about, but it's convenient. You can follow me in your car."

"Fine."

Her little Ford was easy to follow. The place was close by. It was almost as greasy as the diner he had visited that morning. Still, they seemed to draw a fair amount of business for such a small establishment.

However, they were able to get a booth and order coffee right away.

She was the first to speak afterward. "Okay," she sighed. "I'm sorry. Maybe I overreacted a little last night. But, I'm not used to being attacked by ghosts."

"That's perfectly understandable."

"Plus, that place has a bit of a reputation in this town," she added.

"So I've noticed," he said. "Everyone has a lot to say about that house."

"I like you, Russell," she admitted. "I really do. But, I need to be careful. Maybe I'm a little paranoid, but you don't know what I've been through."

"Listen, Heidi," he explained. "I can't begin to imagine what you went through with that scumbag you were with.

But, that's over now. You won't have to deal with him anymore. I can't change your past. But, I can promise you that I won't give you any reason to be afraid. I like you too, honey. And, I'm not going anywhere. I won't be driven from my house by ghosts or demons or . . . whatever! I don't care what other people have done. I'm going to stay there."

"And, what about the Beckenbauers?" she asked.

"I'm working on that," he said. "Ingrid wants me to find her body. She's helping me. She's giving me clues. She's telling me what really happened back then."

"You're talking to a ghost?"

"Not exactly," he said. "She's showing me things."

"Are you talking about Nobody's Grave again?" she asked suspiciously.

"All right, never mind," he said. "That's not important. You don't need to know how I'm dealing with this. You just need to know that I'm working on it. The problems with my house are temporary. I'm not going to leave Autumn. I'm not going to hurt you. And, the situation at my house will get fixed."

"I want to believe you, Russell," she said. "But, you're asking an awful lot. Everything was so great when we started out. I just knew there was going to be a catch. I knew something was going to go wrong. And, you dropped a mighty big bombshell on me last night."

"I'm sorry I didn't warn you about that," he admitted. "I didn't want to scare you. That's why I didn't want to invite you to my house. But when you insisted, I was left with no choice but to hope that nothing bad would happen while you were there."

"Things didn't go as planned, I guess," she reminded with a smile. "Did they?"

"You can say that again."

"How often do you see them?" she asked. "Do you see them every day?"

"I don't really keep track," he said. "Listen. Don't sweat about details. The one thing I want to establish tonight, is that you don't have to worry about me. We'll be fine, if you just give us a fighting chance. That's all I ask. Just give me a chance."

The diner was beginning to get crowded and noisy. Still, two beatiful green eyes were showing him gradual signs of assent.

Finally, she said, "Maybe. I'll have to think about it."

"It's getting kind of loud in here," he pointed out. "Would you like to get a quick drink somewhere? Perhaps Fehr's Steak and Ale? I know Deke would love to see you."

She smiled. "Okay," she said. "Just a quick one. This time, I'll follow you in my car."

He felt much better as he drove to Marshall Ave. It felt as though a two-ton weight had been lifted from his chest.

Of course, Deke was delighted to see them. And, the mood grew more relaxed as they talked further. After a few drinks, she allowed a quick kiss before she left with a smile.

He stayed behind.

"Leaving separately?" Deke observed. "Trouble in paradise, pal?"

"More or less," he said. "We had a bit of a problem."

"What happened?" Deke asked.

"Never mind," he said. "Hopefully, it's over. I'm supposed to call her tomorrow. I think we can work everything out."

"Good luck, Russell," Deke said. "I'll keep my fingers crossed. You two make a nice couple. And, it would be a real shame to let a girl like that get away."

"I hear you," he agreed. "Thanks."

"Would you like another drink?"

"I might as well."

He didn't stay too long. He left as soon as he remembered the cold cuts he'd purchased at The Golden Eagle General Store. He figured the turkey had probably gone bad. It had been sitting in his trunk for a few hours.

He drove home through the crisp, clear night. The air was cooler than he expected. And, it was eerily still. Only the occasional set of headlights marred the unyielding darkness. For a beautiful Sunday night, the streets of Autumn seemed almost deserted.

It wasn't very late when he started his car up the Agnes St. hill. However, he was determined to get home for some well-needed sleep. His weary eyes watched for his home as he continued to drive. He kept watching for his house even as he passed the building.

He was exhausted. He counted the dwellings. And when he lost count, he started again. He didn't even realize where he was until he saw the gate to the Van Pouck mansion growing near.

He slowed as he approached the mansion. He wondered how he had come this far.

Then, he slammed on the brakes when he came up alongside the building. The gate was locked. It seemed like all the lights were on inside.

But, one thing struck him with a deep sense of foreboding more than any other. He stared with a petrifying fear at the message on the front of the decaying abode. It was written in broad, crude strokes. The red, blood-like ink dripped down the faded walls, and over windows and shutters. It matched the writings he had seen in his own house. There had to be a connection. In mysterious, childish lettering, it read:

"OR IT WILL BE TOO LATE!"

He stared at the image with an increasing sense of dread. Then, he felt the need to wipe his tired eyes with trembling hands. When he looked back at the mansion, all the lights were still on.

However, there was no writing on the wall. There were no blood stains smeared over the peeling paint.

He turned away. He knew he had to go to the cemetery. The blood messages must all connected, he surmised. There had to be some sort of warning in those words. He didn't know what it could be. However, he knew he had work to do.

He drove quickly up the hill.

He parked by the gate of the cemetery. He walked down the path to his destination. He marched at a steady pace between the rows of headstones. Even through the unwavering darkness, he could see the neatly dug hole beside Edgar's grave. There was nothing to fear. He felt resolute in his quest to end the nightmares that plagued his new home.

As he neared Nobody's Grave, it grew more difficult to hold back a growing sense of dread. However, he pushed forward, inspired by the knowledge that this was the only way to get back his house.

He stood at the edge of the hole. He glanced bravely down at the bony occupant that he knew he would find resting at the bottom. The skeleton was sprawled lazily across the dirt floor wearing a gold chain with a locket.

It was looking up at him as if waiting for his arrival. It raised its slender, skinless arm. It pointed at him with a long, thin finger. He just stood at the edge of the grave and watched. Even though he knew this vision meant him no harm, it was difficult to suppress the urge to escape.

The clacking sound of bone against bone could be heard as the skeleton's arm fell against the filthy wall of the grave. He was surprised that his gaunt hostess was writing in the dirt before he entered her intended home.

Still, the lanky finger traced the letters in the dirt, as expected. And as he watched, the bloody messages he received earlier became easier to comprehend.

The skeleton wrote the letters "K-A-T-A-L" in the muddy wall that entombed it.

The ground trembled and shook as the floor of the gave fell out beneath its dead hostess. He watched the helpless pile of bones fall and disappear into the mysterious, intimidating void that invited his entry.

The ground continued to tremble as he looked anxiously down into the interminable chasm. The earthquake grew more aggressive until he lost his footing. As he fell, he knew that his alternatives had been removed. He could only keep falling through this chasm of fear, anxiety and hopelessness until he reached the next leg of his harrowing journey.

He kept falling through this unsettling void.

He just kept falling . . .

Then, he found himself in a familiar place. However, it was not the building he had expected to visit.

Even with the outmoded furnishings and decor of the main room, he recognized his own house. He also recognized the two people sitting together on the sofa. The man was impeccably dressed in a tailored suit. The beautiful young woman wore a lovely white dress and a matching hat. Seeing this couple sitting together in his house made him feel edgy. They both seemed a bit nervous.

The man held her hand as he asked, "Why are you doing this, Ingrid?"

"I've explained this to you already, Gordon," she said. "I love my husband."

"But, how is that possible?" he asked. "Admittedly, he's a nice fellow. But, he can't do anything for you. He's a nobody."

"Don't you say that," she averred as she pulled her hand away. "He's a wonerful man who would do anything for me. When I think of the shame and humiliation of what I have done to him . . . and our marriage, I . . ."

She turned away from him and hid her tear-filled eyes in her hands.

"I know how this must look to the rest of the world," he said. "But, you haven't done anything wrong. All you've done is fallen in love. How can that be wrong?"

"I don't love you, Gordon," she reiterated. "I love Edgar. I never should have allowed my head to be turned by wealth and power. But, you lavished so much attention on me. A girl can only resist so much."

"And, that's why you should stay with me, my dear," he coaxed. "I can give you the world. Edgar is a two-bit smuggler with a few impressive connections."

"He's not a smuggler!" she insisted. "He is a legitimate trader and dealer of fine gemstones and jewelry!"

"Of course he is, my dear," he allowed. "Forgive me. Nonetheless, he hasn't the resources to treat you in the manner in which you deserve to be treated."

"I don't need all those things you throw at me, Gordon," she said. "I accepted your frivolous generosity in a moment of weakness. All I really want in this life is love. Edgar's love, to be precise. I know my husband loves me. You throw money at me as if purchasing a trophy. Like you have with your other previous affairs. I am not a trophy to be purchased, Gordon. I am a human being . . . with feelings."

227

"I never said you were a trophy," he argued. "My love for you is genuine. For pity's sake, Ingrid! I killed my wife for you. Do you understand what that means? And, that's not all. I also killed her brother, Phillip."

"Her brother?" she asked.

"Yes, the impertinent fool!" he said. "It was the day after my wife's funeral. Of all the days to be caught without my gun! He accused me of killing her."

"But, you did," she reminded.

"Still," he said. "He had no right to confront me without proof. The little wretch had the audacity to chase me with a knife from the carriage house to the garden at the back of my property. If my careless gardener hadn't left a pair of shears in the tomato patch . . . who knows what might have happened?"

"So, you're a brute and a murderer," she observed.

"Don't you see?" he insisted. "I did it all for you, my dear."

"No, Gordon," she stated. "You did it for the same reason you do everything. You did it for yourself. I made a horrible mistake by being seen with you. And, I made an even bigger mistake by . . ."

She turned away again. She stood and walked to the entrance of the room.

"It wasn't a mistake," he said. "It was destiny. We were meant to be together."

"No," she repeated. "I won't do it. I won't leave my husband. And, I won't bear the shame of being with you ever again. It's over, Gordon. Please just go."

"But, I love you, Ingrid," he declared. "And, I will not be denied. I will ruin Edgar, if you spurn me. I've already taken steps."

She turned to face him. "What do you mean?" she asked.

He rose to his feet. "You'll see," he said with a confident grin.

Then, the front door opened. The man of the house entered with a big smile for his wife. "Hello, Ingrid," he said. "How are you?"

"Very well, darling," she said. "And, you?"

Gordon scowled as Ingrid accepted a kiss from her husband.

"Splendid," her husband replied. "It's been a wonderful day."

However, his smile vanished when he saw the visitor standing by the sofa.

"Gordon?" he said. "What are you doing here? Don't you find it inappropriate to be here, under the circumstances?"

"My apologies, Edgar," he said. "I meant no disrespect. I came over to discuss some business with you. Your lovely wife was gracious enough to allow me to wait for you."

"Oh," Edgar said with a hint of suspicion. "Well, what can I do for you?"

"You might want to sit down, Edgar," Gordon said. "I have some rather distressing news."

Edgar moved slowly over to his favorite chair. He watched his guest with growing concern. His wife's expression disturbed him, as well.

As Edgar sat, Gordon announced, "Since we began doing business together, I've made some inquiries. To put it bluntly, I have built a correspondence and a rather pleasant working relationship with a certain Ronald Higgins."

"Ronald Higgins?" Edgar asked. "From South Africa?"

"The very same," Gordon replied smugly.

"But, how . . .?"

"I have people, my good man," Gordon explained. "I have enormous resources at my disposal. It really wasn't hard."

"Just what are you saying, Gordon?"

"The deal has not been finalized yet," he said. "But, it should only take a phone call or two. I was waiting to see how another situation would play out, first."

"You're squeezing me out?" Edgar asked.

"Let's just say," Gordon said. "That Ronald knows the difference between the big fish in the pond, and the small. And, Ronald prefers to play with the big fish."

"But, you're my main . . ." Edgar sputtered. "If you squeeze me out, it'll ruin me!"

"Tough break, my good man," Gordon said. "Of course, it all could have been avoided. I was willing to make arrangements on your behalf. I was willing to let you walk away with a certain amount of dignity. However, other forces were at work."

Edgar didn't like the way his guest was looking at Ingrid. The way she turned away made him feel a bit queasy.

"What are you implying, Van Pouck?" Edgar said as he stood and stepped away from the chair.

"Would you like to tell him, Ingrid?" Gordon asked. "Or should I?"

"Tell me what?" Edgar inquired. "Ingrid? What's going on?"

She still couldn't face her husband. "Please don't, Gordon," she begged.

"Ingrid?" Edgar said. His confusion was turning to fright.

"Your wife doesn't want you to know," Gordon said. "That I have been cultivating some other more personal relationships, as well."

"What are you saying?" Edgar snapped. "Ingrid! What's this all about?"

When she turned to face her husband, there were tears streaming down her cheeks. "I'm sorry, Edgar!" she cried. "It was a mistake! I don't know what I was thinking. But, I swear it's over, darling! I love you, Edgar! I love you!"

She ran to her husband. He pushed her away.

"Ingrid!" he shouted. "How could you do this to me? To us? Don't you know how much I adore you?"

"I'm sorry, my love," she begged. "I'm so sorry! It was only a few times. It was all a ghastly mistake!"

"You common trollop!"

Ingrid collapsed on the sofa in a fit of tears.

"Apparently," Gordon declared. "Ronald is not the only person who prefers to play with the big fish."

"You bastard!" Edgar snarled. "Not only do you seek to ruin me financially . . . but, you have also sullied my wife? The woman I love?"

"You have been rendered superfluous, dear sir," Gordon stated. "And now, I must bid you good day."

"You unfeeling cad!" Edgar spat. "You won't get away with this!"

He pulled out a concealed knife and went after his guest. However, Gordon didn't move from the doorway. He stood firm. He quickly extracted a pistol from his coat pocket. He fired two shots into Edgar's chest at point blank range.

Ingrid stared in shock, as her wide-eyed husband dropped his knife to the floor. Blood spilled ruthlessly down his suit front.

Ingrid screamed. Her husband dropped to his knees.

"Edgar!" she shrieked. "No!"

Gordon fired a third shot. Edgar dropped to the floor in a huddled, lifeless mass.

"No!" Ingrid screamed. "Edgar, my love!"

She leapt from the sofa and fell on her husband with incapacitating grief. As she wept hysterically over her husband's body, Gordon grabbed her arm. He pulled her up sharply with a merciless tug.

"Let me go!" she cried. "What are you doing?"

"You have no reason to stay with your husband now," he informed her. "He had to be eliminated."

"No! Please! Edgar! My Edgar!"

"I had to kill him," Gordon said. "You saw. He came at me with a knife. It was a clear case of self defense. And, I'm sure any judge in Autumn will see it that way."

She struggled as he dragged her toward the front door.

"Let me go!" she begged hysterically. "What are you doing?"

"You're coming to my house, my dear," he said. "Where we can live happily ever after. And, I can treat you the way a woman like you deserves to be treated."

"No!" she implored. "Please let go of me! I must go to Edgar! I have to help him! For God's sake! I love my husband!"

"He's dead now," Gordon reminded. "I love you, and you love me. You may be angry at me for killing your little smuggler. But, you'll get over that, in time."

"No! Please!"

She continued to scream as Gordon opened the front door. He dragged her out into the unforgiving night.

And, her husband lay motionless . . . curled up on the floor by the entrance of the front room of his house.

When Russell awoke, the sun was shining in his eyes. He sat up suddenly in the grass.

The sweet smells of the dew-filled morning were lost on him. His neck was stiff. His shoulder muscles were sore from sleeping on the hard ground. And, the last images he had seen in his sleep were still reverberating in his troubled mind.

He sat in the grass and rubbed his neck. Then, he stared at Edgar Beckenbauer's grave until he stopped quivering.

CHAPTER 12.....
TRESPASSING_____

He was sitting down to his first cup of coffee. His neck was still sore. He was processing information in front of the television. The morning news reminded him that it was Monday. The weatherman predicted the day would be sunny and pleasant.

The house still needed some work. There were many things he had to do before taking over the store. Still, his connection to the Van Pouck mansion was foremost in his thoughts.

Images and questions replayed in his mind as he watched the news with casual interest. He perked up when he saw the update on the Sharon Kellerman story. The police still had no leads in the case. Her husband was still offering a reward for any information. However, the cops considered him to be the most likely suspect. They were scrutinizing his actions.

He shook his head as he watched the report. "He didn't do it," he muttered to himself. "He's completely innocent."

Just as the sports announcer came on, his cell phone rang. He grabbed it from the coffee table, and answered, "Hello?"

"Hi, Russell," said the caller. "It's Heidi."

"Hi, honey," he said. "It's nice of you to call."

"Well, I had a lot of time to think last night," she said. "I'm still worried about the whole situation, but I don't want to just slam the door in your face. You were right. I should give you a chance."

"Thanks, Heidi," he said with a smile. "That's all I'm asking for."

"Daisy and Tamara suggested that maybe I should even help you," she told him.

"That's a nice thought," he said. "But, I don't know how dangerous it might be."

"Well, I certainly don't want to see ghosts attacking me with knives," she admitted. "But, I definitely don't want to see you get hurt by violent spirits, either. I have the day off, and I wish we could get together and talk some more. Maybe you can tell me what's going on."

"I'd like that," he said. "Would you like to meet somewhere for lunch?"

"Okay," she said. "We might as well meet at Fehr's. Say around noon?"

"That would be perfect."

"Great," she said. "And, Russ? I'm glad we talked last night. I had a good time."

"Me too."

"I'd still like to take it slow," she added. "Especially under these new circumstances. But, maybe we'll be okay . . . if we can straighten out your house."

"I hope you're right," he said. After a pause, he added, "And, I had a good time last night, too."

235

He felt better when he hung up.

As promised by the weatherman, it was turning out to be a beautiful day. The sky was a bright, clean, uninterrupted blue. The sun warmed the sweet air of September like a hug in a freshly-washed blanket.

He rode through the streets of Autumn amid the bustle of Monday lunch hour traffic. He felt a little anxious about his upcoming rendezvous. However, he felt more nervous about the other issues facing his day.

He greeted Amy at the bar before getting a table in the restaurant. He ordered a soda as he perused the menu.

After a few minutes, the waitress came to take his order. He told her he was waiting for someone.

A few more minutes passed before his guest arrived.

"Sorry I'm late," she said. "It's been a hectic morning."

"No problem."

After ordering, she asked, "So, what's been going on at the house? You know, I've heard so many stories about that place, but I thought they were just rumors. Who would have thought that a place like that actually exists?"

"I understand how you feel," he said. "I never would have believed it, either. But, now I'm faced with the fact that I have to get Edgar Beckenbauer back with his wife. I've only been living in Autumn for about a week. And, this situation is cramping my style. I haven't had much of a social life yet, aside from you. Deke is the closest thing I have to a male friend, and he's always behind a bar. I haven't even seen what he looks like from the waist down."

"It must be rough on you," she smiled. "But, what are you going to do about your 'unearthly visitors'? You can't have them attacking everyone that comes to your house. That's a surefire way to ruin any party."

"That's true," he agreed. "But, it has recently come to my attention that Edgar's spirit may not have been attacking us. I've also had a similar situation with another ghost with a knife on the Van Pouck property. It may be that these specters are acting out the last actions they took before their deaths."

"What makes you say that?"

"It's a long story," he explained. "And, I'm not certain, either. This ordeal could very well still be very dangerous. That's why I hate to get you involved. I want to keep seeing you, Heidi. You have no idea how much. But, I've been thinking that it might be better if you stay away from me for a while until I get this mess sorted out."

"Stay away from you?" she asked. "But, why? And, for how long?"

"Because, I couldn't live with myself if you got hurt over this," he replied. "Or, even worse . . . killed."

"I can take care of myself, Russell."

"I know," he said. "But, why take chances? Anyway, it's only for a few more days."

"How do you know?" she asked.

"For one thing," he explained. "I've been getting clues in Nobody's Grave. I almost have enough of the pieces to figure out where Ingrid is."

"So, the children's story is true?" she asked.

"I'm afraid so," he said. "But, that's not all. I may be under a time limit. I received three messages yesterday. They were all written in blood. Two of them occurred on walls inside my house. The third was written on the outside wall of the Van Pouck mansion."

"What did they say?" she asked.

"When you string them together," he replied. "They read, 'Please find me . . .before I spell her name . . . or it

237

will be too late!' I think it refers to Nobody's Grave. Every time I go there, the image of Ingrid's skeleton starts to spell 'Katalina' on the wall of the grave. Each time I visit, she adds another letter to the spelling. So far, she has made it to 'Katal'. I can only guess I have three more visits before it's too late."

"Too late to find her?" she asked. "Why? What will happen if you don't?"

"I have no idea," he said. "Maybe the people who owned that house before found out the hard way. Perhaps, that is what drove them out of town."

"I hope not," she said. "But since none of your predecessors supposedly lasted any longer than two weeks, the time frame fits perfectly."

"That's what I'm afraid of."

"Well then," she said. "You can use all the help you can get. I'm willing to help you look. We can start right after lunch."

"It's not that simple," he instructed. "I don't know where to start. It's like you said earlier. She could be anywhere in the town of Autumn. But, I must admit, I think she's on the grounds of the Van Pouck mansion. After killing his wife and children, Elliott buried them under the floor of the cellar."

"He did?" she gasped. "How do you know?"

"That's another long story," he said. "But, I have to wonder if there's a connection. Of course, not everyone who's been killed in that house is buried under the cellar ... but, I just have a sneaking suspicion about Ingrid. Call it a hunch. Something about love and doubt. I can't say for sure. I just have a feeling."

"So, how do we get into the cellar?" she asked. "If Elliott's as crazy as you say he is, and the place is haunted ... what should we do?"

"*You* don't do anything," he said. "I told you this is dangerous. I can't have you risking your life over this."

"Russell," she averred. "I want to help. I'm not crazy over getting involved in haunted houses. But, I'm not going to sit in my apartment waiting for a phone call. A phone call that may never come. Maybe weeks or maybe months from now . . . where you tell me your house is safe. I'm not going to be watching the news for stories on how the latest resident of the Beckenbauer house disappeared . . . or, went screaming off into the night . . . never to be heard from again. If you want me to believe you're going to stay, then let me help you. I have to do something, or I'll go nuts!"

"All right," he said. "But, we'll have to stick together and be carerful."

"Sounds reasonable, so far."

"We'll have to get onto the Van Pouck property, first," he instructed. "If the front gate is locked, I know where we can find a hole in the fence. It's a little tight, but you can fit through it much easier than I can. That's how I sliced up my upper arm."

"It is?" she asked. "You told me you got that cut while fixing up your house."

"You didn't know about any of this at the time," he said. "I didn't want you to know about my ghost problems. Listen. There are some woods behind the property that lead to a sheer drop some distance from the carriage house out back. I saw some indentations in the undergrowth that looked like recent tire tracks going into those woods."

"Do you think Elliott's been driving in his own woods?" she asked.

"Not his own car," he explained. "He has an old Porsche in the carriage house. My guess is that he almost never uses it. But, I think I mentioned to you that I suspect he may have killed Sharon Kellerman."

"That lady they talk about on the news?" she asked. "The real estate lady? The cops think her husband is responsible for her disappearance."

"I don't want to get into details," he said. "But, I think Elliott killed her. And if she drove to the mansion, he'd have to get rid of her car. Besides, who knows who else might have been over there."

"Why would Elliott want to kill her?" she asked.

"I don't know," he said. "She sold me my house. Perhaps, Katalina doesn't want outsiders to upset her plans for Edgar and Ingrid. But, that's just a wild guess. So far, I can only offer wild guesses about most of what I've seen."

"So, what should we do?"

"I'll tell you everything I know while we eat," he said. "I want you to be prepared for what we're dealing with."

"I can't wait to hear it," she said.

She listened with wide-eyed wonder, as he recounted the unnerving events of his first week in Autumn. Afterward, she was even more determined to help.

"Are you sure?" he asked.

"Positive," she declared. "I'll even go into your house, if that's what it takes."

"Shall we take my car over there?"

"I'll follow you in my car," she said. "We're both parked here at the restaurant. It doesn't make sense to leave my car here, or to make extra trips. Besides, I want to have control over knowing how I'll get home. I still want us to take it slow, for one thing. And, I must admit this adventure of ours still scares me a little."

"I understand," he said.

He drove back to his house. He kept an eye out for her in his rear view mirror. He wanted to make sure he didn't lose her. She had no trouble following him. She pulled in right behind him as he parked in his driveway.

He walked back to her car, as she stepped out onto the pavement. "I'm not sure how you want to proceed," he said. "The mansion is about four or five blocks up the hill. I prefer to walk to avoid detection. I don't want Elliott to look out his window, see my car and figure he has unwanted guests."

"You're too paranoid," she said. "If you park on the street, there's no way he can be sure you're out to disturb him. Get in. I'll drive."

He watched her get back in the driver's seat. Then, he swung around to the passenger's side. As he sat down, he said, "I think you're a nut. We really can't be too careful with that maniac."

"I have every intention of being careful," she said, as she started the car. "Believe me. I'm terrified. But, that doesn't mean I'm going to walk five blocks up that hill."

"It's not a steep hill," he said.

"Just let me know when you see the place," she said.

He watched silently as she drove toward the cemetery. When they reached their destination, he pointed a finger and said, "There it is."

She stepped on the brake. She gazed at the building in amazement.

"Wow!" she gasped. "Just look at the place! What a house!"

"It's falling apart, now," he said.

"That's for sure," she agreed. "But, it must have been gorgeous once. God! It's almost like a palace. You know,

241

I've heard people talk about this place as long as I can remember. But, they were just stories. Seeing the building face to face makes you really stop and think."

"Wonderful," he said. "But, we have a problem. The gate is wide open."

"Why is that a problem?" she asked.

"It's usually locked," he told her. "If Elliott left it open, he's probably expecting someone. I have to hope he's not expecting us."

"This is great," she commented. "I didn't want to climb through a hole in the fence and get all dirty. And if we park outside while the gate is open, it will look even more like we're not visiting the mansion."

She turned off the engine. She anxiously hopped out of her car.

"Are you sure you want to park here?" he asked.

She began to feel a little uneasy as she stared in at the mansion. "Now that you mention it," she said. "Maybe I should move to a better spot. This place scares me. But, where can I park? There are no good spaces on the street."

He got out of the car. "As long as we're here," he said. "You might as well leave it here. You're not blocking the driveway, and there is no other place that's any better."

He escorted her cautiously through the gate. As they approached the mansion, she marveled, "Wow! The Van Pouck estate! I never thought I would be on this property."

"We should be as quiet as possible," he advised. "We haven't literally been invited on the premises."

"What should we do?" she asked.

"I'd be a bit leery of going into the mansion at this moment," he said. "That open gate makes me nervous. Elliott may be dangerously insane, but he's not stupid. It's best not to tempt fate. Besides, I want to check out a few things behind the carriage house. Maybe I can even show you that hole in the fence. You should know where it is in case of an emergency."

"That's not a bad idea," she agreed.

"And, keep an eye out for anything that could be a problem," he said. "I want us both to get out of here alive."

"You won't get any argument from me," she said.

They proceeded quickly and quietly along the side of the mansion. When they reached the parking area in the back, she stopped to stare at the next rotting structure.

"That's the carriage house," he said.

"I can just picture how beautiful this estate must have been at one time," she said.

"We don't have time for that now," he said. "This place is dangerous. I have a few things I have to check out in the back. Then, we have to figure out if it's safe to go into the mansion."

He led her behind the second building and back toward the woods. "I wonder what they keep in that place now," she said.

"Believe me," he told her. "You don't want to know. It's kind of creepy in there. Just before I was attacked, I saw something that looked like a human hand."

"You're kidding!" she gasped. "Could it have been the real estate lady?"

"Mrs. Kellerman?" he asked. "No. It was too old and brittle-looking. I didn't get a close look, but I almost think it might have been another ghost."

"How many people do you suppose died here?" she asked.

"You've lived in this town longer than I have," he pointed out. "You could make a better guess than I could."

"I'd say it was an awful lot," she offered.

243

As they reached the thick undergrowth just ahead of the woods, he glanced around. After a brief search, he said, "See? Over here. Check this out."

She looked over at where he was pointing. "You're right," she said. "They do look like tire tracks."

"Let's follow them, and see where they lead," he suggested.

"Into the woods?" she asked. "Is it safe? Are you sure there are no ghosts back there?"

"I'm not sure of anything," he said. "I told you this could be dangerous. Would you like to leave? I wouldn't blame you."

"No," she said. "I told you I want to help. And, that's what I'm going to do. I just wish it wasn't so dark in there."

"You can still back out, if you want to," he offered.

"No," she repeated. "I'm going to do this. But, I'm going to stick close to you."

They made their way carefully back through the underbrush. They cautiously proceeded deeper into the woods.

* * * * * *

The crowd was beginning to disperse.

Everyone was dressed in black. The coffin was suspended by two supports over the open grave. Someone could be heard crying.

A priest offered his condolences to the departing mourners. And, two men stayed near the majestic, closed casket.

"I don't believe he's gone," he said. "This is our last good-bye. In a matter of minutes, my best friend is going to be buried six feet under."

"I'm really going to miss him," his friend said. "Paul was a great guy."

"A great guy?" he said. "The Sheep Man was the best! Nobody could beat him at anything. Except, maybe driving. Good-bye, my friend. I'll see you on the other side."

"Let's get out of here," his friend suggested. "What do you say, Charlie?"

"All right," he muttered. "There's nothing else we can do here. Besides, we have to have a last drink in memory of The Sheep Man."

"For God's sake, Charlie," his friend observed. "You've been drinking to his memory all week. You couldn't even stay sober for the funeral. It's not even 2:00 in the afternoon, and you're already wasted."

"But, it's started to wear off," he said. "Do you believe the funeral parlor didn't have a bar? They'd make a fortune. What better time to offer people drinks than at a funeral?"

"Give it a rest, Charlie," his friend said.

"You're no fun anymore, Jack," he said. "I miss the way you used to be in the old days. Back before I could say, 'You're no fun anymore, Jack.'"

Charlie began to laugh. Jack just shook his head.

"I'm sorry, Jack," he said. "I'm just really depressed. And, I'm starting to sober up. Let's go drink a toast to The Sheep Man. I'm buying."

They walked back to the car. Charlie bumped his head on the door as he sat down. He swore under his breath. Jack started the car and headed down Agnes St.

A few blocks down the road, Charlie said, "Hey, wait a minute! Stop the car."

Jack slammed on the brakes. "What is it?" he said.

"Isn't that Heidi's car?" he said while pointing out the window.

"You're crazy."

"No," he said. "Look. The little white Ford. Look at that sticker in the window, and the bumper stickers. That's Heidi's car. I'd know it anywhere."

"What's she doing parked outside a big old house like that?" Jack asked.

"That is one monster of a house," he agreed. "The owner ain't taking very good care of it, though. It must belong to that asshole we saw her with the other night."

"Well, it's not your problem anymore," Jack said.

"How can you say that?" he said. "This is almost like Fate playing its hand. On our way home from burying The Sheep Man, we find Heidi's car parked outside the home of an obvious scum bag. I have to save her from this dude. It's the perfect excuse to get her back where she belongs. With me."

Jack rolled his eyes. "Don't start this, Charlie," he said. "Let her go, already. She's not coming back to you. When are you going to get that through your head?"

"Hey!" he growled. "If you were my friend, you'd support me on this. First, I see Heidi right after The Sheep Man dies. Then, I see her car parked outside her slimy boyfriend's slimy house right after we bury my best friend. It's fate, I tell you."

"You're fooling yourself, Charlie."

"I told you I'm going to get her back," he reminded. "This is the perfect opportunity. I'm going in there, and I'm not coming out without my Heidi. And, if I have to beat the crap out of that bastard she's been seeing, so much the better!"

He opened the car door and jumped out.

"Charlie! What are you doing?" Jack shouted. "Get back in the car!"

"It's time for you to make a choice, Jack," he said. "Are you my friend, or not? I'm going in there to get my Heidi back. Are you with me, or aren't you?"

"I'm not going in there, Charlie," he said. "I'm your friend. That's why I'm asking you to get back in the car. You can't win this. If you break into that house, all you'll get out of it is another prison sentence."

"So, you're not coming?"

"No, Charlie," he said. "For God's sake, get back in the car!"

"Fine!" he bellowed while slamming his fist down on the hood of the car. "Don't stand by me! I don't need you! You fucking asshole! Get out of here! It don't matter to me. I'll get a ride with Heidi. Go on, you little bitch! Leave!"

Jack sped away from the curb with a loud screeching of tires.

Charlie glared at the back of the car as it rushed off down the Agnes St. hill. Then, he turned to face the big, gray mansion. He stormed in through the open gate. He marched angrily down the driveway, and across the walk until he stood before the grand staircase.

As he studied the staircase, he observed, "Man! This boy needs some serious carpentry work done here. Maybe after I get Heidi, I can teach this fool how to nail a couple of boards together, using his face for a hammer."

He stomped up the stairs in his quest to reclaim his girlfriend. He could hear his enraged footfalls treading across the sagging wooden steps. When he reached the landing, he noticed the front door was slightly ajar. He rang the doorbell. Then, he pounded on the door.

As the door was pushed open by his effort, he called into the house, "Heidi! Heidi! Are you in here?"

He could hear his voice echo through the house. As he glanced around from his vantage point, he said to himself, "Holy crap! What is this place?"

He walked into the main hall. "Heidi!" he called. "Where are you? It's Charlie!"

He glanced around from inside the room. "Man! This place is filthy!" he said to himself. "It's disgusting! If you're going to own a pad like this, you've got to be able to take care of it. I'm doing Heidi a favor here."

Then, he shouted, "Heidi! Where are you, you little bitch? Don't make me go looking for you. Get out here, Heidi!"

He kept looking around as he crossed the room. Then, he heard the door slam behind him. He turned to look. He was surprised to see the front door had closed. However, he shrugged it off and continued his search.

He noticed the ornate staircase that offered a rickety passage from the main room to the second floor. He noticed the fireplace with a gold candlestick on the right side of the mantle. There was no match for the candlestick on the left side, however.

He passed into the next room. "Where are you?" he shouted. "Heidi! If I have to keep looking for you, you'll be sorry!"

As he turned around, he saw something. The image of a man stood in the doorway he had just passed through. The man looked as if he were in great pain. There was a large dagger protruding from his chest. He opened his mouth.

Then, he disappeared.

He gawked at the empty doorway in horror. Gradually, his gaze softened. He finally allowed himself to smile.

"Maybe Jack was right," he mused. "Maybe I have been drinking too much."

He turned back around and continued his search. "Heidi!" he called. "Where the hell are you? You're only making it worse for yourself!"

He walked into another room. He didn't even notice the old-fashioned furniture or the grime. He only grew angrier as he continued the hunt. "Come on out, Heidi!" he shouted. "You and your wimpy bastard boyfriend can't hide forever!"

He stopped in the middle of the large reception room. He looked around with a grimace. It was getting difficult to ignore the filth.

However, he didn't notice the old man who stood behind him in the doorway. He didn't see the balding man holding the solid gold candlestick in his fist. He didn't see the angry eyes in the pudgy, wrinkled face. He didn't notice the man in the pink robe slip quietly up behind him.

The man in the robe raised the candlestick over his head. When he brought the blunt instrument down, it struck Charlie's head with vicious force.

The intruder fell face first onto the carpet. He had nearly been knocked unconcious. He lay very still on the ground. He groaned as he tried to lift his head. His attacker fell to his knees and beat his unwelcomed guest with a few more savage blows with his solid gold weapon.

When the intruder stopped moving, the man in the pink robe stood. He looked down at his helpless prey. He straightened his robe with his free hand. He was still scowling as he regarded the blood-stained candlestick in his clenched fist.

* * * * * *

They stood at the point where the tire tracks ended. They stood at the edge of the steep drop-off amid the trees which concealed so many sins that transpired on this property. More trees rose up from the banks of the nearly vertical incline below. Despite the natural cover provided by the landscape, a few crumpled and eroded cars could be seen littering the gully beneath the trespassers.

Most of the cars had been there a while. Vegetation had begun to engulf their mangled frames. However, one car looked fairly new. One car appeared to be a recent addition to this collection of demolished automobiles.

"Look down there, Heidi," he said. "See the red B.M.W.?"

"Where?" she asked. Her gaze followed where he was pointing. "I don't see it."

"Just at the bottom," he said. "Between those bent oak trees."

"Oh, I see it," she finally said. "It doesn't look like it's been there too long."

"You're right," he agreed. "Sharon Kellerman drove a red B.M.W."

"Can you read the license plate number?" she asked.

"No," he said. "But, I wouldn't know her license plate number, anyway. I only spoke with her a few times when she was showing me the house, or signing papers. At least, I know my vision told me the truth. Elliott killed her. And, her body must be on this property somewhere. I don't think the old man would have moved her too far."

"That's all well and good," she said. "But, what can we do about it?"

"We have proof," he told her. "Now we can go to the cops."

"What are you going to tell them?" she chuckled. "You were trespassing on private property, and stumbled over a car that might belong to Sharon Kellerman? Once you tell them where you live, you'll destroy all your credibility."

"So, am I just supposed to ignore the whole thing?" he asked.

"You don't have a lot of choices, Russ," she said. "Besides, I thought we were looking for Ingrid Beckenbauer. I thought you had a time limit."

"I guess you have a point," he said. "I just feel a little guilty pretending Sharon's tragedy doesn't exist."

"We'll have to deal with it later," she said. "Right now, we have to get inside the mansion."

"Okay, he said. "But first, let me show you the hole in the fence. You never know when it might come in handy."

He led her along the edge of the steep drop. He took her in the direction of the opening. They circled around trees. They brushed away mosquitos. They trampled through underbrush, until they reached their destination.

"It's not very big," she said.

"If I can fit through it," he said. "I know it's big enough for you."

"I can see how you cut your arm on that thing," she said.

"Like I told you," he reminded. "You should know where it is in case of an emergency. It could save your life."

"Well, thanks," she said. "Now, how are we going to get inside the mansion?"

They began to follow the fence up to the front of the property. "If the front gate was open," he suggested. "There's a chance that the front door will be unlocked. I still don't like the idea of just walking in, though. That's a creepy place. And, Elliott is not a very stable person."

"What are your options?" she asked. "Breaking in through a window? Haven't we broken enough laws for one day?"

"I know," he said. "No matter how you look at it, we're going to have to go in through the front door. I just wish I could avoid bringing you in there. The ghost population can be a bit extreme."

"We'll be all right if we stick together," she said.

The woods were getting less dense. They could see the carriage house up ahead through the trees.

Then, he froze. "Did you hear that?" he asked.

"Hear what?"

He turned to look behind him. He jumped with a start. Then, he pointed a finger and said, "That!"

She turned to see what he meant. Then, she let out a scream.

About a hundred feet or so back from where they had just emerged, an image glowed brightly against the shaded backdrop of the woods. The man scowled at the young couple standing by the fence. He was tall, and muscular. His crewcut and uniform gave the impression that he belonged in the armed services. His posture seemed threatening. Then, he began to approach the couple with malicious intent.

She screamed again as the image trudged toward her. Its feet stomped noisily through the underbrush as he made his way between the trees.

The young couple turned and ran toward the carriage house. They were nearly out of the woods already. It only took a few moments to clear the shade of the many trees behind them. She got her foot caught in the underbrush as she rushed out into the sunlight. Luckily, her companion grabbed her before she fell on her face. They continued to run toward the mansion.

They could hear their pursuer thrashing through the undergrowth behind them. In a matter of moments, they cleared the impediment to their footing. They were able to quicken their pace through a stretch of dry grass as they raced to the carriage house.

Neither of them dared to look back. They just sped away from the certain danger behind them. When they reached the carriage house, they were able to run on pavement. The parking area was cracking and crumbling. Still, it offered a sturdier surface than they had been forced to run on up to that point.

"Keep running," he informed her as he turned his head. "It's still coming."

"What about the mansion?" she asked frantically. "I can't do it, Russ. I can't go in there!"

"Don't worry about it," he said. "Just get back to your car."

They ran along the pavement up along the side of the mansion. They looked up ahead at the open gate. A police car was slowly passing by. It pulled over and parked by the entrance at the gate.

The young couple ran up to the police car, as the uniformed cops stepped out onto the sidewalk.

The older, shorter policeman spoke first. "Hey there, you two," he said. "What's your hurry? Is there a problem?"

"Officer," he exclaimed while trying to catch his breath. "I'm glad you're here. Someone was chasing us."

The cops looked down the side of the mansion. "Chasing you, huh?" the first officer said. "I don't see anybody."

The young couple glanced down the path they had just taken. They stared in shock at the empty pavement.

"I don't believe it!" he said. "The guy was right behind us!"

"It's true!" she added. "He was a big guy in an army uniform."

"Is that right?" said the cop. "Do you hear that, Glenn? They were chased by a guy in an army uniform."

The younger officer replied, "Oh, yeah. That happens all the time, Herbert. Guys in army uniforms chase people, and then vanish into thin air."

"This isn't a joke, Officer," he stated.

"Do you know whose property this is, young man?" Officer Herbert asked. "This house belongs to the Van Pouck family. They were a very powerful and influential force in this town at one time. Old Man Elliott still contributes heavily to the police department every year. And, I don't think he'd take too kindly to a couple of hooligans trespassing on his land. What do you think, Glenn?"

"I don't think he'd like it one bit."

"Please take this seriously, sir," she said. "Our lives were in danger."

"From the vanishing army guy?" Officer Herbert asked. "Well, let's make out a report. Write this down, Glenn. What are your names?"

"My name is Russell Wilburn," he said. "I live at 857 Agnes St. Right down the road."

"Did you hear that, Glenn?" Officer Herbert said. "He lives at 857 Agnes St."

"I sure did," the cop replied as he put down his pen. "That explains a lot. That's a notorious address on this beat. People don't stay long in that house. But, they do seem to see a lot of ghosts. I remember one guy who claimed Elvis stole all the white pieces from an expensive Chess set. He wanted us to go on a manhunt for knights, bishops and pawns."

The cops began to laugh.

"This is no joke," he strongly reiterated.

"Of course not," Officer Herbert said. "I'm sure General MacArthur really was chasing you through the Van Pouck property."

"It wasn't a general," he said. "It really happened. We have real information for you. We found Sharon Kellerman's car. I think Elliott killed her."

"Sharon Kellerman?" Officer Glenn asked. "The missing real estate lady? You were trespassing on the Van Pouck estate and you found her car? Was that before or after The Tooth Fairy stole all the play money from your Monopoly game?"

The cops laughed again.

"Don't laugh!" he demanded. "This is a serious case of murder."

"I don't live on this street," she offered. "And, I saw the car, too. And the ghost."

"You don't live with this guy?" Officer Herbert asked. "But, your boyfriend's got you chasing ghosts, too? Well, I'm convinced. What about you, Glenn?"

"Let's find Elliott and slap the cuffs on him," the cop said sarcastically.

"Listen, kid," Officer Herbert said. "I'll tell you what I'll do. Since you live at 857 Agnes, I'm tempted to forget about your trespassing charge. I'm guessing you won't be in town long enough to pursue litigation. And in return, all I ask is that if you see Santa Claus, tell him my son wants a new bike for Christmas."

All he could do was glare at the cops as they laughed again.

"Look," Officer Glenn offered with a touch of guilt. "I realize the old guy in there is a nut. I think the whole town will breathe a sigh of relief when he's gone. It'll put an end to a lot of rumors and stories that keep circulating around here. Hell, if you could show me Elliott's cold, clammy corpse, I'd probably pin a medal on you myself. I'm sure if we dug up that property, we'd find a lot of bodies that have been there for fifty years or so. But the old guy's a harmless institution in this town. Leave him alone, stay in your own house, and everything will be fine."

"Until you go running out of town some midnight in a fit of screams," Officer Herbert added with a chuckle. "Go home, you two. Find a different hobby."

There was nothing left to do. The young couple got in their car. They each displayed their aggravation by slamming their doors closed.

"I told you it was useless to talk to the cops," she bitterly reminded.

As soon as the white Ford drove away, the cops shared an amused glance. Then, they rode off to protect and serve the public.

* * * * * *

Everything seemed foggy even before he opened his eyes. He felt an excruciating pain in his skull. It felt as though an elephant was mercilessly stomping on the inside of his brain. He groaned meekly beneath the agony.

There was something keeping his chin from resting on his chest. He had a distant notion that he might be sitting upright. He groaned again as he opened his eyes with difficulty. He lifted his head and glanced around the room.

His eyes quickly opened wide in shock. A dim light illuminated only a small portion of what was obviously a large, dusty room. The room was cluttered with old, broken equipment and tarp-covered tables.

"Where am I?" he said as he tried to move. As he noticed that he had been bound to a chair, he shouted, "Hey! What is this shit! Untie me right now, or I'm going to kill somebody!"

His jaw dropped when he saw the balding old man glaring at him from the shadows. But, shock turned to anger as he tried to break free. "Hey!" he bellowed. "What's going on, old man? Did you do this? Untie me, or I'll have your liver for my lunch!"

As the old man stepped into the light, his attire surprised the man in the chair.

"My name is Penelope Van Pouck," he said. "I own this property. You were found trespassing on it. That's why you have been detained. What is your name, young man?"

"You want my name?" he asked. "Sure. It's Charles T. Putnam. Remember that. I want you to know who's going to beat you to a pulp if you don't untie me."

"You are hardly in a position to threaten anyone, Mr. Putnam," Penelope said. "You must be either incredibly stupid, or irreconcilably insane."

"*I'm* insane?" Charlie scoffed. "Look at you. You're wearing a pink robe, for God's sake. I guess Penelope was a good name for you."

Then, he froze. His eyes grew wide with a sudden realization. "Wait a minute," he said. "Did you say your name was Van Pouck? I get it now. This big old house is the Van Pouck mansion. You must be that crazy old man, Elliott. I heard of you. Now it all makes sense!"

"I told you," he sharply reminded. "My name is Penelope!"

"Okay, pal," Charlie scoffed. "Whatever."

"Perhaps you won't be so quick to laugh when you look in the big mirror that's in front of you," Penelope pointed out. "You'll notice the noose around your neck. You see, you are not in the mansion. You are now in the carriage house behind the mansion. And once I release this rope that I'm holding, the platform beneath your chair will lower to the ground floor. You will be hanged by the neck for the crime of trespassing."

Charlie finally noticed the big, dusty mirror nearby. One terrifying glance proved the old man's claim to be accurate.

"Oh my God!" Charlie gasped in alarm. He looked overhead and saw the various ropes attached to the system of pulleys. "Are you crazy, old man?" he continued in a frenzied tone. "You can't do this! Let me out of here!"

"I keep telling you, Mr. Putnam," the old man snarled. "My name is Penelope!"

"Okay!" Charlie hastily agreed. "Sure! Fine! Now, how about untying me, okay? I promise I'll forget the whole thing. Better yet, maybe we can find you a good shrink."

"Do you have any last words before you hang for your crime?" Penelope asked.

He swallowed hard. He could feel the noose around his neck. He could see his horrified expression in the mirror. He struggled in vain to free himself from the bonds that held him in the chair.

"Look, pal," he begged. "This has all been a terrible mistake! I didn't mean you any harm. I was just looking for my girlfriend. Her car was parked in front of your house."

"You're a liar, Mr. Putnam," claimed the old man. "We have received no visitors today."

"I don't know why her car was there," Charlie insisted. "But, it was there! I swear it!"

"I have no more time for this," Penelope proclaimed. "Mr. Putnam, I sentence you to be hanged for the crime of trespassing. May God have pity on your soul."

The old man began to untie the rope that held the platform to the second floor.

Charlie stared in horror, as he realized what was happening. He desperately tried to break free from the chair. The ropes wouldn't budge.

"Please, old man!" he implored. "Cut it out! Get me out of here! I'll do anything! Please! Let me go, you crazy old freak!"

Penelope held the rope in his hand. He slowly lowered the platform beneath the chair.

Charlie's eyes bulged as he felt the noose pull tightly around his neck. He struggled to breathe. He struggled to break free from his bonds. All his struggles were to no avail.

Penelope smiled as he gently lowered the platform all the way to the ground floor. He was amused by the agonized grimace on the face of his prisoner. He listened with glee as the man in the chair gasped and sputtered in a futile attempt to get some air.

He watched the young man jerk and twitch.

He watched the captive squirm helplessly at the end of the rope.

Finally, the prisoner fell silent. His discolored face was frozen in a twisted, wide-eyed expression of panic and anguish. He dangled motionless at the end of the noose.

"I keep telling you, Mr. Putnam," the old man said with an arrogant smirk. "My name is Penelope."

CHAPTER 13.....
QUESTIONS_IN_THE_
CEMETERY_____

The plans were set. They each wanted to go home to shower and rest before dinner. He was to pick her up at 8:00. Under the circumstances, she didn't complain when he was fifteen minutes late.

They ended up back at The Turtle's Nest. They sat at a booth in the back. The waitress had just taken their order.

Her eyes looked tired. Still, he thought they were beautiful in the graceful flicker of the candlelight.

"I guess we're lucky," he said. "We only encountered one angry spirit while we were on the Van Pouck estate."

"I still can't get over those cops," she commented. "I knew they weren't going to believe us. But, the way they mocked us was inexcusable."

"They showed up at just the perfect time, though," he pointed out. "Didn't they? Just in time to miss the action. And, just in time to see us look like idiots."

"We didn't look like idiots," she insisted. "We were being chased."

"Too bad the police didn't seem to notice," he said.

"By the way," she added. "Who do you think was chasing us? Did that ghost look familiar to you?"

"No," he said. "But, that property has got to be crawling with trapped spirits. I keep hoping they're not dangerous. But, every time I meet one face to face, I can't take the chance that I'm wrong. As much as I want to go back into the mansion, it doesn't make sense to go back there until I have a definite location of where to find Ingrid's body."

"How long will that take?" she asked. "You're running out of time."

"I can only hope Ingrid will show me the next time she brings me to Nobody's Grave," he said.

"Did you say she brings you there?" she asked.

"In a manner of speaking," he nodded. "It's hard to explain. I never really choose to go there. Still, I seem to wind up in that grave. But in the meantime, I think you should stay away from the mansion, Heidi. At least, until this is over."

"We've been through this, Russell," she averred. "I'm not going to wait by the phone to hear if you're hurt . . . or dead. And, I'm not going find out the hard way that you skipped town. If I'm going to stay with you, we're in this together."

"Well, at least stay away from my house and the mansion until I have something to go on," he said. "I'll let you know when it's safe. I'll go there with you."

"Fair enough."

"I'll be glad when this is over," he said. "I just wanted to move to a nice little town, buy a house and start a new life. Of course, meeting you has made moving to Autumn so much more pleasant. We should have been able to just go out without having to overcome this kind of a burden."

"It will all be over soon," she said as she took his hand. "I have complete confidence in your ability to put an end to this once and for all."

There was a pause as they gazed at each other in the candlelight.

He finally broke the silence. "Heidi?" he said. "I'm sorry I didn't tell you sooner about the house. We had just started dating. I didn't want to scare you away. I was afraid you would leave before we had a chance to get started."

"I know that now," she said. "And, I'm sorry too, Russ. I shouldn't have automatically flipped out like that. I've just never seen a ghost before. It's not something I could've been prepared for."

"I understand," he said. "I felt the same way when I saw Ingrid for the first time."

"Nobody expects something like that to happen," she admitted. "And, with all the tales that circulate around this town about the Beckenbaurs and the Van Poucks, I was afraid . . ."

She glanced down at the table while suppressing a tear or two.

She looked back up at him as she continued, "I've been hurt a lot, Russ. I just couldn't stand to set myself up again for another painful disappointment. And, I guess since we just started out together, it was easier to bail out before things got . . . complicated."

"I can certainly see how you felt that way," he said. "But, don't worry. I will take care of this little fiasco. You're not going to get rid of me that easily. I promise I'm not going to leave, honey. Okay?"

"Okay," she answered with a sweet smile.

He couldn't resist. He stood, leaned over the table and kissed her on the lips.

As he sat back down, she asked, "Did that make you feel better?"

"A little."

"I just hope you're not hinting around for special treatment," she teased. "I told you I wanted to take it slow."

"It was just a kiss, sweetheart," he replied with a grin. "If you choose to read anything into it . . . that says more about you than it does about me."

There was a playful gleam in her eye. "You sound awfully sure of yourself," she observed. "I knew I should have ordered the lobster."

Later that evening, they were sitting on an old, tattered sofa. She took a sip of coffee. Then, she said, "I think you're starting to like Sky Shards."

"It is a nice little club," he admitted. "But, we didn't have to go there if you didn't want to."

"Don't be silly," she said. "I love that place. Still, I only suggested it because you made such a fuss about not going there a few nights ago."

"I didn't make a fuss," he told her. "I just said that I was surprised that there were so many other things to do in this town."

"But, this is quickly becoming one of your favorites," she said. "Isn't it?"

"As long as I'm with you."

Her delighted smile almost turned into a laugh. After looking away for a moment, she turned those enchanting green eyes back in his direction. One kiss became two. The third kiss was longer and more discernible.

She pulled away. "Deep down," she said. "I think I knew it was a mistake to invite you into my apartment tonight. We're supposed to be starting off slowly again. Remember?"

"If it was such a mistake," he inquired. "Why did you do it?"

"I'm not sure," she said. "Maybe I was testing my will power."

"How's it working so far?"

"Pretty well," she told him. "I think I'll be all right."

"Maybe we should test it a little more," he suggested.

She giggled a little before their next kiss.

Then, she pulled away again. "Okay," she said. "That's enough testing."

"Good," he said. "I prefer practical application, anyway."

He leaned in for another kiss. She backed away just a little. "What about taking it slowly?" she asked.

"I promise," he said. "I'll do this *very* slowly."

He kept his promise. The kiss was slow, sensual and reaffirming. A delicate sunrise brewed between them. The subtle textures of dawn glowed along a vast horizon. And, an awakening was due to follow.

Again she found herself on her back. She looked up at him with a gentle warmth. "You're not taking this seriously, pal," she said playfully.

"Is that what you think?"

"Yes," she smiled. "That's what I think."

"Then, watch closely," he said. "This is me taking it seriously."

They kissed again. The mystic layers of soft lights unfolded and stretched out between them.

"Is that better?" he asked.

"That depends," she said. "What were we talking about again?"

If possible, their bodies pressed even closer together. They blended together like the cocktail of an early morning breeze. Together they invented the sunshine that fed the fields that longed to escape the brutal darkness. They extended the broad reach of daylight over their valleys of seclusion.

* * * * * *

A gentle breeze had picked up in the past few minutes. He could feel it skirting along the ground between the tombstones. He could feel it brush past his hair. A profound darkness veiled the area with the crisp depth of a midnight silence.

The moon looked like a pale, rounded wafer that had been chewed by the Angel of Death. The stars were dim, meek eyes of distant frightened children. The town was asleep below. Everyone else could dream of sweeter things.

He had no idea how he got there. He wanted to leave. He needed to stay.

He stood at the edge of the grave. He was looking down at the skeleton laid out six feet below him. The dingy collection of bones still wore a chain with a locket around its neck. It remained motionless on the dirt floor of its intended home.

He didn't want to be afraid. He didn't want to enter the grave.

He called down into the hole. "Ingrid?" he asked. "Before I move forward, may I ask you a few questions?"

The skeleton slowly turned its head. The eye sockets were deep and vacant. The skull lacked the capacity to show expression. Still, it looked as though it was looking directly at him.

He took a deep breath for courage. He tried to appear assertive as he continued. "You want me to find you," he observed. "Don't you? Those phone calls at your house were not only directed at your husband. They were also directed at me. You have always been trying to help me to find you. Is that true?"

He could hear the eerie sound of bone scraping against bone as the skeleton slowly nodded its head. Then, it lifted its bony arm. With an emaciated finger pointed forward, the arm fell against the dirt wall of the grave. The finger wrote the letter "K" in the earth.

"Will you show me where you are tonight?" he asked.

The skeleton slowly nodded again. Then, its bony finger traced the letter "A" in the dirt.

He needed another moment to summon more courage. He braced himself before continuing, "The spirits who are confined to the Van Pouck property are either members of the family or victims who were killed on the estate. And, they were trapped by the curse that Katalina put on Gordon with the Gypsy Reprisal Beads. Is that true?"

The skeleton nodded again. Then, its slender finger wrote the letter "T" in the mud.

"But, you and your husband are not similarly afflicted," he continued. "Because you were cursed earlier by a different spell. The spell Katalina placed on your necklace. That's why you and your necklace must be found and brought to this grave . . . so you and Edgar can finally be at peace. Is that also true?"

The skeleton nodded slowly. Then, its finger traced the letter "A" in the earth.

"And, on my first visit to this place," he inquired. "I saw my wife because I was still refusing to let go of the past. The very basis of the curse that confines you and Edgar is the spirit's weakness . . . the human unwillingness to release the past and move on. Is that true? Is that the lesson I was to have learned?"

Again, the skeleton nodded slowly. Then, its slender finger drew the letter "L" in the dirt.

He grew nervous as he noticed how much of the perpetrator's name had been spelled. Judging from the pattern so far, he knew there would only be one more question before the grave opened up.

"You told me that I have to find you before you spell her name," he reminded. "Or it will be too late. What happens if I fail to recover you on time? Will I be killed? Will I somehow be driven out of town? Will I be the victim of some sort of tragedy?"

The skeleton did not respond. It seemed to stare at him in a dreadful silence. Then, its gaunt finger wrote the letter "I" in the earth.

The ground shook as the dirt floor of the grave disappeared. He instantly lost his balance and tumbled headlong into the hole that had already claimed the bony specter.

He kept tumbling as he fell through the mysterious blackness. It was difficult to tell in which direction he was falling. The void seemed to push in toward him. The emptiness nearly felt as if it were pulling him apart. He fell into a deep cavern of nothingness and loss. He kept falling through departing seas of misery.

He kept falling . . .

Then, he found himself in a room. This room was familiar. It looked bigger and much nicer when the furniture was new. The room looked splendid when it was clean. This was a beautiful reception chamber not far from the grand front room.

"Please, Gordon," she begged through a wave of tears. "You can't keep me here forever. You must let me go."

"Why do you insist on denying what we have, my love?" he said. "How many times must I tell you how much I adore you?"

"You killed my husband," she reminded. "You deliberately set out to ruin him financially. And then, you killed him right in front of me!"

"I did it all for you, darling," he said. "I did it for us. Now you see that I will stop at nothing to win your love. I will treat you like a queen for the rest of your life."

"When are you going to realize that I don't love you?" she implored. "I will never love you. I will love Edgar 'til the day I die."

"But, Edgar is dead."

"And, I died with him," she declared. "Everything I am is still back in my house. You have held me here against my will for two days, Gordon. For two days I have begged for my freedom. And, you refuse to relinquish me. I'm not even allowed to use the phone! Can't you see how wrong that is?"

"If you weren't so stubborn," he snapped. "I wouldn't need to take such drastic measures. You refuse to admit your love for me. You didn't mind my company last winter. You didn't mind the fancy dinners and expensive presents."

"Don't, Gordon!"

"You didn't mind when I lavished my attention on you," he continued. "You didn't mind sharing my bed!"

"Gordon!" she gasped. "Is such language truly necessary?"

"What made you turn your back on me, Ingrid?" he asked. "Why did you suddenly spurn me, in favor of your husband?"

"I've told you," she reminded. "I always loved him. I was a silly fool to allow my head to be turned by flattery and useless trinkets. You had to have known that I would come to my senses eventually."

"Nonsense!" he insisted. "You love me! I demand that you stop denying me! I demand that you stop denying our love! And, take that blasted necklace off! I can't believe you continue to flaunt that insult in my face!"

"No!" she snapped. "I'll never take it off! It's the only keepsake I have to remind me of my beloved Edgar."

"Fine," he grumbled. "Keep your cheap costume jewelry, if you must. Perhaps Katalina was right. Perhaps you will never be more than a common tart and a smuggler's wife."

"Katalina said that?"

"Just before I killed her."

"And, do you agree with her now?" she asked.

"You give me reason to consider the notion," he allowed.

"Then, you give me reason to take my leave," she declared.

She turned and stormed off toward the door.

He grabbed her arm. "You're not going anywhere," he told her.

She screamed as he pushed her down into a chair.

Then, a voice came from nowhere. It said, "You know she's going to leave you, Gordon. She'll never stay. Not unless you force her."

"Katalina?" he asked. "Is that you?"

"Yes."

"Damn you, woman!" he growled. "Get out of my head! I don't believe in you! You're dead! You can not taunt me like this!"

"Hurry, Gordon," she continued. "She'll leave if you don't stop her. Even a cheap tart like that would never stay with a miserable wretch like you."

"Stop it!" he shouted as he grabbed his head. "You can't be talking to me. You're dead! I killed you myself!"

"You can't keep her, Gordon," the voice said. "That little trollop will never stay with a fool like you."

She sat upright in the chair. She stared at her kidnapper with fear in her eyes. "Who are you talking to, Gordon?" she asked. "There's noboby here."

"Leave me alone, you devil woman!" he shouted while clutching his head. "You are dead! You can't make me listen!"

"She's going to leave you," the voice repeated. "Do you think your money can disguise what a horrid little weasel you are?"

His face was turning red as he yelled, "Shut up, Katalina! Shut up!"

She was turning pale. She stared at him as his rage grew more apparent. She quietly slipped out of the chair. She snuck over to the door.

"She's getting away, Gordon," said the voice. "See? I told you she would never stay."

He glanced over in time to see the woman run through the door.

He chased her into the grand front room. "Come back, Ingrid!" he called. "Don't run away! Don't let Katalina win!"

She ran as fast as she could in those shoes. But, he caught her before she got very far. He spun her around and grabbed her shoulders. She was crying hysterically when she begged, "Please don't, Gordon! Please let me go!"

"I told you she would never stay with a simple idiot like you!"

"You have to stay, Ingrid!" he commanded. "I love you! And, I'm not an idiot!"

"I never called you an idiot," she wept. "Please let go of me! You're hurting me!"

"See how she's looking at you, Gordon? She has nothing but contempt for you."

"I'm not a fool!" he shouted. "And, you won't leave me, Ingrid! You will never leave!"

She was crying as she struggled to break free of his grasp. She was pleading with him to stop.

"She still wants to go, you worthless little leech!"

"No!" he shouted. He pushed her to the ground. Her head struck the stone hearth.

She fell silent. She lie motionless on the floor. A small trickle of blood spilled over the hearth from the back of her head.

He looked down at her unmoving body. "Ingrid?" he called. "Ingrid? Are you all right, darling?"

"You see, Gordon?" said the voice. "Now she isn't causing trouble. Now she's not trying to leave."

"But, is she . . .?

"The important thing," the voice said. "Is that she's not trying to leave. If you want her to stay, you have to keep her. You must keep her where you can watch her. You must stay in complete control."

He was still looking down at the woman lying very still on the floor. "How can you say she wants to leave. She seems so docile."

271

"You made her that way, you fool," said the voice. "If you want her to stay with a simpleton like you, you must keep her here. You must control her."

"Control her?" he said. "Make her stay?"

"Why else would she stay with a fool?"

"Enough, Katalina!" he averred. "I'll teach you to insult me! I'll show you that I am not to be mocked! I killed you, and I can control Ingrid."

He marched over to the body lying still on the floor. He lifted her up. He slung Ingrid over his shoulder and carried her out of the room.

As he passed confidently from room to room, he averred, "So, Katalina! You don't think I can keep her? You don't think our love is strong enough to withstand your meddlesome interference? I know how Ingrid feels about me, and I'll show you that we can overcome your childish pranks."

He strode through the large, immaculate kitchen. He opened the door to the cellar and turned on the light. He carried the limp body down the stairs. "You think I feel guilty about what I did to you, my dear wife?" he asked. "You think I hear your voice as some manifestation of negative emotion? You think your stupid gypsy beads will make me believe in your spirit . . . haunting me forever? I have news for you. Your feeble attempts to control me can never work, my dear. I am too strong a man to be taken in with such foolishness."

He turned on another light in the clean, tidy cellar. He carried Ingrid over his shoulder to the east wall. There was a painting on the wall. It pictured a stream in a springtime meadow. He didn't even need to shift Ingrid's weight. He just moved the painting a few inches to the left.

The painting acted as a lever. With a heavy scraping sound, a portion of the brick wall swung open. He walked into the secret brick chamber. It was only about 10 feet by 15 feet long. "This chamber hasn't been used in almost a year. I knew it would come in handy again someday."

He lowered the limp body and placed it carefully against the wall inside the chamber. When he returned to the doorway, he turned to gaze at his motionless prize. "That should hold her," he said.

He stepped out of the chamber. He shifted the painting back to its original position. The wall closed noisily to form a secret, air-tight seal. "You see, Katalina," he proudly declared. "My love is going nowhere. And, I didn't need your help."

"You will have to keep her there forever," the voice told him. "She will never stay with you otherwise, you pompous clod."

"I don't need your advice," he insisted. "I know how to keep Ingrid so she will never leave me."

"She will never stay with you, Gordon."

"Enough, Katalina!" he snarled. "I can keep her here as long as I choose. Our love will prevail!"

"She'll never stay with you . . ."

"Leave me alone, Katalina!" he cried. "My love for Ingrid will sustain us forever!"

He woke up in a cold sweat. He was shivering. The sun was warm. The sky was blue and inviting. Still, he was cold. He recognized the familiar aches in his neck and shoulders. He recognized the hard surface on which he was resting ... and the smells of wet grass in the morning. The fact that he could see the sun directly overhead alarmed him. He quickly sat up. He frantically glanced around.

He was surrounded by tombstones.

"What happened?" he asked himself desperately. "How did I get here? I was at Heidi's place! I should be with Heidi!"

He looked around again. His stomach seemed to leap up into his throat.

"Oh, God!" he gasped. "She's going to kill me!"

CHAPTER 14.....
SPECTRAL_
INTERFERENCE_____

When she opened her eyes, she was looking up toward the ceiling. Her head rested comfortably on soft pillows. A smile of contentment graced her lips. She didn't want to move. However, she rolled over in her bed.

Her smile disappeared.

Covers and sheets had been tossed aside. The space beside her was vacant. She lifted her head. She glanced around the room.

"Russ?" she called.

There was no reply.

She got out of bed. She walked out into the living room.

"Russ?" she called again.

No one was in the living room or the kitchen. The bathroom door was open. The light was out. There was still no reply to her call.

Her eyes narrowed. "Did that little bastard take off on me?" she muttered to herself.

She slammed a few drawers and cupboard doors as she began the ritual of making a pot of coffee. As she filled the pot with water, she considered different suitable punishments for his behavior.

Then, her gaze softened. "The house!" she gasped. "It must have something to do with his house!"

Her head started reeling. Her eyes grew wide as they filled with tears. "Oh my God," she said. "He promised he wouldn't leave town suddenly. He promised he wouldn't be like all those other people in that house!"

She placed the coffee pot on the counter. She sat at the table as tears spilled down her cheeks. "I knew it was a mistake to take him back," she sniffled. "I'm glad I was at least smart enough to avoid any emotional attachment. I'm glad . . ."

She stopped. She paused to consider a notion. "How could the house reach him from here?" she asked herself. "What could it do to drive him away without even waking me up? Why go after him, while leaving me alone?"

Her eyes dried as they filled with wonder. "Maybe the Beckenbauers drew him away," she conjectured. "Maybe Nobody's Grave beckoned him, or something. Perhaps he just went over to the mansion on his own to keep me out of danger."

Her gaze grew more certain. She jumped up and retrieved her purse from the bedroom. She sat at the kitchen table as she fished out her cell phone. She pushed a number on her speed dial.

She heard the number ring on her phone. She also heard a phone ring in her apartment. She looked up in surprise. Both phones rang again. She glanced down under her kitchen table. The cell phone on the floor was ringing in unison with her phone.

She hung up. Both phones stopped ringing.

"Damn!" she muttered. "What's Russell's phone doing on the floor? Now I know something is wrong."

After a pause, she concluded, "I have to find him."

She bent down and picked up the other cell phone. She placed the two phones on the table beside her purse.

She ran to the other room to take a shower. She washed up as quickly as she could. However, she was in the shower long enough to miss the ringing of her phone. Her phone kept ringing, but she couldn't hear it from the shower.

A few moments after her phone stopped ringing, Russell's phone started. His phone rang five or six times. Then, it stopped.

Five minutes later, she turned off the water in the shower. She dressed as quickly as possible. She grabbed her purse and headed out the door. She hopped in her car and sped off toward Agnes St.

She left so quickly, she didn't notice the two cell phones sitting on her kitchen table.

* * * * * *

He was a little sore and dirty from sleeping on the ground. He wasn't surprised that his cell phone was not immediately at hand. He hurried out of the cemetery. As he figured, his car was parked right outside the front gate.

Still, he stopped. "Oh, crap!" he said with sudden realization. "Did I drive here last night? How did I get here? Who's responsible for this? And, how did they . . .?"

After a moment, he mumbled, "Never mind. I have more important things to worry about. I've got to reach Heidi."

He opened his car door and hopped in. He glanced around for his cell phone.

He couldn't find it.

He searched under the seats and in the back. He even checked the trunk. "Where the hell is my cell phone?" he asked desperately.

He ran back into the cemetery. He checked carefully along the path. He searched the whole area around Edgar Beckenbauer's grave.

The phone was nowhere to be found.

He hurried back to his car. He raced back over to his house. He cleaned up, showered and dressed. Then, he ran out of the house. He drove off down Agnes St. toward the town. He needed to find a pay phone. There was an apology he needed to make.

Luckily, there was a little corner store not far from the bottom of the hill. A pay phone was right outside. He stopped his car on the corner. He scooped some change out of his pocket along with a phone number.

He dialed the number. He listened to the phone on the other end ring.

It kept ringing. No one answered.

As it continued to ring, he made a face. "That's strange," he commented. "I wonder what's wrong. I hope she's not furious with me. I wonder if she has my phone. Maybe I left it at her place, and she grabbed mine by mistake."

He hung up and dialed his own number. He let it ring five times. As he hung up, he mumbled, "I didn't think that was very likely. But, I have to reach her."

He jumped back in his car. He turned the key in the ignition. The engine whirred and sputtered. Then, it stopped. He tried it again. The engine still wouldn't catch.

"Come on, you piece of junk," he complained. "You're less than a year old. And, I don't have time for this."

He tried again. The car started up, and he pulled away from the curb. Just to be safe, he stopped at the nearest gas station for a fill-up. Then, he rushed his car across town. He knew the quickest route to his girlfriend's house. And, he was determined to get over there as quickly as possible.

The situation at the Van Pouck mansion was on his mind. He finally had an idea where to search for Ingrid's body. However, his new lover would have to come first. Even though he would prefer to keep her out of this, he could not just disappear without a word.

He knew how she would worry . . . that is, if she wasn't angry at him for leaving her in the middle of the night.

* * * * * *

She sped through the streets of Autumn. She needed to find him. She had to help him. She had to return his phone.

The subtle Agnes St. hill was easy to find. Traffic was fairly moderate. The Tuesday morning rush hour was winding to a close. She slowed a bit when she started up the hill. She was anxious to reach her destination. However, she wanted to watch for a house that she had only seen twice.

She drove at a hastily prudent speed while scanning the properties along the way. The first few blocks were easy to ignore. She knew she still had a way to go before finding the house. After that, however, she began to pay attention.

She grew nervous as she approached the house. She hoped he would be there.

Finally, she saw the dwelling in question. Her heart sank as she noticed that the garage and driveway were empty. She pulled in anyway. She ran out and rang the doorbell.

Nobody answered.

She rang again.

There was still no reply.

Her stomach was in knots when she sat back down in her car. "Is he really gone?" she whispered to herself. A tear formed in her eye. She was staring at the steering wheel.

Suddenly, she looked up. "The mansion!" she gasped.

She backed out of the driveway. She drove farther up the hill. She searched for a sign of his presence as she neared her new target. She didn't see him . . . or his Monte Carlo.

When she reached the Van Pouck estate, the tears welled up in her eyes. The gate was locked. Plus, there was no reason to believe the mansion had received any uninvited guests.

She continued driving up to the cemetery. It was difficult to feel optimistic. Still, she didn't want to leave any possibility uncovered.

As she suspected, a quick scan of the cemetery grounds proved fruitless. The tears were getting harder to control as she sat in her car outside the open, rusty gate. "I knew it," she said as she wiped her eyes. "The house got to him. I don't know how, but these sons of bitches drove him out of town."

She began to cry. "I didn't even get to give him his phone back," she wept. "And, I know he must be gone. Even without his phone, he would have at least tried to call me. Even if he needed to use a pay phone, he wouldn't let me worry like this."

She reached for a tissue in her purse. She was wiping her eyes when something occurred to her. She froze. Then, she looked back in her purse.

"My phone!" she gasped. She started rifling through the handbag as she said, "Where is it? I know I brought it. And Russell's, too. Where are they? They must be in here somewhere. Unless . . ."

She stopped. She looked up with wide eyes. "My kitchen table!" she muttered. "Don't tell me I forgot to bring the phones. What happens if Russ tries to reach me? He might have been calling for the last half an hour! And, I'm out here without a phone. That's it! I have to go back!"

She turned the car around. Then, she raced off toward home.

* * * * * *

Her car wasn't anywhere near the building. He rang her doorbell four or five times. There was no answer.

"I guess she's not home," he surmised. "But, I've called her from two different pay phones. Why won't she pick up? She must be furious at me for leaving last night. I wish I could see her. She has to let me explain."

He got in his car. He tried to start it. Again, the engine wouldn't catch. He swore at the worthless machine. Then, he turned the key again. It started with some coaxing.

"I've got to get this thing to a mechanic later," he told himself.

He took off out of the parking lot with screeching tires. Then, he headed for Agnes St.

About halfway home, he decided to stop at another pay phone. He popped the coins in the slot. He dialed the number. He let it ring eight times. Then, he hung up.

He got back in his car. He'd left the motor running. He thought about Heidi. It almost felt like a bucket of acid was eating out his insides. He took his time driving back to the house.

He was about to turn into his driveway, when he was struck with an idea.

"She's been here," he whispered. "I'm not sure how I know. But, I know. She was here. She wants to see me."

There was a smile on his face. However, it quickly vanished.

"The mansion!" he gasped. "She promised she wouldn't go there without me. She wouldn't. Would she?"

He drove up the hill. He hurried to the place where he hoped he would not find her.

He stopped outside the locked gate. He regarded the mansion with a touch of fear. It looked ominous and forbidding even in broad daylight. Luckily, he saw no sign of the girl. There was no car, no muddy footprints . . . nothing.

For some reason, he felt compelled to step out of the car. He opened the door. He got out and stood on the pavement. He looked at the mansion. Even with what he knew, this building scared him. He wanted to enter this mysterious domicile, recover Ingrid's body and end his spectral nightmare. Unfortunately, he had a more immediate nightmare with which he must contend.

He got back in the car. Then, the engine stalled.

He rolled his eyes and swore under his breath. Then, he tried to start the car. It didn't work. He tried again. He still had no luck.

"Come on, you piece of shit!" he yelled. "I don't have time for this! Start, already!"

He tried a few more times to no avail. He banged the steering wheel with his fists while shouting, "Damn! It's like the whole world's against me today!"

He took a moment to calm himself.

He got out of the car and popped the hood open. He played with a few wires and tried again. The car just wouldn't start.

He leaned back in the driver's seat. There were so many things on his mind. He needed to talk to Heidi. He needed to get into the Van Pouck mansion. He finally had a good idea where to find the body that would end his house problems. Of course, there were other problems with the house . . . and the store. His cell phone was missing. It could be anywhere in Autumn. And now, his car wouldn't start.

He turned his head and stared at the mansion. That was his most troubling concern. How would he get past Elliott and an untold number of ghosts to get to Ingrid? And, how would he get a pile of bones out of the mansion once he found her?

He needed to cool off. He had tools at the house. If he could fix the car, it would save him a fortune in garage bills and towing costs. He had to get away from the car at the moment, though. He just couldn't face it. He slammed the door shut after stepping out onto the pavement. Then, he walked home.

As he stood at the end of his driveway, he thought of something. He strolled a few doors down the road. He looked at the mailbox that read "The Burgdorfs" in bold letters. He looked at the quaint little abode behind the trees.

He took a deep breath. Then, he walked up and rang their doorbell.

She opened the door and greeted him with a smile. "Russell?" she said. "What a delightful surprise. What can I do for you?"

"Hi, Maria," he said. "I was hoping your husband was home. My car broke down a few blocks up the road."

"Oh dear," she said with a worried frown.

"I'm not sure what's wrong with it," he said. "I have an idea or two. And, I have a few tools at the house. But I must admit, I'm not prepared for what I'm facing."

"Well, I'm sorry, dear," she said. "But, Jerry's not home. He's working today. And, I haven't a clue as to where his tools might be."

"That's all right," he said. "I'm sorry I bothered you."

"You're no bother, Russell," she said. "As a matter of fact, you're welcome to come in for some lunch, if you'd like. I was thinking about making something for myself, but I'm not very hungry. I seldom eat anything at lunchtime."

"No, thanks," he said. "But, I'd appreciate it if I could use your phone. I lost my cell phone this morning. It's been an unpleasant day."

"I guess it has," she said. "You're having all sorts of troubles. Of course you may use our phone, dear. It's right this way."

She allowed him to enter. She escorted him to the nearest phone.

"Thanks," he said. "I need to call a cab so I can run an errand or two in town."

"Why call a cab?" she suggested. "Since neither of us feels like eating, I could give you a ride into town. I have an errand or two of my own to take care of."

"You wouldn't mind?"

"Not at all."

"Thank you, Maria," he smiled. "That's the best news I've heard all day."

As they rode into town, they enjoyed a meaningless, idle conversation about nothing in particular. But during an awkward pause, she cautiously approached a delicate topic.

"Russell?" she asked. "Tell me honestly. Is that house really haunted?"

He was slow to answer. After consideration, he said, "I don't mean to be impolite, Maria. But, I don't like talking about my house to anyone in this town. People tend to think you're crazy if you say anything. Deep down, everyone wonders. A lot of people even believe it, to some extent. But, almost everyone will call you a nut right to your face."

"I used to be like that," she admitted. "I mean, who believes in ghosts? In all my years in my house, I never saw or heard anything. And, all the people who bought your home, and then ran away . . . I thought they were kooks who spent too much time listening to local gossip. But, you seem like a sharp young man."

"Thank you."

"And, when I was in your house the other day," she continued. "And, the unplugged phone rang. And, the look on your face when you answered the call . . . it was the spookiest thing I've ever experienced. And, I started to think that all those people couldn't have been crazy. Something must be wrong with that house."

"There is definitely something wrong in there," he told her. "But, I wouldn't worry about it. I think I solved the case. I know where Ingrid's body is."

"Really?" she said. "Where is it?"

"It's in the Van Pouck mansion," he said. "I think I know how to find it."

"But, how?" she asked. "People in this town have been pondering that mystery for over seventy years."

"It's not important right now," he said. "But, I know I'm going to have to enter the mansion and get her out of there. That's going to be tricky. Everything's going wrong today. My car broke down. My phone disappeared. I woke up in a different place than I went to sleep. It's almost like the forces of Nature are against me. It seems like there's some sort of spectral interference trying to keep me from succeeding."

"That sounds scary," she said. "Is the mansion really haunted, too?"

"Yes," he nodded. "Very much so. That's one of my biggest fears about going in there. Elliott is dangerously insane, and those ghosts don't seem very hospitable."

"What are you going to do?"

"I wish I knew," he admitted.

"Can I help?" she asked.

"This ride to town is help enough," he smiled. "But, thanks for asking."

* * * * * *

For some reason, she looked down when she stepped out of her car. She didn't know why. She just did. There were fresh skid marks in the parking lot.

"Russ?" she whispered to herself. "Was he here?"

She shook her head. There were a number of apartments in her building. Anyone could have made those tracks.

She was uncertain and confused about everything when she entered her apartment. She placed her purse on the kitchen table beside the two cell phones.

"I knew that's were I left them," she muttered.

She picked up her phone. She dialed a number.

Nothing happened.

She hung up. She couldn't get a dial tone. She pushed a few buttons. She tried to get the phone to respond. But, nothing worked.

"Don't tell me the battery's dead," she said. "Of all the days this could happen!"

She plopped herself down in a chair. She leaned her elbows on the table. She put her face in her hands to cover a fresh stream of tears.

Even if she didn't want to admit it, she was going to miss him very much. She had promised herself that she wasn't going to care. But, it was too late to keep that promise. There was no proof yet that he was gone for good . . . but, the chance that she would see him again diminished with each passing minute.

And, all she had to remember him by was a cell phone he'd left behind. He left Autumn in such a hurry, he forgot his cell phone.

She stopped crying. She lifted her head. She grabbed his phone from the table, and dialed a number. Luckily, his phone was working.

"The Golden Eagle General Store," said the voice on the other end. "May I help you?"

"Yes," she said anxiously into the phone. "Is Daisy Nakajima there, please?"

"Just a moment, please," said the voice. "I'll see if she's available."

Her stomach was doing somersaults as she waited. A minute later, she heard a familiar voice saying, "Hello. This is Daisy Nakajima."

"Hi, Daisy," she said. "It's Heidi."

"Hi, honey," Daisy said with a smile. "What's going on?"

"I'm sorry to bother you at work," she said. "I know Bill hates it when people get personal calls."

"I know," Daisy said. "I still can't believe he won't let us have cell phones at the registers. What a bunch of crap!"

"Listen, Daisy," she said. "I asked for you, because I trust you more than Tamara or Stacy. Have you seen Russ over there today?"

"No," Daisy said. "Why? Did you lose him?"

"I can't find him," she said. "I have his cell phone. I'm calling from his phone because mine's not working. The battery's dead."

"So, you can't find each other," Daisy laughed. "And, you can't even call each other?"

"It's not funny, Daisy," she snipped. "He disappeared . . . like all the other people who owned that house."

Daisy stopped laughing when she heard the tone in her friend's voice. "I'm sorry, honey," she said. "I didn't mean anything by it. Do you think he's . . .?"

"I don't know," she said shakily. "I can only hope not. But, do me a favor, okay? If you see Russ, tell him I have his phone. He can't reach me unless he calls his number."

"Okay," said Daisy. "But, do you think he's still around? Did you two patch things up, at least?"

"We did plenty of patching," she said. "But, now . . ."

Daisy still didn't like the sound in her friend's voice. "Don't worry, Heidi," she said. "If I see him, I'll tell him."

"Thanks," she said. "I might even swing over to his house one more time, just to be on the safe side. Later today, maybe. He might still come home."

"Wow," Daisy commented. "You sound a little desperate."

"You'd be desperate, too," she said. "If you thought Ken was gone forever."

"Yes," said Daisy. "But, Ken's my husband."

There was an awkward silence.

"I've got to go," she said. "I've been on Russell's phone too long. 'Bye."

After hanging up, she made sure she put both phones in her purse. Then, she sat for a moment. She puttered around the apartment for a while. She found one or two things to clean. Then, she grabbed her purse and hurried out the door.

She had to stop for gas on her way to Agnes St. Still, she made good time as she raced across town with a purpose.

Again, she grew jittery as she drove up the road leading to the cemetery. She had a feeling. She just knew he must be home. She was certain that he had not left town. The knots grew tighter in her stomach as she neared his house.

Then, she suddenly felt as if a two-ton weight had dragged her heart to the bottom of the ocean. His garage and driveway were still vacant.

"Damn!" she cried. "This is the second time I wasted over half an hour driving over here! And, it was all for nothing!"

She parked in the driveway anyway. She ran out and rang the doorbell. A few more tears fell each time she rang it.

Nobody answered. No one was going to answer.

She got back in her car. Her heart was still heavily weighted down as she wiped her eyes again. She knew it was useless, but she had to make one more swing up toward the cemetery. She just couldn't leave any possibility unexplored.

She tried to stick to the speed limit for this residential neighborhood. She tried to avoid having expectations. She kept telling herself it was a waste of time as she watched the houses pass by. She braced herself against the inevitable disappointment.

Then, she saw something as she approached the 1100 block. Feeling much lighter, her heart leapt up to her throat. A delighted smile brightened her face, as she stepped on the gas. She raced up the road and slammed on the brakes behind a familiar sight.

She recognized the black Monte Carlo. She had ridden in it many times. A sigh of relief brought forth a few tears of joy.

Then, she looked up. The smile slowly disappeared from her lips. She noticed that his car was parked near the locked gate of the Van Pouck mansion.

The same weight dragged her heart down again. She stared through the bars of the gate with trepidation. She suddenly felt very cold.

The chill wouldn't go away as she stared at the intimidating structure. She thought about the man she had searched for all morning. She could almost picture him in that treacherous building all alone . . . facing the terrible ordeal that confronted him.

It made her shiver with fright.

Finally, she managed to look away. She took another minute to sort her priorities. Then, she grabbed her phone from her purse. When she couldn't get a dial tone, she tossed it back in with an aggravated grunt. Then, she took the other phone from her purse and dialed.

After a few rings, a voice on the other end said, "Golden Eagle General Store. May I help you?"

"Hello," she said. "May I speak to Daisy Nakajima, please?"

"Just a minute, please."

She stared at the mansion from the driver's seat as she waited. She grew more anxious with each passing second. Her courage was fading as the interminable wait dragged on.

Then, a voice finally broke the phone silence. "Hello?"

"Daisy?" she said. "It's Heidi again."

"For God sakes," Daisy said. "You know I can't keep getting these calls. This is the second one today."

"I know, honey," she said. "And, I'm sorry, but this is an emergency. Believe me. Russ is going to kill me, too. This is the second time today I've used his cell phone without asking. That is, he'll kill me if . . ."

She needed to pause for a moment. Then, she continued, " . . .If he's all right."

"Oh," Daisy gasped. "I forgot about that. How's the search going?"

"Well, I found his car," she said. "Unfortunately, it's parked right outside the Van Pouck mansion."

"It is?"

"Yeah," she sighed. "He must be in there trying to find Ingrid Beckenbauer's body. That's the only way to stop his house from being haunted. He told me he had an idea where to find her. Maybe he got some more information last night. That has to be why he disappeared."

"So, what are you going to do?" Daisy asked.

"Well, I can't let him face this mess by himself," she explained. "I have to go in there, so I can help him."

"You're going into the Van Pouck mansion?" Daisy asked. "Alone?"

"I have to," she replied. "That place is extremely unsafe. I was only on the estate once with Russ. And we got attacked by a ghost. According to Russ, the place is crawling with spirits. And, Elliott really is insane to the point of being dangerous."

"Aren't you scared?"

"I'm terrified," she admitted. "That's why I called you. I'm so scared, I can hardly talk myself out of leaving my car. But, I'm still not as scared as I was this morning. When I woke up and saw Russ had disappeared, I thought he took off out of town in the middle of the night. If he had vanished like all the other people who had owned the Beckenbauer house, I'd . . ."

She had to stop talking. She knew she could hold back the tears.

Hearing the tone in her friend's voice, Daisy said, "It's all right, honey. Everything's going to be fine. If you have to go into the mansion, I support you."

"Thanks."

"Just be careful," Daisy added. "That place can be hazardous to your health."

"I know," she said. "Thanks for everything, Daisy. You're a good friend."

"That's okay," Daisy said. "Are you sure it's all right to go in there by yourself, though? I'm worried about you."

"I'm a little worried, too," she admitted. "But, I'm a big girl now. I can take care of myself. And . . . I really have to do this."

"Okay, honey," Daisy said with a knowing smile. "Good luck. Be safe."

"I will. 'Bye."

She hung up the phone and glanced back at the mansion. She took a few deep breaths for courage. She hid the cell phones under her front seat. She decided to carry her purse, however. A few items in there might come in handy.

She stepped out of the car and closed the door. She regarded the huge building with a growing sense of fear. The gate was locked. However, she remembered the alternative entrance that Russell had shown her.

She glanced around. A car or two passed by. Then, the street fell silent. She hurried down the side of the estate. She followed the fence back to the wooded section of the hill. She wasted no time finding the hole in the fence near the steep drop.

She made a face. Crawling through that hole was not a pleasing notion.

However, she took a breath and sunk to her knees. Slipping through the hole was easy enough. Still, it was as messy as she had presumed.

She got up and brushed the dirt from her clothes. As she surveyed the landscape, a chill went up her spine. The realization that she was standing alone on the Van Pouck estate filled her with a sudden wave of fear.

Cautiously, she stepped away from the fence. She knew enough to keep a constant watch on her surroundings. Her eyes kept moving as she walked carefully through the underbrush. Aside from the gentle crunching beneath her feet, everything was eerily silent.

The woods were very still. Only scant beams of sunlight escaped through the leafy branches overhead. It was as if nature provided occasional lamp posts to break the mysterious darkness.

While she was here, she decided to cover all her options. She gathered her courage. Then, she called out in a timid cry. "Russ?" she called. "Russ? Are you there?"

No response broke the belittling stillness.

She kept moving. She kept looking around for signs . . . either good or bad. She kept watching for clues as to how to proceed.

She was heading in the general direction of the mansion. However, she continued to look everywhere, just to be safe.

When she reached a respectable distance from the fence, she called out again. This time, her voice was louder and stronger.

"Russ? Are you out here?"

There was still no reply.

She glanced around again as she took another step toward the mansion.

Then, she saw a flash of light. She jumped with a start. She turned toward the object. She saw a figure illuminated in the shade of the trees. It was in the form of a man. He was located over by the sheer drop-off. He moved slowly toward her.

A gasp nearly turned to a scream. She covered her mouth to stifle the sound. This glowing figure was advancing on her in a slow but steady pace.

She turned and ran toward the carriage house. She ran between the trees toward the clearing. She was too scared to watch the underbrush. She just had to hope her footing was sure as she raced for freedom.

She refused to look behind her. She didn't want to waste the time it would take. Plus, she was afraid of what she might see. She was afraid of how close her pursuer might have gotten.

Her heart was beating like a drum roll as she sped out of the shade of the trees. The sunlight was warm and refreshing, but she didn't have time to notice. She sprinted over the top of the remaining undergrowth. She refused to stop running until she passed the carriage house.

As she stood at the edge of the parking area, she looked over her shoulder. When she saw no threat behind her, she stopped. She kept an eye out toward the woods as she caught her breath. She needed a minute to calm her nerves.

However, she knew that it wasn't safe to just stand out in the open. So, she began to walk toward the mansion as soon as she was able. She was still breathing heavily as she made her way up the drive. Apparently, exploration was not a good idea. She decided to stick with a sound plan. If Russ was most likely to enter the mansion, then that's where she should go as well.

When she reached the grand staircase in the front of the building, she stood and looked up. It was a longer climb than she would have imagined. And the stairs didn't look as sturdy as they once were.

She glanced around. All was quiet. Still, she didn't want to spend any more time here than necessary. So, she began to walk up the stairs.

They creaked and sagged beneath her feet. However, she continued to climb up the paint-faded path to the front door. And as she neared the entrance, her heart and stomach both jumped up into her throat.

Every muscle in her body tensed as she approached her destination.

The steps creaked menacingly beneath her as she climbed . . . one step, then another. She continued to glance around her until she grew close to the landing. The front door loomed ahead of her like the entrance to Hell. She had to fight back the fear that boiled inside her as she forced herself to move forward.

Finally, she reached the landing. She stared at the door as if it were a jungle animal ready to strike. This was the passageway to a legend that had terrified the people of Autumn for generations. She was about to walk into a living nightmare of unknown proportions. She didn't want to continue. But, she knew it was imperative!

Knocking would be a mistake. So, she slowly reached out and grasped the cold doorknob in her trembling fist. It turned with ease. The door slowly opened with a loud, horrific squeak that made her jump.

She took a deep breath. Then, she leaned inside. She saw no one. So, she crept into the grand hallway as quietly as possible. She cautiously surveyed her surroundings as she stepped deeper into the great room.

She made a face as she saw how filthy everything was. The smell of decay made her wince. "Disgusting!" she commented to herself. "This must have been a gorgeous place a hundred years ago."

She took a few more cautious steps into the room. She noticed the great stairwell on one side of the hall. She saw the grand fireplace on the other side.

"That's a nice candlestick," she said to herself. "I wonder where the other one is."

The silence was daunting. She didn't want to draw attention to herself. Still, she had someone to find. "Russ?" she called in a shaky voice.

The echo bounced just as shakily through the house.

It frightened her. She decided that calling out was not an attractive idea. However, there didn't seem to be many options when it came to finding someone in a house this size. She took a few more steps.

Then, she heard a loud slam. She jumped nearly ten feet in the air.

She turned around with her eyes wide open. The front door had slammed shut. However, nobody was anywhere near the door.

Her skin was crawling like a nest of fearful centipedes. She was shaking like fine China during an earthquake.

She turned around. She saw the body of a man lying at the foot of the stairs. The knife in his chest had ruined his shirt with blood.

She screeched at the top of her lungs.

The echo of her scream hadn't even died down when she looked back at the closed front door. That's where she wanted to go. However, an image suddenly emerged from the wall right beside it. This blurred man was standing. And, he seemed to be looking right at his uninvited guest.

She screamed again.

Her exit was blocked. She turned and ran deeper into the house.

She passed through a few rooms before she was able to stop. She was constantly searching for Russ, but she didn't see him. When she stopped running, she was able to look around with greater care.

This room was big and beautiful, too . . . except for the layers of grime and decay. She kept glancing around. She was lost. She had no idea where she was. She had never been so frightened in her life . . .

. . .That is, until she saw the next ghastly spirit. This image of a gentleman seemed to be bleeding from what appeared to be bullet holes in his lapel. He sneered at the woman in the center of the room. He took a threatening step toward her.

She shrieked with unimaginable fright.

Then, she turned and raced hysterically from the room. She crossed three rooms before she could stop. Her wide eyes were streaming with tears of horror. She was struggling to catch her breath. After glancing around the empty room, she turned her attention to the door she had just passed through. She wanted to be sure that the menacing ghost had not followed her.

Therefore, she did not notice someone entering through the other door. She took a cautious step backward. She did not see the balding older man in the pink robe. She didn't notice as he snuck quietly up behind her. She did not see him raise the solid gold candlestick above his head.

However, she felt the forceful blow of the implement as he viciously struck her on top of the head.

She fell forward like a sack of groceries. She lay perfectly still on the carpet in the center of the room.

The old man looked down at the motionless body on the floor. He watched the woman lie unmoving between to chairs.

She didn't budge.

However, her blood stained the tarnished candlestick in the old man's hand.

* * * * * *

"Thank you for the coffee, Russell," she said. "That was very sweet of you."

"You're welcome, Maria," he said. "It's the least I can do to repay you for driving me into town today. I only wish I could have added lunch to the occasion."

"You're too kind," she said. "But, as I mentioned before, I seldom eat lunch. This does look like a nice place, though. What was the name again?"

"Fehr's Steak and Ale," he said. "I'm becoming a regular customer here."

"I can see why," she nodded. "It has a pleasant atmosphere. I'll have to get my husband to take me here sometime. I usually have to twist Jerry's arm to get him to take me anywhere. He's such a stick in the mud."

"He seems like such a nice man."

"Oh, he is," she admitted. "He can be a little cheap, though. Oh well. Are we done here? I'd like to get home this afternoon. I have to make Jerry's dinner."

"Yes," he nodded. "I have to get home, too. I have to quit stalling. I have to get into that mansion today. I just wish I was better prepared. I don't know how to attack the situation."

"I wish I could help you, dear," she said. "But, I'd be scared silly."

"Don't worry, Maria," he said. "It's not your problem. Besides, you've helped me today more than you can imagine. Just let me make a quick call, and we can get going. Can I use the bar phone, Amy?"

"Sure," Amy said as she handed him the receiver. "But don't tie up the phone too long. You can never tell when the boss will turn up."

"Thanks," he said.

He dialed the number. After a few seconds, he said, "That's odd. I'm not getting anything at all. Maybe her battery ran out. That's just my luck. Everything's going wrong today. And after last night, I really need to get a hold of her. Maria? Just on a whim, do you mind if we stop at The Golden Eagle? It's not far from here. Maybe someone there will know how else to reach Heidi."

"Okay," she said. "It might be fun. I haven't been there in ages. I thought it was closed down already."

"Thank you," he said. He handed the phone back to Amy and threw a tip on the bar. "Thanks, babe," he told her. "Have a good day."

"You too," said Amy. "Drive safe."

As they headed out the door, Maria observed, "The way you describe her, your lady friend sounds like a wonderful girl."

"She's a sweetheart," he said. "I'm sure you'd like her."

"So, tell me," she inquired. "Is it true love? Do I hear wedding bells in the future?"

"I've only known her a week, Maria," he said. "But, don't worry. If it ever comes to that, I'll reserve you a seat at the head table."

"You're a peach," she said with a laugh.

It didn't take long to reach the store. He tried not to rush Maria as they entered the building. He immediately walked up to the cash registers. All three registers were attended by cashiers. With no customers, they were engaged in idle chatter.

"Hello, ladies," he greeted.

The three women said hello.

"Russell?" Daisy asked. She pointed to the pretty young blonde woman in the center. "Have you met Stacy Constantine? She's another one of your cashiers. Stacy? This is Russell Wilburn. He's the new owner."

"Yes," he smiled. "I believe we met once before."

"The pleasure was all mine," Stacy said with a disarming smile.

"So, Russell," Daisy added. "Did you find Heidi at the mansion?"

"What?" he asked. "I don't know what you're talking about. I've been trying to reach her all day. That's the main reason I'm here. I can't even get her on the phone."

"She called on your cell phone because her battery died," Daisy explained. "She told me she found your car parked by the mansion."

His eyes grew wide with fear. "She saw my car by the Van Pouck mansion?" he asked.

"Yes," Daisy continued. "She figured you were inside. She said she was going in to find you."

He turned completely white. "Did you say Heidi went into the Van Pouck mansion?" he gasped. "Alone? Looking for me?"

"Yes," Daisy nodded with a distressed look in her eyes. "She told me she wanted to help you."

"Oh shit!" he exclaimed. "I've got to get her out of there! Maria! We've got a change in plans. I have to get home right away! It's a matter of life and death!"

"I heard," Maria said. "And, I understand completely. Let's go."

"Good-bye, ladies," he said. "And thanks, Daisy."

Russell and Maria rushed out the door as the girls said good-bye.

When they were gone, Stacy commented, "So, Heidi got to him first, huh? I've got to give her credit. He's a good-looking guy. When she jumps back in the game, she really jumps back into it."

"Don't do it, Stacy," warned Tamara. "Heidi really likes this guy a lot. And, she needs this more than you do right now."

"Don't worry," Stacy sighed. "You're right. I'll behave. I'm certainly not going to cheat on Tony, anyway. Not after he just took me to Florida. And, I know Heidi needs to have something good happen in her life. The poor girl's had a rough couple of years. She's my friend. I love her to pieces. And, I'm glad she finally found somebody. I'm just saying she's a lucky girl. That's all."

"She's not that lucky," Tamara said. "Not if she's in the Van Pouck mansion all by herself."

The three women shared a concerned glance.

CHAPTER 15.....
KATALINA'S_REVENGE_____

The car raced toward Agnes St. as quickly as traffic would allow.

"Sorry we can't make better time," she said. "I don't know why there are so many cars on the road today. Of course, this old Chevy of mine has seen better days."

"That's all right, Maria," he said. "Just do your best. I'm sorry if I snapped at you back at the red light a few blocks back."

"It's perfectly understandable, dear," she said. "You have every reason to be upset."

"But, I shouldn't take it out on you," he told her. "You have been very kind, driving me around like this today. Frankly, I'm mad at myself more than anything else. I never should have left my car in front of the mansion. I should have seen something like this coming. It's just my luck Heidi would come looking for me. And, why didn't I buckle down and take care of my business at the mansion while I was there?"

"Well, it's not as if you could just march in there," she justified. "That's against the law. And, Elliott wouldn't stand for that. And, even if you were able to get Ingrid's body out of there, it wouldn't help your lady friend now. Whoever is haunting the mansion would still be there. And, Elliott would still be there, also."

"But, maybe if I could have gotten in there," he argued. "Perhaps I could have talked to him."

"What would you say?" she suggested. "'Sorry to trespass on your land, but don't let your ghosts kill my girlfriend if you see her?' That's absurd."

"Still," he insisted. "There must have been something I could have done to prevent this. At least, I should have gotten my car back to my house."

"Don't beat yourself up, Russell," she imparted. "What's done is done. All you can do is move forward. Who knows? Maybe she left when she saw you weren't there. Maybe Elliott invited her to stay for tea."

"That's highly unlikely."

"Well, we won't know until we get there," she said. She turned the car onto Agnes St., and drove up the hill. "This girl of yours sounds like she's something special. I'd love to meet her sometime."

"Let's hope you get the chance," he said.

"That's a dreadfully morbid attitude, Russell."

"That's the sort of day I'm having."

They didn't say much else as they headed in the direction of the cemetery. The uneasy silence made the tense ride seem even more unbearable. As they neared the mansion, his heart dropped into his freshly churning stomach. He saw the little white Ford parked directly behind the black Monte Carlo.

"I knew it!" he grumbled. "That's Heidi's car! I have to get her out of there!"

As she pulled over to the side of the road, she asked, "Is there anything I can do?"

"No," he said. "You've helped me so much today already. You have no idea how valuable you've been. Thanks, Maria."

He opened the car door. He leaned over and kissed her on the cheek. Then, he hopped out of the Chevy.

"It was no problem," she said. She blushed with a nervous giggle. "By the way, you still have a few bags of things in my trunk."

"I'll get them from you later," he replied. He closed the door. "Thanks again. Wish me luck."

"I wish you all the luck in the world, dear."

As she pulled away, he muttered to himself, "Let's hope that's all I need."

He watched the car drive off. Then, he turned to face the gray mansion. The gate was still locked. So, his first move was clear. He took a deep breath to steady his nerves. Then, he hurried around to the side of the house. He followed the fence all the way back behind the carriage house and into the woods.

He continued to follow the fence until he found the hole near the drop-off. He wasted no time slipping through the hole in the fence.

However, his path was not as obvious once he got inside. He knew that she could be anywhere on the property.

He took a quick tour through the woods. He was determined not to be afraid of anything. Finding Heidi was the only thing that was important. He called out her name as he ran between the trees.

There was no response.

He glanced around in a rapid search through as much territory as he could cover. He found nothing in the dismal shade of the area.

Again, he called out, "Heidi!"

Once again, he was met with only silence.

He moved swiftly through the woods. It didn't take him long to decide that he was more likely to find her in the mansion. However, something caught his eye. An illuminated figure stepped out from behind a tree by the sheer drop-off.

It startled him. Still, he refused to retreat. The figure walked slowly toward him. He took a few steps to back out of the apparition's way. But, he was not going to run.

Every muscle in his body tensed as the image drew near. He thought its vacant eyes were staring at him. He braced for whatever confrontation he might have to face.

However, the ghost walked past him. It disappeared as it neared the sunlight.

He breathed a sigh of relief. Then, he decided to get out of the woods. He marched through the undergrowth with a definite purpose in mind. If nothing else, he was going to get Heidi out of this madman's house . . . alive!

The trees grew fewer, and the sunlight was just ahead. The thick undergrowth still hampered his mobility, but he persevered.

Suddenly, he tripped and fell to his knees in a reasonably fresh mound of dirt. He rose back up to his feet. He looked behind him as he brushed himself off. He wanted to see what he had tripped over.

A chill went up his spine as he saw something that vaguely reminded him of the carriage house.

"Oh my God!" he gasped. "Is that a human hand? This one looks a lot younger."

A terrible pain curdled inside him, as he feared the worst. He dropped back to his knees and began scooping the dirt away with his hands.

His fears grew darker as he desperately brushed the dirt away. He was obviously uncovering a human body. It was a female. And, her body was cold.

When he revealed enough of the face, his eyes grew wide with fright.

"Sharon Kellerman!" he gasped.

He quickly jumped up to his feet. Various insect life had already begun to feed on her flesh. Still, you could recognize who she once was. The deep knife wounds in her chest looked like a cafeteria for parasites.

He backed away slowly. His heart was racing with a new desperation. He turned and ran away from the woods. He stopped when he reached the carriage house. He considered searching that building as well. Then, he remembered that he told Heidi that he was focusing his attention on the mansion. He figured he would have better luck if he continued his hunt up there.

He ran to the front of the mansion. He stopped at the foot of the grand staircase. These stairs used to scare him a little. However, he had no time for fear at this moment. He charged up the stairs and through the front door.

Luckily, it was not locked.

He immediately glanced around as he entered the grand hall.

"Heidi?" he called out.

He walked further into the room. He continued to survey his surroundings as he listened to the echo from his voice die down.

No response was offered.

He called out even louder. "Heidi?" he shouted. "Are you in here?"

He considered his options as his voice repeated through the eerie echo in the building. He knew that he'd told her to aim for the cellar. However, if Elliott had gotten to her first, she could be anywhere.

Then, he heard a loud slam. He turned to see that the front door had closed behind him. No one was there to close it. His eyes narrowed. He became more resolute in his quest to find his girl.

He decided his voice could reach a greater area inside the building if he called out from the second floor. Perhaps he just had a hunch that she was upstairs. Either way, he began to run up the stairs.

But when he neared the top of the staircase, a spirit stepped out from behind a door to greet him. He recognized the illuminated image of Gordon Van Pouck. The vision startled him. He took a step backward in his surprise.

Being on a staircase, he missed his footing. He tumbled backwards down the grand stairwell. He rolled head over heels until he hit the first floor. He was severely jarred from the fall. He was groggy from having hit his head a number of times on the way down.

He didn't even see the balding old man who was standing over him at the foot of the stairs. He was visibly shaken from his unpleasant descent. He didn't even notice the old man in the pink robe clutching a gold candlestick.

The next thing he knew, he was regaining consciousness. His head felt as if it had been used by a professional baseball team for batting practice. It even hurt to open his eyes. He was vaguely aware of the fact that he was sitting upright. And, it felt like something was wrapped around his neck.

When he finally managed to open his eyes, everything looked blurry. There didn't seem to be much light in the area. He began the excrutiating task of raising his head.

Then, he heard a familiar female voice calling, "Russ? Russ? Are you awake? Are you all right, honey?"

It sounded as though she had been crying quite recently.

It gave him added incentive to get up. He tried to look around and see where he was. His vision had not yet fully returned. "Heidi?" he called. "Is that you?"

"Yes," she said. "Oh, Thank God! Russ! You're alive!"

"Of course I'm alive," he said. He tried to move. He couldn't budge. "Why wouldn't I be?" he continued. "Hey! What's going on? Where am I? Where are you?"

"I'm over here, Russ," she directed. "We're on the Van Pouck estate."

His gaze followed her voice. It took him a few seconds to focus. The first thing he saw clearly was his girlfriend tied to a chair with more thick rope than was necessary. She was about fifteen feet to his left. She looked terribly frightened in the scant light of the large, filthy room. Only one or two lights were on. Most of the room was still shrouded in darkness. Heidi sat near the dwindling edge of the shadows.

He tried to move again. It quickly became obvious that he was also bound to a chair with any abundance of thick cord. "What the hell is happening?" he asked while continuing his useless effort to escape. "Are you all right, Heidi? You're bleeding!"

"I'm okay, Russ," she said. "Don't move. Please stop moving."

"Why?"

"That certainly seems like a fair question, Mr. Wilburn," said an eerily calm male voice.

He looked up and saw a familiar old man step out of the shadows. The man was wearing the same pink robe with white fur trim. The look in his cold eyes was confident and unsettling.

"The answer to that question," the old man continued. "Can be seen in the mirror directly in front of you."

He looked into the dirty, large mirror before him. He recognized this mirror from a previous visit. However, the reflection that awaited him was gruesome. His pounding headache suddenly seemed unimportant when he saw that he had a bigger problem than being tied to a chair. The noose that was fitted around his neck seemed to be strung up through the rafters overhead.

"I'm sure you know where you are, Mr. Wilburn," the old man said. "You've been here before. This is the carriage house behind the family mansion. You have trespassed here before. But, I will make certain you never trespass here again."

He knew he had to act rationally. He had to swallow his fear. The old man had the advantage. Plus, the man was insane. Diplomacy and tact seemed to be the only cards he had to play.

"Am I addressing Penny?" he asked.

"Goodness, no," scoffed the old man. "You mean Elliott's wife? The little tramp who married my husband's grandson so she could get her hands on the family fortune? You insult me, sir. My name is Katalina. Katalina Van Pouck."

"And, do you plan on killing us both?" he asked.

"Can you think of a reason why I shouldn't?" said the old man. "You both have gained unlawful access to my property through a hole in the fence on more than one occasion. That level of transgression is punishable by death. After all, I must ensure no such behavior occurs in the future. Don't I?"

"We meant you no harm," he explained. "We were only looking for Ingrid."

"As I recall," the old man reminded. "Ingrid left you a message that you were no longer welcome in her house."

"Penny gave me that message," he said. "But, I have corresponded directly with Ingrid since then. Apparently, Penny was misinformed."

"What?" growled the old man. The anger in his eyes grew visibly deep. He stood manacingly over his captive as he ranted, "Do you intend to correct me, sir? In my own house? I will not stand for such impertinence! Why would Ingrid even waste her time corresponding with a man like you?"

"We share the same house."

The old man took a step back as he smiled. "I see," he said. "You believe Ingrid can be located in your house?"

"Her spirit spends a lot of time there," he explained. "Of course, you know where her body is . . . as well as I do."

"You plan to win your freedom with feeble trickery, do you?" the old man asked. "You think that if you stir my temper, it will somehow give you an opportunity to get away. I should have expected nothing less from a common criminal. Do you know what will happen when I release this rope, Mr. Wilburn?"

He looked at the beam where the rope was tied.

"When I release it," the old man continued. "The platform beneath your chair will drop to the ground floor. And you will be hanged by the neck until dead for your crimes against this household."

"Do you plan to hang us both?"

The old man looked over at the chair to which the girl was tied. "No," he said. "Somehow, hanging doesn't seem like the appropriate punishment for a lady. I have entirely different plans for Miss O'Dell."

He pointed toward a nearby table that stood partially hidden in the shadows. Both prisoners had to crane their necks to see the long, sharp knife which rested near the edge of the moldy wooden table.

"Please don't kill us," she sobbed. "We don't deserve to die! We'll never bother you again! Russ can move to another house! We can all put this behind us! We won't say a word to anyone! I promise. Just please let us go!"

"It almost seems unfair to make the lady watch you die first," the old man said. "But, it's the only way she can learn the true depth of her offense."

He grew angry as he watched her cry. The sound in her voice filled him with rage. She said, "Please don't kill us! Please!"

He was on the verge of an outburst of fury. He needed to control himself. As calmly as he could manage, he said, "How many people have to die, Katalina? You have taken vengeance against three full generations of this family for a single act of indiscretion by one man. How many countless others have died? How many people have you driven out of my house? When will it be enough? When will you let it go, so you can be at peace?"

"That was an eloquent speech, Mr. Wilburn," said the old man. "And, a fitting comment for a man's last words. But, I grow tired of our conversation. It is time for your punishment to commence."

He began to panic as the old man reached for the rope tied to the wooden beam. "No!" he cried. "Don't do it! This won't solve anything!"

"Good-bye, Mr. Wilburn," the old man said. He began to untie the rope.

His captive struggled frantically to free himself from the chair.

When the rope was untied, the old man slowly began to unwrap it from its metal post in the support beam.

The captive had no luck in his desperate effort to break free.

"Enough!" shouted the girl. "I will not have this! Tie that rope back to the support beam!"

The two men froze. They stared at the woman who was tied to her chair.

"You heard me," she ordered. "I told you to tie that rope back up!"

It took the old man a moment to respond. However, with a curious smile, he finally replied, "My dear girl, whatever will you do if I refuse?"

"You should know by now, you insolent fool!" she snapped. "You have disobeyed me too many times in the past, and look where it's gotten you! I punish you and punish you, and still you never learn! And now, you have the audacity to try to assume my identity? How dare you tell these people you're me! I am Katalina Van Pouck! And you will suffer for your misbehavior!"

"What?" scoffed the old man. "You must be joking. I would be angry if your claim wasn't so ridiculous."

"Don't mock me, Elliott!" she warned. "You know what happens when you mock me."

The smile instantly vanished from the old man's face. Curiosity quickly turned to outrage. "Don't call me Elliott!"

he shouted. "I'm not Elliott! And, you're not Katalina! *I* am Katalina Van Pouck!"

"No!" she shouted. "I will not allow you to take my identity, you pathetic little man!"

"How dare you call me a man!" he bellowed.

"You are a man," she insisted. "Do you think wearing my favorite robe transforms you into anything else? Tie that rope back to the support beam, and look in the mirror. Go on! Look at yourself!"

He thought for a moment. In a moment of uncertainty, he tied the rope back to the support beam.

"I'm a woman," she said. "You think you can get away with pretending you're me just by tying me to a chair? You know that will never work, Elliott! No matter what you do or how you try to hide, you can't escape me. I will always find you, and I will always make you pay!"

"Don't call me Elliott!" the old man screamed. He stormed over to the table. He grabbed the knife. In no time, he was holding the blade to her throat.

"Tell me why I shouldn't slice you to ribbons right this second," he threatened.

She was trembling as she felt the cold steel pressed again her flesh. But, she knew she had to remain strong. "You can't kill me!" she told him. "You're grandfather already took care of that! I'm already dead! If you stab me, you'll just make me mad. And if you think I have haunted and tortured you before, just wait 'til you see what I'll do if you don't put that knife down!"

His mouth fell open. He looked into the girl's eyes. He saw a determination that scared him. He backed away.

"You can't torture me," he said. "I'm not him! I'm not!"

"Of course, you are," she persisted. "You can't hide who you are by wearing my robe, you meaningless little boy! You are Elliott Van Pouck! And you are a disappointment to everyone in your family! No wonder you wish you were me."

"But," he said in a worried voice. "I am Katalina!"

"You're not even a woman, little boy!" she shouted. "Look in that mirror! Take a look at yourself!"

He walked over to the mirror. He gazed at his reflection with a hint of confusion.

"Look at you, you fool," she pointed out. "You're going bald! I could never go bald."

The old man felt the top of his head as he continued to watch himself in the mirror.

"Feel your face," she instructed. "You have razor stubble. You're a man, for God's sake! I could never grow a beard!"

He looked closely at himself in the mirror as he felt the coarse hair growing along his jaw. "But, how . . .?" he stammered. "But, I . . ."

"Don't stutter," she ordered. "People will know what a worthless man you really are."

"But, I can't be Elliott. I can't be!"

"You are Elliott!" she insisted. "You only pretended to be me so you wouldn't have to face the fact that you killed your wife and children!"

"My wife?" he said with wide-eyed innocence. The old man almost looked like a child waking up from a long sleep. "Penny?" he asked. "My wife, Penny? Where is she? Is something wrong? What did you mean?"

"You killed her, you buffoon," she informed him. "Her and the kids."

"You lie!" snapped the old man. "Penny and the children mean the world to me. I would never harm any of them."

"You killed them," she continued. "Because I told you they would never stay with a pathetic little man like you."

"I'm not pathetic!" he argued. "You always call me pathetic, but I'm not!"

"I told you they would never stay," she pressed. "But, I never told you to kill them. You did that on your own, because you're weak!"

"I'm not weak!" he argued. "They would've stayed! They would've! You never had any confidence in me, Grandma Katalina! You always had to knock me down! But, I don't care what you say! I would never hurt Penny or the kids!"

"Then, where are they?" she inquired.

"They're . . ." the old man began. "They're in the cellar . . ." His voice trailed off.

"They're under the floor," she told him. "That's where you buried them. You piled the children neatly one on top of the other. They never make a sound."

"They never make a sound," the old man repeated slowly.

"Because you killed them!" she told him.

"I would never kill my Penny!"

Both of the captives suddenly stared at the mirror. The ghostly reflection caught them by surprise. The old man stared directly at the vision of a woman he hadn't seen in a long time.

"Penny!" he gasped. "Is that you? How are the kids?"

The image vanished.

"No!" cried the old man. "Don't leave me, Penny! Don't go! Don't leave me! You can't be dead! I would never hurt you!"

Elliott dropped the knife to the floor. He fell to his knees and wept into his hands. "Penny!" he sobbed. "I wouldn't! I could never kill you!"

Even as they sat tied to their chairs, the captives felt a certain sympathy for the man who knelt blubbering before them.

However, the old man looked up after a minute or two. He pointed a finger at the girl. "You!" he accused. "You made me do this! You told me to kill her!"

It was difficult for her to be cruel. But as she saw the rage in his eyes, she knew that her very life was at stake.

"I told you she would never stay with you," she corrected. "But, I never told you to kill her. You chose to do that on your own because you're a weak, pathetic man! You always have been! And, you always will be!"

"No!" Elliott bellowed. "You can't say that anymore! I won't stand for it!"

"You'll take it and like it!" she demanded. "I have haunted you your whole life. I have lived to tell you what a disappointment you are to me! And, I will always be there to remind you of what you truly are!"

"No!" Elliott repeated. "You can't haunt me anymore. I know how to stop you."

Elliott removed the noose from the young man's neck. He moved the chair off the platform. "I know how to keep you from taunting me," he said. "I know where I can go so you can never hurt me again! I know where I can join Penny and my beloved children. You can't hurt me anymore, Grandma Katalina! I finally know how to stop you!"

Elliott stuck his own head in the noose as he stepped on the platform.

"You think you're better than me, Katalina?" he inquired. "You think you can stop me from being happy?

Well, I've got news for you. I will never be unhappy again! Not for you or anybody else! You can't stop me from being happy! You can't touch me anymore! And, you can't keep me from being happy with my wife!"

Elliott pulled the knot from the rope that was tied to the support beam. The rope quickly unraveled from the handle. The platform dropped out from beneath him. It fell to the ground floor with a loud crash.

The two prisoners gasped as they watched the noose pull tightly against the old man's neck. He flailed his arms wildly as his air passage was cut off. His face turned red . . . then purple as it contorted in anguish.

She screamed in horror. Yet, she couldn't bring herself to look away. The young couple stared with wild-eyed terror as the man in the pink robe gradually lost his struggle for oxygen.

The young man had to look back into the mirror as something caught his eye.

Did he see the image of a familiar woman in the mirror? Was she smiling as the old man bobbed, gasped and gurgled at the end of the rope?

"Katalina!" the young man whispered.

But then the image was gone.

The old man's arms grew useless. They fell helplessly to his sides. His whole body became motionless. The eyes that were bulging out of his discolored face became lifeless. He hung heavy and still . . . wearing a pink robe while dangling from the end of a noose.

Moments after he stopped moving, she wept, "Oh my God! Is it over? Is he dead?"

"It certainly looks that way," he said.

"How do we get out of here, Russell?" she asked. "I've got to get out of here."

"That's a good question," he asked. He looked down at the knife. It was on the floor, not far from his chair. "I'm sure we'll work something out."

He rocked his chair, hoping to tip it over.

"Be careful," she advised. "You're not very far from that hole in the floor."

"Don't worry," he said as he kept rocking. "I'm being real careful about that."

Suddenly, his chair fell on its side. The knife was only a foot or so away from his bound hands. He struggled to maneuver the chair into a position where he could grab the knife.

"I have to ask you," he said. "How did you decide to pretend to be Katalina? It was a brilliant strategy."

"It was sheer desperation," she said. "He was about to kill you. I couldn't just sit there and watch that happen. Especially, since I knew that I was going to be next."

"Well, it couldn't have worked out any better," he said as his fingers wrapped around the knife on the floor. He immediately began to cut through the ropes that held his hands tied behind the chair.

"Of course," he continued. "You could have told him to untie us before he killed himself."

"I didn't mean for him to kill himself," she said. "I just didn't want to die. I didn't want either one of us to die."

"Well, I certainly have to thank you, Heidi," he said. "You saved my life."

She didn't reply. Tears flooded her eyes as she watched him cut the ropes behind his back.

"How did you even know what to say?" he asked.

"I just remembered what you told me," she explained. "I tried to remember everything you said about your experiences here . . . and in Nobody's Grave and your dreams. Basically, it was all desperate babbling."

"Well, it sure did the trick," he said.

The knife finally tore through the rope. He got his hands out from behind the chair. It was much easier to either cut through or untie the rest of the ropes.

"I thought I was going to die," she said. "I thought *you* were going to die. I really thought we were both dead!"

"You don't have to worry about that now," he said as he freed himself from the last of the ropes. He jumped up and hurried over to untie his girlfriend. "But, why did you come here in the first place?"

"You disappeared last night," she said. "At first, I was just mad. But, I knew you wouldn't just leave. I thought something happened. I thought that maybe you left town like everyone else in your house. I thought you were gone."

She was weeping again by the time he untied her from the chair.

"Then, I saw your car," she said. "I had to find you."

She leapt up into his arms. "Then, I almost had to watch you die," she said. "And, I almost lost you again! I couldn't do it, Russ! I just couldn't do it! I love you!"

He smiled as he held her quivering, sobbing frame. "Sshhh," he whispered in her ear. "Everything's all right now, sweetheart. I love you, too."

They held each other for a minute.

He looked into her beautiful green eyes. "I'm sorry about last night," he said. "I don't know what happened. I don't know how I woke up somewhere else. It was because of Katalina. That's all I know. But, you don't have to worry anymore. I told you I'm not leaving Autumn. Not while you're here."

She looked up at him with a precious smile. They shared a long kiss of many needs.

Then, she pulled away. She winced as she saw the lifeless body hanging from the rope about twenty feet from where she stood.

"Can we please get out of here, Russ?" she asked. "This place is giving me the creeps."

"Sure," he said as he looked over at Elliott's corpse. "I know where there's a staircase in the corner."

He led her down the stairs and out of the carriage house. "Now that the last of the Van Poucks is dead," he told her. "We shouldn't have to worry about ghosts around here anymore."

"I hope that part of the legend is true," she said.

They walked in the sunshine along the parking area behind the mansion.

Then, he stopped. "Wait a minute," he said. "Get out of here, Heidi. Go somewhere safe. I have one more thing to do before I leave."

She watched him run toward the back of the mansion. "Russell?" she called after him. She followed behind him as she continued, "Where are you going?"

"Just go, Heidi," he told her. "I'll be out in a few minutes."

She followed him to the back door of the mansion. "No, Russ," she said. "I'm not leaving without you. Where are you going?"

He checked the back door. Luckily, it was open. He ran through the door and directly into the large kitchen. "Ah," he smiled. "Just where I wanted to be."

He found the door to the cellar. He bounded down the old creaky stairs to the cellar as soon as he found a light switch.

"Russell?" she asked from two steps behind him. "What are you doing?"

When he reached the bottom of the stairs, he turned on another light. It didn't offer a lot of help seeing in the dusky, dank cellar. However, it allowed him to find the wall with the picture of the stream. The room was still filled with canned goods stacked in tall piles.

She looked around with growing fear at the eerie spectacle all around her. "Do we really have to be here now?" she asked.

"I told you to go," he said as he walked over to the picture. "I'll be out in a minute or two. I have to do this right now."

"What are you doing?"

He tried to shift the picture to the side. The picture wouldn't move. The wall wouldn't budge. "Damn it!" he muttered.

He tried to find a seam in the wall. "Shit!" he cried. "It's sealed tight!"

"What are you trying to do?" she repeated.

He remembered something Elliott had said to him when they first met. He ran over to the adjacent wall. Just as Elliott had indicated, there was an axe and a sledgehammer leaning against the bricks.

He grabbed the sledgehammer and ran over to the picture. He swung the hammer at the wall. The bricks began to crumble. He swung again.

"Russell?" she asked. "What's going on?"

He kept swing the sledgehammer until he cleared through about a three-square-foot space in the brick wall.

The horrific odors knocked her back from where she stood. "My God!" she complained as she covered her nose. "What is that terrible smell?"

He was impervious to the odors. He just kept swinging the sledgehammer until he broke a big enough hole through the obstacle. Then, he stared through the hole.

"Oh my God," he gasped. "It's her! It's really her! And, she wasn't even dead when he sealed her up in here."

"What?" she asked. "What are you talking about?"

She covered her nose as best she could as she went over to look through the hole in the wall. She gasped when she saw the skeleton curled up near the wall Russ had just broken through. Dust and pieces of brick littered the floor around the fetid pile of bones.

"Who is that, Russ?" she asked.

"It's Ingrid," he said.

"Ingrid Beckenbauer?" she asked. "Are you sure?"

"Believe me," he nodded. "I'm absolutely certain. I'll explain everything when we get back to my place. After we call the cops. Now that Elliott's dead, they'll have to listen to us. I believe Officer Glenn owes us a medal."

They stood and stared at the bony resident of the tiny secret room for a minute.

Finally, she said, "Let's get out of here, Russ. I'm scared."

He just stood there and gazed through the hole. "Don't worry, Ingrid," he whispered. "I'll make sure you get where you belong."

Then, he offered her a knowing smile. He placed the sledgehammer against the wall.

"Please, Russell," his girlfriend begged. She was still protecting her nose from the awful smell with her hand. "I'm frightened!"

After a respectful silence, he turned and said, "Okay, Heidi. You're right. Let's get out of here."

He put his arm around her as they walked through the dusky cellar to the stairs.

They left the end of an era behind. It was wearing a pink robe. It was hanging lifelessly at the end of a rope in the carriage house.

They hurried up the stairs.

The odors they left behind were atrocious.

The skeleton they left behind still wore a gold chain with a locket around her neck.

ABOUT THE BOOK

Russell Wilburn moves to a seemingly quiet small town to start a new life. He buys a house that appears to be the ideal setting to begin this new venture. Unfortunately, strange things begin to happen. Mysterious phone calls and ghostly visions lead him to believe the house is haunted. He quickly develops a facination with an old mansion a few blocks away, and a cemetery further up the road. It doesn't take long to discover that the mansion is inhabited by a crazy old man who is the only living descendant of a once rich and powerful family. Everyone in town knows the horrific legend of the mansion. Everybody knows of the tales that tie the mansion and the cemetery to Russell's new house. On the surface, no one admits these places are really haunted. However, everyone is still afraid of them. The notorious spot in the cemetery is considered a childrens' story of a grave that doesn't exist. Still, he must go there to answer the questions that will rid his home of its supernatural inhabitants.

Russell struggles to begin a normal life. He thinks he can save the floundering store he purchased. And, a beautiful cashier named Heidi O'Dell cautiously agrees to start dating him, despite an ex-boyfriend who doesn't want to let her go. He becomes acquainted with the mansion and its dangerously insane sole occupant. And, a message in blood warns him that his time to rid his house of ghosts may be limited. Now he must keep Heidi safe from his perilous secrets. He must brave the infamous cemetery and the haunted mansion (with its deadly resident) in order to save himself from the unwanted guests in his new home. The police won't believe him. No one else in town will help. There is only one person who is willing to aid in his fight to save his house and survive! Unfortunately, that person is already dead!

ABOUT THE AUTHOR

Donald Gorman was born on September 25, 1961 in Albany, NY. An almost fatal desease during infancy left him partially paralyzed on the right side of his body. He grew up in the nearby small town of East Greenbush, and graduated from Columbia High School in 1979. He attended a few local colleges, and now works for the State of NY in Albany.

He enjoys art and music. He has done some painting, drawing and he plays the piano fairly well for a guy who can only play with one hand. He's also done some cartooning. But, his main love is still writing. And the horror genre has fascinated him since the first time he saw his first slasher film in the theater. His first three books "The Brick Mirror", "The Waters of Satan's Creek" and "Macabre Astrology" are great examples of his work as well.

Printed in the United States
52226LVS00001B/5